Enlightened

Billie Kowalewski

Copyright © 2016 Billie Kowalewski

All rights reserved. No part(s) of this book may be reproduced, distributed or transmitted in any form, or by any means, or stored in a database or retrieval systems without prior expressed written permission of the author of this book.

ISBN: 978-1-5356-0804-6

This book is dedicated to my father
Timothy W. Kowalewski
See you when I get home from school

Contents

Chapter 1 6
Chapter 2 22
Chapter 3 36
Chapter 4 53
Chapter 5 67
Chapter 6 77
Chapter 7 89
Chapter 8 105
Chapter 9 118
Chapter 10 140
Chapter 11 156
Chapter 12 162
Chapter 13 177
Chapter 14 186
Chapter 15 202
Chapter 16 219
Chapter 17 237
Chapter 18 249
Chapter 19 261
Chapter 20 272
Chapter 21 285
Chapter 22 294
Chapter 23 303
Chapter 24 317
Chapter 25 332
Epilogue 342

My world is your world, only you can't remember any of it. A barrier exists between what you think is real and what you know to be. It was put in place during the transition into the world you currently know, and will be removed upon your return.

In other words…this is not your real life.

My name is Harmony, and I'm gonna let you in on a little secret.

I am a student at the *biggest*, most *famous* school ever known.

And so are you!

Earth.

Yep, Earth is school. Are you shocked? If you are, it's okay. This is the most common and expected reaction to this news. I'll give you a moment to let that sink in…

Just kidding! Based on the fact that you've chosen to read this, I'm gonna bet that you're a lot like me. You're probably fine, and not shocked by this at all. If you do,

1

however, find this news to be at all surprising, perhaps it would be best if you stopped here. This story is based on an alternative viewpoint, and I'm not looking to upset anyone's beliefs. I do understand that this story may not be for everyone. Our extreme diversity is an important part of what makes up who we are. So this may be where we will agree to disagree, and possibly part ways. Hopefully as friends. For everyone else, we will move on.

Yes, life is about learning, and Earth is the school. I'm sure you've heard someone on Earth say this before. I know when I'm there I hear this often. People know, and it's not because they remember that it is. They know because you cannot get through a single day there without learning something, somehow. It was set up to be that way. On Earth, learning some type of lesson is unavoidable.

If you're sitting there right now searching your mind for a tiny clue that this is true, you're wasting your time. You won't be able to find anything. Please don't be mistaken—your memories are there. You carry them along with you, buried deep within your subconscious, hidden by a special barrier. This barrier will remain in place throughout your entire life, and it is what is keeping you from being able to remember the world from which you came. Not to worry—you'll get your memories back, along with your new ones, once you… *ahem*…return home.

Enlightened

No one knows why we need this barrier, but we all have our theories about it. Personally, I think it's because it gives us a chance to start off life with a clean slate. We can let go of our fears and opinions about things. We can forget about any mistakes that we've made, too. I also think this teaches us how what we think we feel about something can change depending on the situation. Of course, these are just my theories. I'm sure you probably have your own. One thing I think we can all agree on is that birth is the only time that we can truly forget about the past.

For obvious reasons—and perhaps ones not so obvious—most don't like the barrier, and think school would be a lot easier without it.

"How do you succeed at something when you can't remember why you need to?" they argue.

I do see their point. If the barrier wasn't there it would certainly make learning on Earth easier. *Maybe*. I'm not in full agreement on this. These select few do not fully understand the barrier, or how it works. They just haven't been enlightened yet. Once you figure this out, though, it's your ticket to shine.

Of all the things you will end up taking away from this story, the most important thing to remember is that there is *always* an exception to every rule. All of them. Using this logic, I have discovered that there are ways of getting things through and around this barrier. Yes, that's right—I said *through*. It is a common misconception that the barrier blocks everything. It doesn't. You can compare it to a coffee filter. It keeps the bulk on one side, while only allowing what is important through. So it's not that we can't remember *anything*. We only remember what we need to, or have to. And if you concentrate hard enough, you can get vital information through that will help you succeed in ways you never thought possible. Nothing can completely hide who we truly are, and that's the point. That's all that really matters.

My classmates don't think that this is possible, but I'm determined to prove to them that it is. I want to show them that anything is possible with hard work and determination. That believing in yourself really is the key, and that anyone can hold on to all the information they need to be successful in life. We all possess the courage we need to face anything and to be what we want to be. It is up to us to use it. It really is that simple. It's time for us to show my classmates and everyone else that they can do this too. With your help, together we can. Our life and education stretches far beyond Earth, and will continue on forever. Damaged relationships will be mended, unresolved conflicts will be settled, and all new lessons learned will be acknowledged. The time has come for you to see beyond the barrier. The time has come for you to become enlightened.

Enlightened

A wise person once told me: *All good things must come to an end.* Respectfully, I have to disagree. All stories have a beginning, but the best stories start at an end.

Chapter 1

June 1980

The silence that followed after shutting off the car hit me in the face like a sack of bricks. It may as well have been a bolt of lightning, the way it jolted through me and sent my body skyrocketing out of control. Suddenly my heart was beating in my ears, and my breaths were coming out in quick, frustrating gasps. My hands started to sweat now too, and were gluing themselves to the steering wheel. This made me feel more like a prisoner strapped into an electric chair than a young girl with a fancy rental car who thought she was strong enough to visit her best friend. I started to wonder if coming to see him was a big mistake.

Maybe I am insane, I thought to myself as my heartbeat continued to consume me and I fought to steady my breathing. Whether or not I was insane had been an ongoing internal debate for me for the last

Enlightened

five years. I've often wondered how someone would determine such a thing about themselves. I have yet to find anyone brave enough to step up and say, *"We're so sorry, Veronica. We have to commit you now, you're a crazy person."* Too bad there isn't a test you could take at home that alerts you to something like that. Not only would I have taken that test…*several times*…but I would be seriously questioning its accuracy right now. Especially if it came back that I wasn't.

I do know there is a difference between being insane and simply being sad. But often enough I have found that line tends to blur occasionally. Sitting there, I couldn't help feeling this way and thinking that my plan was stupid. Perhaps this was that final straw that would break the camel's back? Maybe this plan of mine would send me right over the edge for good, and there wouldn't be any way to return. I imagined an idiot slamming his sledgehammer against the wall of a dam. Is it wise to do such a thing? If it cracks open, how do you stop the water? But then I thought, if it was already drained of all the water, it wouldn't matter if the idiot cracked it or not. Because if there was nothing left, there would be minimal damage.

The minutes felt as though they were dragging on like hours as I continued to fight my body for control. I started to wonder how long it might be before someone would notice me here. Thankfully, this place wasn't known for frequent visitors—at least not of the *live variety*. I shuddered as I thought about what kind of wreck that poor soul might find. A young brunette, sitting alone in a black Ford Mustang convertible, having an unexpected nervous breakdown in the middle of a cemetery.

I thought about leaving and forgetting this whole thing. But I couldn't. I couldn't forget; that was the problem, and why I'd come. I wasn't able to come up with a better way to deal with all of my feelings. I started to wonder if anyone in their right mind would do something like this. Then I thought, if they were in their right mind, they probably wouldn't have thought of it at all.

Slowly, I felt myself starting to gain control with each intake of breath. My heartbeats were starting to settle now too, slowly winding down. Each one beating a little softer than the last. I kept myself still, and my eyes shut, just breathing steadily until I felt better. Then, suddenly, I was just really pissed at myself.

I was so sure before I came here, so confident in my plan. Not a single butterfly in my stomach right on up until I got here. Then it all went out the window the second I turned the key.

"You're tougher than this," I grumbled under my breath.

I took in a slow, deep breath and exhaled fully. Gradually, I started peeling my fingers away from the wheel, one by one. I took my time, going slow, not wanting to risk starting round two of another monumental nervous breakdown. My hands trembled at first once they were free, causing me a little concern. I took in another cleansing breath, and let it out. Slowly, I began to realize that I felt okay. I gently placed my hands in my lap, trying to stay as calm as possible.

I have to do this, I reminded myself. My plane leaves tomorrow to go back home. I don't know if I'll ever get another chance to come back to Connecticut. I might not get this opportunity again. If I don't do this now, I know I'll kick myself for not trying. Especially if I continue in the way that I have been. I don't have another choice—it has to be today.

I opened my eyes and reached for the rearview mirror. I gasped the second I turned it and saw myself, horrified by my own reflection. My wide brown eyes were puffy, and the whites had turned a bright red. My hair was blown wild, sticking up all over my head in a crazy mess. I quickly glanced around and sighed in relief that no one else was here, thankful I'd come alone. I quickly went to work trying to fix the disaster I had become. I felt confused as I wiped under my eyes, removing the tears that were clinging to my lashes and hanging in the corners. How does crying go by unnoticed? I wondered. My fingers were met by large, tight snarls and knots, when I tried to comb them through. I failed miserably to smooth down the windblown strands. I had severely underestimated what driving here with the top down would do to long curly hair. I sighed in frustration. "*Ugh*…I don't give a crap," I grumbled, quickly giving up. I know he's seen me way worse.

I took in a swift, cleansing breath and grabbed my bag, slinging the strap over my shoulder. When I moved my bag, I uncovered a couple of mementos his grandfather had been nice enough to let me take from his room when I'd visited him earlier. His Led Zeppelin T-shirt and a pair of sunglasses that he always wore. My heart skipped a little when I saw them, as it always does, still, whenever I think of him. Of course, it's not the wild frenzy it used to be. Now it's more like a dull thud.

I paused for a brief moment, savoring the emotions I felt as I ran my fingers across the print on the tee. I grabbed the sunglasses, and then stepped out of the car before I could give myself a chance to have second thoughts.

My legs wobbled a little as I started to walk. A breeze that I could barely feel howled eerily through the trees. I paid no mind to the clear blue sky overhead, or the warm June air. All I focused on was putting one foot in front of the other as I made my way along the row of headstones over to his.

I don't think I know anyone who doesn't feel just a little uneasy walking through a cemetery. I can't say that I am any different. All those bodies lying underground tend to create such an awkward feeling, and I always end

Enlightened

up walking as gently as possible on the tips of my toes. I know it sounds silly, but as I walked through, I felt like I was stepping on people, disturbing all those poor souls who were trying to get some rest. If this were any other occasion, under different circumstances, I would be apologizing.

I felt my heart thump hard against my ribs once his stone came into view. Suddenly, I kept having to swallow because a dry lump was starting to rise up into my throat. I became a bit worried about passing out when I felt my head swirl some. I paused for a moment and took in a deep breath and let it out.

"Get a grip, Veronica!" I harshly whispered to myself.

A strange feeling slowly came over me as I moved closer to where he was. It was confusing, because suddenly I felt oddly calm for no real reason. The feeling seemed to follow me, becoming stronger the closer I got, and the walk became easier. I began to worry that this good feeling wouldn't last, and that it was just temporary. But no sooner had I thought this than the worry was gone, and a sense of enthusiasm took its place. Now, I couldn't move my feet fast enough.

Once I finally reached where he was, I put on his sunglasses and smiled.

"Honey, I'm home!" I announced as cheerfully as I could, throwing my hands out.

Billie Kowalewski

I knelt down in front of his headstone, and placed my bag on the ground beside me. I began clearing away a few leaves that had gathered in front as I read the names.

Seth Chase	Joan Chase Wright
August 28, 1956 –	July 24, 1933 –
August 11, 1975	April 17, 1967

The memory of the terrible accident we were involved in slowly crept into my thoughts. The very one that took his life and spared mine. I still suffer with heavy guilt over it, always wondering what could have been. I miss him terribly.

I was quiet as I traced along the letters in his name, and then his mother's. There are no words good enough to describe how genuinely wonderful both of these people were to me. It's disappointing to know that the world is without two very good souls.

"*Hi, Joan,*" I said out loud, continuing with my cheery tone. "I hope you don't mind that I came to visit your son today."

I began nervously picking at the grass once my attention turned toward speaking to him.

"Seth, it's me… *Veronica,*" I said softly. Finally saying his name out loud after so many years tugged at my heartstrings.

"I'm sorry that I haven't been able to visit you until now. I moved to San Francisco after *you…*" I stopped myself out of habit, before just stating the obvious. Even

Enlightened

though so many years had gone by, I still had trouble saying it. "*Left*.

"I hope things are going well for you wherever you may be, and I hope you've found happiness there," I said with the utmost sincerity.

"As you may or may not know, a lot has changed for me since then. I live with my father now, and his wife Linda.

"Do you remember that she had just found out that she was having a baby before you left?" I asked him and then paused, as if he could reply. "Well, she ended up having a son, whom they named Joshua Seth Edwards." I said his name proudly.

A soft smile slowly began spreading across my face as I continued to talk. I started to relax a little, and my one-sided conversation slowly became easier.

"I couldn't believe it when she asked me about using your first name for Josh's middle one. Of course, I proudly agreed. Linda is the warmest person ever, and a wonderful mother. She barely knew me, and she did that." I chuckled. "She makes Donna look like crap.

"Josh is just so adorable. I know you would have loved him as much as I do. I play with him all the time…I teach him things, and I spoil him every chance that I get." I spoke happily.

"I have been very focused on going to school, too… I just finished, and I know you'd be proud to hear that I was offered a job teaching kindergarten at an elementary school in the fall."

I could feel my emotions beginning to churn in the pit of my stomach as I slowly approached a more sensitive topic. I continued to pick at the grass and fidget with my fingers while I spoke, in an effort to help keep myself talking. I wanted to get everything that I needed to say *out*. There was no way I was going to let myself lose it just yet.

I took in another cleansing breath and let it out before trying to continue. But my emotions were still taunting me, causing me to fidget even more. I started to ramble, and my voice became high pitched and speedy.

"I stopped by your house today to visit George… I am sure you probably know he's doing well… Do you remember the roses we planted out front? They look so good! *See*? I told you planting them was a good idea… *Ooh*…I should confess, I went into your room while I was there. As you can see, I took your sunglasses, and I hope you don't mind." I ducked, and made a face. "…I also took your Led Zeppelin shirt."

My nerves were beyond frazzled, and I was feeling so overwhelmed that I almost forgot a small part of my plan. I jumped up, excited suddenly, and started digging through my bag.

"*Oh*, I almost forgot! I brought you a little treat."

Enlightened

I pulled out a cassette player and placed it on the ground. Then I went through my bag again and dug out a cassette and held it up toward the headstone.

"Look, Seth, music is on cassettes now."

I put the tape in the player, and pressed play.

"*Ooh*…what's this? A little…'Toys in the Attic?'" I said, sounding dramatic. I smiled. "I knew you would love this."

I placed my back against the headstone, making myself more comfortable. I closed my eyes and started to sing along to some of the songs. It was enjoyable at first, and, as intended, it started to bring memories to the surface from our time together. Any nervousness I'd felt before was long gone, and I wasn't fidgeting anymore either. The idiot succeeded and cracked that dam *wide* open. Tears were streaming down my cheeks now. I knew it was time to get out the rest of what I really needed to say.

"It's so hard not being able to talk to you, and it's just so unfair. I've watched people who didn't love each other half as much as we did get to be with each other for years, while you and I only had five months—unless you start counting from when we met in the third grade."

I felt cheated. "*Really*…that's all we get?!" I shouted angrily, tossing my hands up. I hung my head down, cupping my face in my hands, and sobbed hard. "Just five months of happiness…*and then it was gone*," I said through the tears.

"*I'm…not…ungrateful*," I struggled to get out at a barely audible level. I felt like I was choking as I pushed each word out through the gasps and sobs.

I wiped under my eyes and took in a breath, trying to calm down.

"I'll never forget how you and I met," I managed to say, barely above a whisper. "Bumping into you while getting my lunch on my first day of school here was the best thing that has ever happened to me in my whole life," I whispered again. The memory caused me to chuckle a little. No matter how miserable I am, I still can never resist a little joke to help lighten a mood. "…Even if it did land me on my butt.

"Not too many people can say they found their soul mate when they were eight years old. I can say with absolute certainty that I did. I know for a fact that if you didn't have to move away for the time you did, our love would have blossomed so much sooner. It would have been nice to have you that whole time then, to be able to love you longer. I will always be grateful that you came back at all.

"I miss you so much, and it's just so hard. I've been trying to keep going, but that's tough to do when a big piece of your heart is missing.

"My stepmother suggested to me a year ago that I should *'get back out there.'* I know she means well, but I almost threw up right there." I shuddered. "And until she

Enlightened

said something, that thought never once crossed my mind." I shook my head, and had never sounded more serious.

"I've had a few guys ask me out at school too, and I kindly told them all no. I just can't do it, and I don't think I'll ever be able to. I know it sounds crazy, but I can't love anyone else the same as I love you. So I decided…I'd rather live the rest of my life alone loving you, than try to pretend with someone else. That's why I came here, because I wanted to tell you that." I wiped under my eyes and sucked in a jagged breath.

I shrugged. "Who knows, maybe I'll be one of those ladies with, like, forty cats."

The image of me being surrounded by a house full of cats suddenly filled my mind, and then I started to laugh.

"*Uhh*…on second thought, I think I'll minus thirty-nine of those." I chuckled again.

"I'm going back to California tomorrow. I'll be getting ready to start my new job soon… I'm looking forward to that… The kids have always brought me joy."

Suddenly, pain was shooting across my forehead. I quickly clutched my head, leaning forward in agony as the pain traveled, wrapping right around my skull. Shortly after I moved to California, I began suffering from severe headaches. They came on suddenly, and were so sharp at times that I could barely move. It seemed to be occasionally at first, but lately I'd been having these headaches much more frequently. I was surprised that this was the first one I'd had today. I'd been to several doctors about them, and none of them could figure out what was wrong.

I rummaged through my bag and grabbed the Tylenol and the Coke I had brought with me, and took two pills. I carry these things with me everywhere I go now. I pinched the bridge of my nose and leaned forward, resting my head against my knees.

"*Ugh*, and these headaches just won't stop... What am I gonna do when I have a classroom full of kids?" I spoke through the tears, just above a whisper.

I sat there for a while, waiting for the pills to dull the pain just enough so I could function. I had one more stop to make, and then I was going back to my grandparents' house to spend the night.

Once the pills began to kick in, I started picking up my mess on the ground. I stood up, brushed the back of my pants off, and smiled.

"I'm going up to Devil's Hopyard now to go sit by the falls. I would have done it before while I was up that way, but I wanted to see you first, so I could invite you to come with me... I hope you follow me there... I love you so much, and I'll never stop."

I cried on the walk back over to the car, and while I started it. I tried to stop while I was driving, but I couldn't.

Why did I do this to myself? I thought while I drove. It had taken me five years to pull myself as together as I

Enlightened

was, and just a few short hours to undo it all. It would probably take me another five years to fix what I'd just done to myself—*I feel like such an idiot!*

I turned onto the road that ran over the top of the falls, pulled into the parking lot, and parked the car. The sound of rushing water greeted me the moment I turned off the engine. I smiled; it felt like the falls were welcoming me home, and it made me feel a little better.

Seth and I spent a great deal of time visiting Devil's Hopyard State Park. It just seemed like a good way to cap off my visit, and hopefully bring me the closure that I'd been looking for.

The falls sounded energetic. I crossed the road, and walked along the cedar fence that ran alongside, and then stopped to watch the water cascading down. I took in a deep breath. The scent of the honeysuckle growing by the fence hit my nose, and then suddenly I felt amazing. To my intense surprise, I actually felt relieved and happy. And more alive right here than I had in the last five years. Maybe doing all of this really was what I needed to do after all? I was now convinced that I'd done the right thing.

I walked down the path that ran alongside the falls, over a small wood bridge, just like we did the last time we were here. I followed it down to that secluded little spot he and I shared that day he asked me to be his wife.

I sat down on the rock and curled my knees in, just staring down at the water. I caught sight of the red and blue friendship bracelet with the little white beads that I was wearing. A gift from Seth when we were eight. The day he and I decided to be best friends. It was a little tattered-looking now. The little white beads were a bit scuffed and had darkened with time. The red and blue woven threads had darkened too, but remained strong and had never frayed. I'll never forget how big it was when he'd tied it on then. Now it fit perfectly, and served as a brilliant symbol of our everlasting friendship.

I ran my fingers across the weave, feeling the beads, the way I always did whenever I thought of him. Instead of the sadness I was feeling at the cemetery, I was filled with happiness from my memories of him, and the memory of that last day that he and I were here.

This was our place, and I could not think of Devil's Hopyard without thinking of him.

It was starting to get late. I decided to head back to have dinner with my grandpa. I stood up and brushed off the back of my pants. When I turned around to start walking up the path, intense pain shot forcefully across my head. It brought me to my knees, and tears to my eyes. I quickly clutched my head in my hands, doubling over in agony. I fell to the ground, crumpling up on the rock, cursing myself because I knew my bag with the pills was in the car…

Enlightened

The pain intensified, paralyzing me against the rock. My vision went askew suddenly, and then I heard a loud pop inside my head.

Chapter 2

I'VE OFTEN WONDERED IF I am the universe's personal court jester. Like maybe I'm someone they toy with all the time because they think I'm funny when I get mad. When I look back over my life, it seems like it was an endless parade of infuriating situations brought on by the crappiest people. I swear, if the *Guinness Book of World Records* dedicated a book to unfortunate souls, I'm sure my picture would be in there somewhere. There is no way the staggering amount of aggravations I've endured have all been a coincidence, and this is why I believe that someone in the universe finds this amusing. I am convinced that if I do have a guardian angel, he has a twisted sense of humor.

I know it sounds like I am exaggerating, but this is how I feel. I have yet to come up with another logical reason for the amount of bullshit I've encountered in my lifetime. How else might someone explain this? By simply saying that life is unfair? Possibly. Or more logically, maybe someone in the universe just thinks it's funny when I swear?

Enlightened

I believe I can prove that someone in the universe is picking on me, all while sparing you from the tragic details of my so-called life. Sleep is proof positive that the joke is on me. How is it possible that something so wonderful can be just as aggravating as the meanest person? Without fail, it seems that I go through the same annoying routine every night…

First, I have to find my sweet spot. You know, that certain position you toss and turn just to find that makes you melt into the bed. This feat alone can take me a good twenty to thirty minutes, and nine times out of ten, it is usually the exact same position that I fell asleep in the night before—*you would think the tossing and turning wouldn't be necessary.*

Even if I'm lucky enough to find my sweet spot right away, it doesn't help shut down my overactive brain! It amazes me how many things can occur to me at bedtime that never once entered my mind at a more convenient time. Like, say, for example, *during the day!*

Yes, sleep can be such a frustration for me. Especially since once I'm asleep I love it so much. *Oh*, expect to lose a limb or walk away with a black eye if you're the one waking me up before I have to. That has got to be one of my biggest pet peeves. I can't stand that.

Once I'm asleep, I just can't seem to get enough. Morning seems to come sooner than I would like. This time can be just as dangerous for anyone badgering me.

Billie Kowalewski

Leave me alone until I've showered and brushed my teeth at the very least—*unless you don't really like seeing out of that one eye!*

I wasn't always like this. There was a brief time in my life when I looked forward to waking up. But just like all the other good times in my life—which proves my point—no sooner had that time come it spun away quickly, coming to a crashing halt.

I'd be kidding myself if I said this "particular time period" wasn't the real fuel behind why I have trouble sleeping, or why I struggle to get out of bed in the morning. That time is something I try hard not to think about anymore. The pain from losing him has left a permanent mark on my life. If I were being honest with myself, I would say that this time period is the true reason behind my gripe with sleep. But I would rather lie. It's so much less painful, and sleep is the only break I ever get from the truth.

The worst part is I just never feel rested. No matter how much sleep I get, I always feel so tired still.

So I'm sure you can imagine the slight guilt starting to trickle through me right then, as I was just beginning to wake up. For the first time in years, I felt rested. An incredible sensation of relaxation and peace was flowing through me. I couldn't stop the happiness I was starting to feel, or the smile that was beginning to spread across my face.

Enlightened

Light started filtering in through the darkness as the sun began to rise. Gradually the light grew, becoming stronger and brighter. It shined brightly against my lids, twinkling through them in a way that I had never seen before. I let out a giggle when I felt it tickle my nose, enticing me into awareness in a playful manner. The light continued its peculiar dance across my face, and flowed down the length of my entire body. The sun felt warm and strangely inviting as it radiated through me, energizing me from head to toe. It was filling me with love and happiness, and I could feel that it was all for me.

I took in a breath through my nose, and I was greeted by a familiar fragrance that I truly missed. A scent so sweet it smelled like the most succulent honey. I inhaled deeply, savoring my guilty pleasure for a moment, and then I could have sworn I'd just heard the most incredible sound.

"Veronica."

Ahhh, there it was again! Spoken like a gentle whisper by a uniquely familiar deep voice—*the deep voice of an angel.* Oh please, sweet lord, let me hear it again.

"Baby."

Excitement began coursing through my veins after hearing the term of endearment he used to call me. I giggled, giddy with delight, and I savored the sound of the heavenly deep voice that had been awakened from my subconscious memory.

This must be a dream. That sound…*his* voice…could only be a dream.

The heavenly scent became much stronger, surrounding me, and I felt someone gently touch my cheek. My whole body tingled when I felt his breath against my ear.

"It's time to wake up, Veronica," he whispered.

I must be dreaming. I feel way too good.

"Aren't you gonna get up?" he asked, sounding puzzled.

I held my eyes closed.

"I'm having a good dream, and I don't want to get up," I replied to my heavenly angel—*I hope he speaks again.*

I heard the delightful sound of him chuckling.

"Baby, you're not dreaming. You're home now."

I stretched my arms up above my head while trying to inhale as much of his heavenly sweet scent as I possibly could. I felt my body relaxing even more the deeper I inhaled the delicious scent, and I could feel it tingling through, all the way down to my toes. I was trying hard to hang on to as much of the dream as possible. This was the closest I had felt to him in such a long time. But with my playful sun still dancing brightly against my lids the way it was, I knew sleep would be impossible for me now. I was so disappointed with myself. I was about to ruin the best dream I'd had of him in years. I tried to open my eyes, but it was so bright that I had to shut them again quickly. I lay there processing for a

Enlightened

moment. I was confused. Because I could have sworn that I was in my bed at home. But then more confusion set in, because I couldn't recall where I was last, or where I was now. Slowly, I began opening my eyes, blinking them. Trying to adjust them to the overwhelming light that surrounded me.

"I'm home?" I questioned, glancing above me.

I was still feeling very confused. I'd never seen anything like it. There were no defined walls or ceiling. Just never-ending bright white all around me.

"This doesn't look like home…it's too bright," I stated.

"Yes," he said on an exhale. He sounded so happy.

I became even more puzzled when I placed my hands on my chest and felt the silky-smooth material that I was wearing. I glanced down at my hands and saw that I was lying on a tan leather cot. Then my eyes took in the long, silky white robe that I was dressed in. I ran my fingers along the coils of the gold-colored rope that was around my waist, following it down to its fringed ends.

It was the most confusing sensation when the fear I started to feel didn't make my body react in the same way it normally would have. There was no heart pounding, or blood racing, just calm and peace. As if it were a controlled emotion.

Slowly, I began catching on to where I may be. I turned in the direction of where I heard his voice. My eyes widened, and I gasped.

Billie Kowalewski

He was sitting right next to me. Looking more glorious in death than in life, than any angel had any right too. His chin-length jet-black hair was shiny, and hung down, framing his handsome face. His lips were turned up into a carefree smile, rounding his cheeks and lighting up his gorgeous green eyes. They were sparkling, and full of such warmth and joy, just as I remembered him. The only difference was the two overlapping purple scars that ran the length of his left cheek were now gone.

"Seth!" I shouted.

Tears began flowing uncontrollably from my eyes. I was elated, and jumped up quickly from the cot and threw myself at him. I felt the chair sway back as the force of my leap almost knocked him over, causing him to chuckle lightly. His deep, throaty tone sent my heart into an all-too-familiar, extremely missed frenzy.

Tears were streaming steadily down my cheeks. I felt like a dam that had burst open after years of extreme pressure. These were tears of ultimate joy. I'd held in the pain of missing him for so long, and now it was suddenly gone. I'd never felt such relief. But these tears were also contradictory, because a small part of me was sad. I now know that I must have died.

I sat back to look at him, not daring to let go of the hold I had around his neck, and he was smiling at me ear to ear. I was flowing with overpowering joy in this moment. I desperately pressed my lips to his, eagerly gripping his shirt up by his collar. My instinct to grip his shirt tighter and pull him closer was reawakened by the taste of his sweet lips. I could feel his strong arms wrapping snugly around my waist, pulling me closer. Sounds of contentment were escaping from his lips as he eagerly kissed me back, just as desperate for me as I was for him.

I truly was in heaven.

I became distracted by a strange noise to my left. It sounded like static, as if someone had turned on a television in here.

Seth and I turned toward the direction of the noise. Instantly, I became captivated by a static image that was playing, like a television that was floating in midair.

The static changed, and numbers began counting backward from five…four…three…two…one.

A movie started to play, centering on a familiar-looking young couple. It was clear that the woman was pregnant. She appeared distressed, holding on to her rounded belly. The man held on to her tightly, helping her through what looked like a hospital entranceway.

The scene changed, focusing on the woman. She was soaked with sweat. It glistened on her cheeks and dripped from her hair. She panted and screamed while she clutched the rails of the hospital bed she was lying in. The man paced back and forth just outside the room, in front of gray double doors, anxiously wearing a path into the floor.

The doctor leaned in, and the wail of a newborn baby echoed all around me. I blinked, and leaned forward when I started to realize the young couple was my parents. The doctor held up the tiny screaming infant and I gasped in shock. I'd just witnessed my own birth; that baby was me.

Images from my life began unfolding before my eyes. One by one, I relived it all. My heartaches, and my struggles. My triumphs, and my milestones. Each image unfolding faster than the one before it, right up to my collapse in the woods, which I now knew was my death.

Before I had a chance to react, my vision went askew suddenly. I became very dizzy, and started to sway backward. I felt Seth's arms tighten protectively around me as a flood of information came rushing into my mind all at once like a wild torrent.

I was Veronica Edwards when I was on Earth, but that was not my real life. My real life is here; my true name is Harmony.

The bizarre television quickly inverted on itself, disappearing, and then all was silent. Earth's effects had completely worn off, and I could now remember who I really was.

Not all of my reality had sunk in right away. I slowly began to realize that my hands were still gripping tightly

Enlightened

on a soft cotton T-shirt, so I turned back around. Instead of the chin-length, jet-black hair and green eyes I was expecting, I was greeted by short, sandy-blond hair, and my brown eyes met his blue.

The moment our eyes met, I went into shock. Because it wasn't "Seth" sitting there anymore. It was a guy from my class named Kaleb.

I jumped up, startled, quickly releasing my grip on his shirt, and removing my arms from around his neck. I stumbled back in my haste, catching my foot on my robe, flipping myself backward over the cot.

Kaleb stood up quickly. He leaned over the cot, trying to offer me his hand.

"Harmony, are you all right?"

Am I all right? As I stared into his eyes, I couldn't help questioning this too. During my acrobatics over the cot, and as I sat there on my transition-room floor, countless memories from past lives on Earth, along with my life here, continued to fill my mind.

Situations that happen here are not forgotten simply because we go to Earth. More often than not, we pick right back up where we left off.

I started to become angry as tiny details began to fall into place. I'd been angry with him before I left, and I was remembering why.

Unexpected death, also known as "accidental death," whichever you would like to call it, isn't all that uncommon. We've all become victims of it at one point. With the way Earth is set up, no one can completely control the things that occur there, so it does happen occasionally.

See, there is the key word…*occasionally*.

Most wouldn't see this as a big deal, but for me it was. I'd died accidentally more times in a row recently than I would really care to admit. It was occurring to me that I'd died young —*again*. Accidents do happen. But dying over and over unexpectedly the way I had was not normal.

All of those times had had one thing in common. *Well*…more like *someone*. I was mad at him before the life of Veronica Edwards for all those accidental deaths, and he knew this. And I was just as furious now regarding this one. I couldn't recall Kaleb being involved with my death this time, as he was in the others. But I couldn't dismiss the fact that it had happened again, and he was here now. I felt like there had to be a connection somehow. I stood up from the floor, not bothering to take his hand.

"*You!*" I pointed right at him. "This is *your* fault!" I snapped at him.

Confusion quickly swept across his face, and he took a few steps backward. "My fault?" he questioned, sounding surprised.

"YES, *your fault!*" I continued to point angrily at him.

He looked down at the floor, his eyes shifting from one side to the other as he searched his mind for the

Enlightened

possible answer. His brows were heavily creased when he finally looked back up at me.

"What's my fault?" he asked, sounding more confused than before.

"It happened again!" I threw my hands up. I was so mad.

"Harmony, what are you talking about?" It was clear in his tone that he was growing frustrated.

"I'm home early again! I know you had something to do with this, *didn't you?!*" I shook my finger at him.

"No, how could I?" he huffed, defensive. "I was already here when you died."

I could see his point, but I wasn't letting him off that easy. He was here now, in my transition room. As far as I was concerned, I'd died young again, and with all those other accidental deaths this couldn't be just a coincidence. Perhaps he'd done something while I was asleep? That had happened to others before.

"What did you do?!" I shouted at him with clenched fists.

"I didn't do anything!" he shouted back.

Which now begged the question, "Why are you here?" My tone was bossy and I crossed my arms. *This should be interesting*, I thought to myself. This isn't Earth. Lying is impossible here. He wouldn't be able to lie his way out of *this* like he could there.

"Luke told me to come," he replied simply.

Billie Kowalewski

I was shocked, and I'm sure it showed.

Luke is my spirit guide. A spirit guide is very much like a teacher. When I go to Earth he stays behind watching over me, and helps to guide me through everything I experience there. Then once I'm home he helps me with understanding all the lessons I encountered so I'm less likely to repeat them.

Why would he do this to me? I wondered. I had made it very clear to Luke how I felt about all of this before the life of Veronica Edwards. He knew how mad I was about all of those accidental deaths, and he knew I was avoiding Kaleb because of them. Of all the souls he could have had help transition me back to reality, he picked the one he knew I was angry with. None of this made any sense. He was my guide and was supposed to be on *my* side.

I pressed my fingers against my temples and shook my head, as if it ached like it would on Earth. Trying to understand what Luke was thinking, I sighed out of pure frustration. "And why would he do that?"

"Because I am in love with you," he replied.

I was stunned. He caught me so off guard. Did he really just say that? Perhaps I didn't hear him correctly. "What?"

Kaleb carefully studied the expression on my face before trying again. I'm not sure exactly what he saw there, but his stance made him look like he was facing a

Enlightened

wild animal and was trying to figure out whether or not he had to run.

He took a breath before trying again. "Harmony, I'm in love with you." His voice sounded shaky and unsure.

This was not what I was expecting at all. After everything that had happened between us, that was the last thing I wanted to hear from him. I felt betrayed and angry, and more confused now than ever. But worse than that, I felt exhausted from just waking up from Earth, still dealing with him, and this whole situation. I lost it.

"Enough!" I snapped at him. "Get out!"

His eyes were wide, and he just stood there, frozen.

I narrowed my eyes at him. "Get…out…*Kaleb*," I told him sternly with clenched fists.

He looked away, trying to hide the pain as it quickly moved across his face. I watched as he faded away, disappearing before my eyes.

Chapter 3

It became eerily quiet in my transition room. Normally, we are required to sit and wait for our guide to come and check on us. They look us over, answer any questions we may have after Earth, making sure we transitioned well, before they release us to go home.

I was *way* too angry to deal with any of that.

I closed my eyes, caring very little about the rules, and allowed the image of my home to fill my mind, to take me there.

I felt the shift in the atmosphere as it changed. The stark quiet was quickly replaced by the sound of a stream flowing by. A woodsy pine fragrance filled the air, greeting me like a warm welcome as I breathed in. I wiggled my toes, feeling the mossy soil under my bare feet. I opened my eyes, filled with relief to be home.

Yes, I live in a forest. I can feel your questions starting to surface as I continue through the story. I know you have a lot of questions about home, and I promise to do my best to answer as many of them as possible as we move along. Please try to understand that, because of

Enlightened

reasons that are unknown to you right now, I won't be able to answer them all.

Obviously, there are a few things about home that are very different from Earth. We have unlimited use of our imagination here. We can use it in ways that your Earth mind won't be able wrap itself around. We use it to create things, to live, and to travel. Exercising your imagination on Earth is a highly underestimated but important part of your journey. Never stop using it.

Naturally, not everyone lives in a forest. Some do, some don't. Each one of us has a home that fits us and what we like. I like living in the woods. I find peace and tranquility here that I cannot get anywhere else, and that's why I picked it. It suits me. If I ever feel like it, I can change it to something different. Every single soul here lives in a home that suits them, just like you would. Would you like a beach or a tropical island? Or maybe you'd love a simple raised ranch, or a huge castle? The sky's the limit.

Now where was I?

I was so mad. When I opened my eyes, I began hastily pulling on the gold rope that holds my robe closed. As far as I was concerned, in that moment, I was done with school. So done, in fact, that there was a good chance I was never going back. As I opened the robe and started to shrug it off my shoulders, I was quickly reminded of what I'd chosen to wear under it. A black T-shirt and a pair of blue jeans. The T-shirt was a present from my spirit guide, Luke, and had the logo "The Legendary 7" printed across the front in shiny silver. The letters and the number on the shirt were jagged, making them resemble lightning bolts. The Legendary 7 is the name of the coolest nightclub here. Only the best rock bands that have ever existed get to play there, and Luke just so happens to be the proprietor. I was so thrilled when he first gave this to me. Seeing it right now, though, I felt like it was the icing on top of a very crappy cake.

Feeling very mad, I took that robe, crumpled it up, and chucked it to the ground. I stomped my way over to an enormous flat rock that was wedged up against a tall oak on the bank of the stream and sat down. I felt so relieved to be home, and that I was able to travel by thought to get here. If I were stuck using any of Earth's usual limited methods right now, I think I'd scream. I hugged my knees to my chest, still fuming, and just stared down at the water. It's a common misconception on Earth that "home" is this magical oasis, one overflowing with blissful never-ending happiness, where nothing ever goes wrong. Sure, it is much better than Earth in many ways, but it is not without its own set of difficulties. With the amount of diverse personalities constantly mingling and interacting with each other, who don't always agree, there can and will be problems. I'm sorry I have to be

Enlightened

the one to break it to you: you can't escape that kind of thing here either.

I couldn't stop thinking about this whole situation. But my problems with Kaleb seemed trivial now compared to what Luke had just done. Why in all of heaven would my guide do this to me? Why would he send someone he knew I was angry with to help transition me back to reality? No one I know would want to be woken up like that, and certainly not me. Despite my problems with Kaleb from before the life of Veronica Edwards, this was the part that bothered me the most. I felt betrayed in the worst way by my own guide. The soul who is supposed to be looking out for my best interest. The one who knows me inside and out. The one I trust with all of my most intimate secrets, and who is supposed to be watching over me. That's what a spirit guide does. They take care of you. They help steer you in the right directions, and guide you through everything. Both here, and especially on Earth.

Luke isn't what most on Earth would expect a spirit guide to be like anyway, and he certainly doesn't fit the stereotypical description either. Most on Earth would picture long white beards, flowing robes, and wise old men. I know I can't speak for all the spirit guides here, but I don't know too many guides who do fit that depiction. All the spirit guides here are just as unique as the souls they guide. They have their own likes and dislikes just like anyone else, and, naturally, their own sense of style.

Luke definitely does have his own style. While most of us travel to the school by thought, he rides up on a black motorcycle with orange flames down the sides. He's often tying back his long dirty-blond hair as he's coming up the front steps of the school, because he typically prefers to wear it down. He wears tight-fitting T-shirts, which are usually black. A chrome-plated angel-wings belt buckle shines brightly from the waist of his blue jeans, too.

While this in itself would be enough to define Luke as a unique individual, it is his towering size and bulky, muscular physique that sets him apart from the rest of the guides, making him seem rather intimidating at first. I know I felt this way when I first met him. Of course, that quickly changed once I began working with him. He is the wisest soul I know, and is how I learned to never judge a book by its cover.

Normally, I feel that Luke is an outstanding guide. He and I have always worked well together, and have an excellent relationship. That's a big factor in why I have always done so well in school. It is his dedication and his unwavering support that has always made the difference. This has always been the way up until my problems with Kaleb, and all those accidental deaths started. But

Enlightened

as of right then, still feeling the sting from his possible betrayal, I was having my doubts.

"I think someone I know is in need of a few classes."

I glanced up, and Luke was standing just a few feet away, glowering at me. His big muscular arms were crossed and maxing out the sleeves on his snug-fitting black T-shirt.

I let out an exasperated sigh. I knew it wouldn't be long before he showed up. I should have figured as much. Fat chance he'd ever let me get away with escaping a situation like this without talking about it at some point. I was still just way too mad and wasn't ready to yet.

I narrowed my eyes at him. "Me too," I snapped, my tone snotty and dripping with sarcasm. "When Kaleb finishes, let me know how he did."

Luke's heavy black boots clanked loudly against the rock, echoing through the trees as he started to walk toward me. He was staring me down with his eyebrows raised in disbelief, not saying a word.

"He has a lot to learn," I added, breaking the silence.

He let out a quick, disbelieving chuckle. "*Oh-ho*, and you don't?" he barked back.

"No, I don't," I stated with confidence.

"I'll be the judge of that," he replied. Looking me in the eyes, he started ticking the list off on his fingers. "I think we'll start with, Compassion and Understanding…The Dangers and Illusions of Jumping to Conclusions…It Takes Two…*oh*, and let's not forget, Anger Management."

I rolled my eyes and groaned. "I don't need classes."

He just glared at me.

I pounded my fists on the rock. "I am a good student," I huffed at him.

"Your behavior in your transition room a moment ago says otherwise."

I stood up from the rock and crossed my arms, staring back at him in disbelief. "*Oh*…like you had no role in any of that!" I snapped at him.

He narrowed his eyes in confusion. He seemed surprised by my accusation.

"Of all the souls you could have sent to help transition me back to reality, you picked the one you knew I was angry with… Why didn't you just send Anna? I know she's home. If you had just sent her, this wouldn't have happened… What were you thinking?"

"I was thinking my student would conduct herself in the levelheaded, compassionate way she is known for, no matter who I send."

"It's hard to stay levelheaded when one of your classmates is constantly creating situations that cause your *untimely death*."

It was during this sentence that I noticed a slight shift in Luke's eyes. I've known Luke long enough to know when he's dodging answering a question, and this

Enlightened

was certainly the case. This is a common tactic used here, because once we are home, we are not capable of lying like we can on Earth. Yes, that's right, lying is impossible here. Souls will use a different truthful answer to avoid giving the actual one. Most of the time, it's just the guides who do this. They want us to learn and discover things on our own, in our own time, the way that we are meant to. Knowing full well that he just did this had me really paying attention now.

Now, I know what you're thinking: "But isn't *that* lying?" Do you remember what I said in the beginning? *There's always an exception to every rule.* This a prime example of that.

If you do decide to press on a little harder, you will get the correct answer. Just make sure you are ready for it before you do. Sometimes the truth can be a hard thing to handle.

Luke continued his effort to misguide me away from why he'd truly sent Kaleb.

"There are two sides to every conflict; both always have their faults," he replied.

"You're kidding me right now, *right?!* How can you think this?" I asked him. Still really mad, I tossed my hands up. "I didn't start any of this… Surely, you can see that. You were there when this whole thing started…"

✦ ✦ ✦

We sat poised with our legs crossed in a wide circle on the grass, under the shade of an enormous maple tree in the center of our classroom. Luke's favorite setting for when it's his turn to lead our discussion. It was me and the seven souls that make up the rest of my class: Anna, Gwen, Jaire, John, Kaleb, Maggie, and Robin. These seven individuals always end up playing some type of supportive role in my life on Earth, just like I do with them. Usually the role will be some type of family member, or really close friend. Yes, you have this too. Though they will come in and out of your life at different points, most of the souls who are in your class surround you now. They are your support system, helping you through your toughest challenges, all while you are helping them with theirs. I'm sure if you gave it a little thought, you could figure out which ones they are.

Behind us are nine freestanding doors that are arranged in a wide circle. Each door is decorated in a manner that suits the soul it is intended for. Mine is weathered blue with black wrought-iron hinges. Each door leads to our own personal room for going to Earth, except for one. The ninth is an open doorway that leads to a courtyard. When you look through the doorway from our classroom, it just looks like a doorway to the night sky with its darkness and twinkly stars. Once you walk through it, though, it's a whole other matter, which we will discuss later.

Enlightened

We had all just finished another life on Earth. A few of us were more successful than others. I was the one who'd had the most success. My classmates were convinced that I was on some type of lucky streak, because this was not always the case for me. Not that long ago, I struggled with life on Earth just like the rest of them. One life in particular scared me so bad I almost quit school entirely. Then Luke talked me into trying one last time. I was so afraid before that next life that when it was time to go I kept repeating to myself "*I have to be stronger, I have to be braver,*" over and over in my thoughts. To my surprise, in that next life, I actually was.

It was after that life that I recall making the connection between what happened on Earth and what I was telling myself to do. It was as if I remembered to be, I recall thinking. Then I connected something that Luke was constantly telling me over and over: there is always an exception to every rule. Up until this point, I believed that, as with so many others, the barrier blocked everything. So I decided to test this theory and tried it again. Except this time I concentrated on something else that I wanted to do, and then that worked. Over time, I began to realize that the barrier doesn't block everything, and with Luke's help, started inventing new ways of getting the information I needed to be successful in life. Each time I went to Earth after that became easier, and easier. So after yet another successful life on Earth for me, they were all curious. And because they asked, I was explaining how I was doing it.

"If you concentrate hard enough on what you want to achieve on Earth before you leave here, you can pull it through the barrier and make it happen," I told them.

They were all looking at me with doubt in their eyes. It was obvious that this was not the answer they were expecting. It was too simple sounding. It was clear from their faces that they did not agree, but I held my ground.

"That can't be," Robin said.

Her tone made her statement sound more like a question, or maybe she was thinking this but accidentally said it out loud. Though I'm not quite sure. I was surprised that she spoke up as quickly as she did. Robin is the shyest one in our group, and usually avoids conflict however possible. She tends to go along with what others think or want, trying to avoid problems. Which doesn't always work. This is probably the biggest reason she has such a hard time on Earth. Robin is also our musician. Her door to Earth is white and covered in musical notes. She has the ability to be able to play any instrument handed to her, and she writes beautiful songs. A gift that would shine more if she would let it.

She toyed with strands of her long, curly ginger hair as she continued to speak. "If it was that easy, everyone would already be doing it," she added.

Enlightened

"But that's how I have been doing it," I said with a light shrug. "Seriously...I just concentrate on what I want to do on Earth before I leave here...then when I get down there I can't help thinking about it often. I can never remember where the thoughts come from, or why I am thinking them. But they end up bugging me so much that I end up doing it just to shut it up."

Jaire started laughing. "There's no way that's what you're doing!" he blurted out. "The barrier makes that impossible!"

He's the tall, thin one with the short, wavy dark-brown hair. He's also our carpenter, which is evident from his door as well. According to Jaire, his door is made of "*solid hardwood cherry*" and has "*a rich honey-stain finish.*" He is also the comedian of our group—or so he thinks—usually cracking jokes at my expense. For once, he actually sounded serious.

"No it doesn't." I shook my head. "Harder, yes. But impossible, no."

"Maybe she's onto something?" Gwen spoke up.

She is the slender petite one, with the long blond braid, and she is also my closest friend. I can always count on her, no matter what. Her door to Earth is teal and is covered from top to bottom with black flowers and paisleys. "It's not like any of us have ever tried to do anything like that before. If Harmony says that's how she's doing it, and it works, I think it might be worth trying next time."

Gwen looked over at me and smiled wide. "I got your back, chickie! Love ya!"

I smiled back. "Love you too," I said, and then we high-fived each other.

"No one has really told us much about the barrier... actually, it's been next to *nothing*," Anna added.

She's the tall one with the long, straight black hair and wide hazel eyes. She is also our artist. She paints and sews, making clothing and furniture beautiful. She is also a mother type; she takes care of all of us, and has been a mother figure to me many times on Earth. Her door is an interesting mix of reds, greens, and yellows. Sections of paint on the door have been rubbed away to allow different colors of paint to shine through each other. "All any of us ever knew is that when we get to Earth we won't be able to remember this place or who we are. Even if that's possible, it would be extremely hard to do. I'm sorry, Harmony, I can't say that I'm not a little skeptical too."

I smiled at her sympathetically. "It's okay."

I could tell that John and Maggie still weren't sold on how I was doing it either. John is the stockier one, with short light-brown hair and round freckled cheeks. John is similar to Robin in the way that he tends to avoid conflicts, and often has a hard time on Earth as well. He is not shy like Robin is, but tends to run from even the tiniest amount of distress. He reads a lot, too, and frequently has his nose buried deep in some type of science-fiction novel. His door looks like it came out of a spaceship. It's made of shiny silver metal, and trimmed all the way around in rivets. A keypad is in place where the knob should be.

Maggie is a whole different ball of wax. Putting it mildly, she can be a strong personality. Her door is made of obscured beveled glass, with a sleek black lever handle. She tends to be competitive in everything, from sports to the latest trends. She wears a lot of athletic clothing, and always has her strawberry-blond hair in a tight ponytail. She and John hang out a lot, and typically side with each other.

Not surprisingly, Maggie was the one who spoke up. "I think you're probably just mistaking what is really going on for this whole"—she paused for a moment as she searched for the right words—"*concentration thing.*" She waved her hand dismissively as she spoke. "I just can't see how that would work either."

"So let me get this straight," Kaleb interrupted suddenly. He put his hand up, cutting off my chance to reply to Maggie. His door looks like it is made from old wood planks that are fastened together lengthwise, and is arched at the top. A small circular window is in the center. Kaleb has a strong, passionate nature, and is often overwhelmed by his emotions, especially on Earth. Like John and Robin, he tends to avoid conflicts too, but to a much lesser degree than they do. Every once in a while,

Kaleb will find something that he feels strongly for, and will speak up about it. So naturally, I was pleasantly surprised by his interruption, and hopeful that he was lending his support.

He combed his fingers through his wispy, feathered sandy-blond hair before looking me square in the face and continuing, "So you're saying that if I concentrate hard enough, I can do anything that I want?"

Immediately, I felt disappointed. His tone had a skeptical edge, just like the rest of them.

I smiled warmly at him anyway before I replied, "Yes."

"And you're certain of this?" His eyes were narrowed and still locked on mine, and it was making me a little uncomfortable. I felt like someone who was undergoing questioning in a police station down on Earth.

"Yes, very," I replied.

"Can you use this method of yours in *other ways*?" His tone had a teasing edge to it, and he was trying to stifle a smirk.

I was on full guard now, not quite sure where this line of questions was leading. "What do you mean?"

"Well…I was wondering if you can do this to find people on Earth?"

Immediately, I was intrigued by his question. I pressed my fingers to my lips while I thought about what he'd asked. I had never thought about doing that before. So far, I had been able to achieve so much on

Enlightened

Earth by simply concentrating on what I wanted to do that I didn't see why this wouldn't be possible. Perhaps you could find someone on Earth if you thought about them hard enough.

"…because there have been countless times where we didn't find each other on Earth before," he added, interrupting my thoughts.

"I can't see why you couldn't," I replied.

He rose to his feet from the floor with a noticeable bounce and smiled. "I think this would be an excellent test!" he said, facing the group.

"What would be?" I asked him. My brows were narrowed slightly in curiosity.

"You say that we can do anything we want on Earth as long as we concentrate hard enough before we leave here…*right*?"

"Yeah."

"Well then…*come find me*," he said on an exhale. He smiled at me, placing his hand on his chest, and then bowed. "If Harmony finds me then we'll know what she is saying actually works."

Jaire and John exchanged a quick glance and then immediately started clapping, both of them appearing to be very impressed with Kaleb's idea. Jaire stood from the floor, smiling and continuing to clap. "That is an *excellent* idea, my friend!"

"Thank you," Kaleb replied with a smug smile, and then they bumped their fists together. I'm sure you can tell by their exchange that Jaire is Kaleb's best friend.

Everyone exchanged quick glances with each other, but all eyes were focused mainly on me as they waited for my decision. I didn't see the problem in trying what he had asked. If concentrating on finding Kaleb on Earth worked and I did find him, and that would help to prove that my method did work, then why not? It would only serve to benefit all of them in the long run anyway. I glanced around at the faces of my classmates, one by one, and smiled at each one of them. It was my job to help them on Earth, just like it was theirs to help me. I would like to think they would do the same for me if the tables were turned.

I glanced up at Luke, who was just standing by, quietly watching all of this unfold. If I didn't know better I could swear that he was stifling a smirk too. "Do you have any objections?" I asked him.

"*Nope*…not at all," he replied coolly.

I rose from the ground to my feet. Smiling, I held out my hand to Kaleb. "Challenge accepted." He placed his hand in mine and we shook on it. "…You have yourself a deal."

Chapter 4

KALEB AND I STOOD IN the center of our classroom, surrounded by the rest of the souls in our class. We were all dressed properly in our standard-issue white silk robes, secured at the waist with a gold-braided rope, a tradition held here since going to Earth began long ago. We are only required to wear our robes when we are going to Earth; casual attire is permitted the rest of the time.

Though the doors in our classroom will always remain the same, our surroundings are changed before each time we use it. Instead of being under an enormous maple tree like the last time, we were now in a wide-open field of tall grass with snowcapped mountains in the background. A soft breeze was blowing through, providing serenity before we embarked on our next journey.

The decision to go ahead with our challenge had been made, and now Kaleb and I were discussing the finer details. Since I had experience in achieving what I want on Earth by simply concentrating on what I wanted to do, I was explaining to Kaleb how to do it so we had a better chance at success in finding each other once we were on Earth. Squaring this up now was important if we wanted it to work, because once we were there, we wouldn't remember that this conversation ever took place.

"It's simple really…all you have to do is think about finding me. *Really* concentrate on it, especially once you're on the cot…that's when it's most important…and try not to think about anything else. If you think about something else it may not work as well."

Kaleb's expression was serious, and his arms were crossed. "Don't worry, I will."

"And just to be on the safe side, I will concentrate on finding you. I'm thinking since we are both concentrating on the same thing, there's *no way* we're gonna miss."

"You really think this is gonna work?" he asked. His skeptical tone was back, but I shrugged it off.

"Of course I do… I'll bet we find each other within the first ten years," I said with a confident grin. "If you concentrate on what you want before you leave here, you can accomplish *anything*."

All of the doors opened, signaling that it was time to go. I turned around and started walking toward my room, as did the others.

"See you soon," Kaleb called after me. I turned around and he was standing at the foot of his door. A wistful expression was in his eyes.

I smiled back at him. "Just concentrate on it… I will find you," I assured him.

Enlightened

As he turned and entered his transition room, he muttered something. It kind of sounded like *hope so,* and then he closed the door behind him. I shook my head, dismissing what I thought I had heard.

"Harmony, it's time," Luke called from behind me.

I walked into the bright, stark-white transition room, closing the door behind me, and hopped up onto the cot. Playfully swinging my legs, I looked up and smiled at Luke. "Okay, let's do this."

Keeping up my end of our deal, I lay back on the cot, thinking about finding Kaleb. I held his face in my mind and kept repeating "*I have to find Kaleb*" over and over in my thoughts.

Luke smiled at me. "Have fun," he said with a wink. He waved his hand over me. "And remember…I'll be watching you."

How exactly we travel to Earth is shrouded in secrecy. All we really know is that when it's time, we go to sleep, and when we are done, we wake up. That's it in a nutshell. I wish I could tell you some other, fancier, more interesting way that it happens. Like we're shoved down some rainbow-colored rabbit hole, sliding down through a long, winding kaleidoscope tunnel. Then shrunk down to the size of a grain of sand, and then shoved into a baby or something. To me that would be way more interesting. Sadly, as far as I know, that's not what happens.

Billie Kowalewski

In the interest of keeping this story at a reasonable length—and not boring you with countless past lives—I have chosen to share with you the more relevant parts of our story. Just the accidental deaths, and some of the reactions from my classmates. Don't worry, we will explore what happens after a life later in this story, but just one. I know if it were me reading a story like this, no matter how long or short they were, I would be drooling all over myself and falling asleep if I had to read through ten entire past lives. Plus all the lengthy discussions and classes that go along with them afterward. *Boring*! That would be way too much, and I have zero interest in boring anyone that way. So without further ado…*here we go*.

✦ ✦ ✦

Sarah Shaw
May 1875, Georgia, USA

Today seemed like as good a day as any other, but slightly better. The sun was shining brightly through the tall windows of our quaint little schoolhouse. The weather was warm too, which always made me happier. I smiled as I placed my pencil in the groove at the top of my desk,

Enlightened

feeling pretty confident about the quiz I'd just finished. I glanced over at my friend Clara, who was sitting in the seat next to me. She had a look of serious concentration on her face, and a strand of her blond hair in her mouth. She was chewing away on it while she busily scribbled on her piece of paper, figuring out the math problems the teacher had written up on the blackboard.

I glanced around the room, checking on the six other students in our grade who were taking the same quiz. I quickly became disappointed that the only other student finished was Jacob, the new kid who had started today. I groaned to myself as quietly as I could, not wanting to upset the teacher. She had a tendency to react harshly to even the slightest interruptions.

The teacher had told us that once we were all finished with our quiz we would be dismissed for the day. One would think this little fact would be enough to motivate them to finish their quiz faster. I know it certainly motivated me.

I started bouncing my foot while I waited, growing more impatient by the second. *Why do I have to wait for everyone else to be finished before I can be dismissed?* I wondered. It would have been nice to be able to leave ten minutes ago instead of wasting more time just sitting here doing nothing. Out of pure boredom, I started looking for patterns in the cracking plaster walls.

Billie Kowalewski

I became excited when out of the corner of my eye I noticed Clara suddenly place her pencil at the top of her desk. We both looked at each other at the same time and smiled wide, and then my boredom vanished. Clara was, without a doubt, my closest friend ever. I couldn't imagine what my life would be like without her in it. She and I had been such close friends for so long that we seemed to have a way of telling each other things without ever speaking a word. And I could tell by the gleam in her eye that we were getting into some type of trouble right after school.

The other students finished, and the teacher finally dismissed us. I quickly gathered up my books and my lunch pail and then headed out the door as fast as I could. Normally I would wait for my friend, but I was slightly afraid that the teacher might change her mind.

I sat on a rock by the horse trough while I waited for Clara. A few leaves from the oak trees that hung above my head had fallen in, and a small black beetle was clinging to the edge of one of the leaves. I watched as the little guy struggled to climb aboard the leaf, and then, once he did, start floating around the trough. My mind was quickly swept away, and I was now imagining the beetle on his own little green-leaf boat. I was imagining what it must be like for the beetle. How the leaf boat must be so big to him. Not to mention the horse trough. That must seem like a lake to him too. I wondered if

Enlightened

the current in the water seemed faster to him at his size than it did to me as he floated by. I started dragging my fingers through the water to change the direction of the current while I was now imagining myself as the beetle.

I leaned forward a little and my eyes refocused as I caught my reflection in the water. Strands of my brown hair had come loose from my braid and were curling up around my face from the humidity. Instead of focusing on fixing my hair, like most other girls would do, my thoughts drifted off again. I was seeing the clouds floating by overhead, reflected by the water in the trough, and then a strange feeling suddenly came over me that things were about to change. I shook my head, dismissing that strange thought as soon as it happened. My imagination was seriously out of control lately. I often find my mind wandering off to parts unknown every day— especially in school—and it always gets me into trouble.

A few students were coming down the stairs of the little red schoolhouse and Clara was right behind them.

"Sarah!" She had a huge grin as she ran over to me. "Everyone is going over to the bluffs right now…do you want to go?"

Going to one of my favorite places…with one of my favorite people…why did she even think she had to ask? Of course I did!

I smiled at her. "Yeah, sure."

Billie Kowalewski

The bluffs were a level grassy field on the edge of a very high cliff that overlooked a beautiful ravine. One of the greatest views in our area, and a very popular place for picnics and bonfires.

Clara and I strolled happily along the dirt road toward the bluffs, talking casually. We chatted happily about the fact that we were having such nice weather, and we talked briefly about the math quiz we'd just taken as well. Clara was convinced she didn't do very well, and naturally, I reassured her that she probably did just fine. Of course, neither one of us can resist sharing a little gossip along the way, too.

"So the word around town is that his family has *lots* of money," Clara continued. She was giving me the small-town-circulated gossip about the new kid, Jacob, and his family. "His parents owned some kind of bank in New York City and sold it. Now they are retired."

I narrowed my eyes at her. "Why would anyone like that want to retire here?" I couldn't help but question. It didn't make any sense to me. We live in a very underprivileged area. Small farms and limited means are the way of life here. People like that don't come here unless they are collecting taxes.

"Are you sure they are not tax collectors?" I asked her. I was very puzzled by this. Jacob and his family must be *weird* people, I thought to myself.

Enlightened

She laughed at me. "They're not tax collectors!" She started bouncing and skipping as we walked, growing more excited as she continued to talk about the new kid. "They built a huge house on the other side of town too."

"Oh…is that the one at the end of Grove Street?" I asked her.

"Yep, the one with the long winding driveway."

"My father was one of the workers who was helping to build it… He never told me who it was for."

"Well now you know… Did you see Jacob's shoes?!" she exclaimed suddenly, slightly changing the topic. "They were shinier than that ten-cent piece Pa showed me a year ago!"

"I didn't look at his shoes."

"Did you at least look at his face?" She gave me a sideways glance. "He's kind of cute."

All of the boys around here were the same to me. They all wore the same style of brown overalls, and a white cotton long-sleeve shirt. Same short haircut, and they were all usually dirty.

"He's definitely cleaner." I shrugged, indifferent.

"Oh come on, Sarah!" She nudged my shoulder as we continued to walk. "Don't tell me you didn't notice him! I'm your best friend—I'll know if you're lying."

"Honestly, I was very preoccupied with getting out of school early today…*sorry*."

"Well, that figures. He's going to the bluffs too. I overheard Leo and Sam invite him."

"*Ugh*...Sam is going?" I was complaining a little. I didn't really mind Sam, but he could be annoying sometimes. He was a tall skinny kid with dark-brown hair and a big mouth. He found a way to make a joke about everything, and often his jokes were about me. Leo, on the other hand, wasn't so bad. He was a quiet kid with red hair and freckles. He read a lot, and he was always very polite.

"I did say that everyone is going," she reminded me.

"I know...I just didn't really think about it."

She suddenly gave me that sideways smirk again. "How could you not notice those dimpled cheeks? Or his hair!" She was swooning. "His blond hair is speckled with strands of brown...and those eyes!" She started fanning herself. "My, *my*, they are a deep, dreamy blue!"

"Okay, *okay*!" I put my hands up as if to stop her. "He is a little cute," I admitted, before I shrugged. "I'm just not into those fancier types, I guess."

When we finally reached the bluffs and entered the field, I was surprised by how many kids were already here. There were kids gathering wood for the firepit. Some were just standing around talking. A few of the boys, including Leo, Sam, and the new kid Jacob, were running around, tossing a leather ball and tackling each other. Then there were the few brave couples that were

Enlightened

sneaking off into the woods together. I shook my head at them.

I crossed my arms. "They are going to regret that," I whispered softly to Clara.

"*Yep*…they're stupid," she agreed.

Clara and I walked closer to the edge of the cliff to admire the view, being extremely careful not to get too close. The drop to the ground below had to be a good three hundred feet down, or more. Neither one of us liked heights very much, but we did enjoy the view.

I didn't know too many people who didn't like admiring the jagged snowcapped mountains in the distance, or the wide-open sky. White fluffy clouds glided over the canyon, casting shadows on the ground below. Trees that looked like little green puffs grew out of the rocks across from us down along the rock face. Hawks were circling and swooping down into the ravine as they spotted their next meal. The best part was the shimmering blue river that flowed along the bottom.

Clara and I jumped when a group of boys suddenly tackled each other at our feet. Even though we had some distance from the edge, we were still close enough that if someone had knocked into us hard enough, it would have been a bad situation. In our eyes, they'd created a close call.

"*Hey*!" Clara shouted at them, shaking her finger. "Watch what you're doing!"

"You guys need to be more careful!" I shouted at them too.

The boys all started to get up, dusting off their clothes. Sam and Jacob helped Leo to his feet.

"You shouldn't be standing so close to the edge," Sam commented. Unsurprisingly, his tone was quite bossy.

I crossed my arms, staring the boys down. "You guys are idiots… Everyone knows you shouldn't be throwing a ball near a cliff."

"We were being careful. We had already decided that this was the limit. See?" Sam pointed to a line that someone had drawn in the dirt. "This is our line. It's not our fault you're standing on it."

"*Fine.*" I rolled my eyes. Already I was sick of arguing with him. "Clara and I will move."

Clara and I were just about to walk away when Jacob suddenly spoke up.

"That's a pretty dress you're wearing," he said.

I was surprised to find that he was staring right at me with a dazed look in his eyes and a dumbfounded grin. His comment confused me because my dress was nothing special. It was a simple blue dress with little white flowers all over it. The cuffs and collar were made of eyelet lace. My mother had made it for my older sister, and I had gotten it as a hand-me-down two years ago for my fourteenth birthday. Regardless, I smiled and accepted his strange compliment. "Thank you."

Enlightened

"You're welcome." He was beaming. He placed his hand on his chest before continuing to speak. "…I'm Jacob."

"I'm Sarah," I replied.

He took a few steps forward, holding out his hand to shake mine. I don't know if he was the one leaning too far forward, or if it was me, perhaps it was both. Or maybe he tripped, though I'm not really sure. The moment I took his hand we knocked our heads together hard. The pain sent stars swirling around my head, and blurred out my eyes. He stumbled, tripping over his own two feet, shoving me backward onto the ground. With his hand still in mine, he tumbled over me. He dragged me to the edge, and was now dangling off the cliff. Instantly, I was horrified.

It never ceases to amaze me what people do during intense situations. While I struggled to hang on tightly to Jacob and pull him up—along with trying not to go over the edge myself—kids were coming from everywhere screaming and yelling. They stood there and watched as I grabbed him with my other hand and pulled him with all of my strength. Not one of them thought about helping us in any way. Fear often keeps us from doing the things we know we should.

I felt like I was starting to lose my grip on him. "Climb up!" I was shouting at Jacob. "Find a place to put your feet, and *climb up*!"

"I'm trying! I haven't found anything!" He sounded frantic, and was swinging his legs, trying hard to find a place in the rock to put his feet. Rocking his body the way he was made him feel like he weighed a million pounds. It was hard, but there was no way that I was letting him go.

"I've got you!" I shouted at him. My heart was pounding in my chest. "I won't let go!" I shouted again.

The look in his eyes changed from horror to hope when he finally found a small lip of jagged rock to put his foot on, and he started to climb up.

I pulled as Jacob pushed, both of us struggling but slowly making progress. I managed to get onto my knees, and was working on getting to my feet. Jacob found a lip in the rock for his other foot and was now nearly waist high. I could feel now that it was almost over.

I managed to drag one foot forward, hoping that getting to my feet would give me some leverage to pull him up. Suddenly, the lip Jacob was standing on gave out under his feet from the weight. His eyes went wide and were filled with horror as he fell backward, and pulled me off the cliff with him.

Chapter 5

DYING ACCIDENTALLY DOESN'T COME WITH quite the same fanfare as living a full life would. It's not because nobody cares. It's because it was not expected. Yes, the guides are watching us, but it's not always easy for them to tell. There is always that chance we will survive a fall, a crash, or that bump on the head. It's a lot like watching a movie where the character is all mangled after an accident. You're on the edge of your seat, trying to figure out whether that character is going to make it or not. The best part for them is when you pull through, but sometimes that just doesn't happen. They get the news when you suddenly wake up, and the screen they were watching you from turns to static.

Waking up after an accidental death is naturally very disorienting. You wake up alone—thinking with your limited Earth mind—in a bright, stark-white room with no walls or visible doors, which does not exist where you just came from. You may as well have just woken up on Mars. Panic sets in pretty fast at this point. It isn't until a moment later when your memories return that you realize what's happened. That's about the time when your guide will enter…

…*coward*. (Yes, I'm kidding. I'm sorry, I couldn't resist.)

Again, it's not that nobody cares. The guides have limits that are set on them in regards to how they can interact with us. They have no choice but to wait until our memories return before they can enter our room. Human beings tend to scare very easily. I wish I knew why we are like this as humans. Maybe it's some kind of side effect from the barrier, or a part of how we are meant to learn? That part I don't know, but I do believe that knowledge is power.

Yes, your guide interacts with you all the time. *How* is the only question about this that I cannot answer,—the reason? It's because it all varies widely as to how they do it. What works to guide you will not always work for another. What I can tell you is that they are very creative and inventive when it comes to guiding us in the right directions. This will become evident the more we pay attention.

When I woke up after the life of being Sarah Shaw, I, of course, had no memory of the deal that I had made with Kaleb, or of who "Kaleb" was. I didn't even know that "Kaleb" existed. I had no idea that my real name was Harmony, either. All I knew was that I was in a very strange place, in a white silk robe that I couldn't remember putting on. Somehow I didn't cry or scream, and managed to stay calm the whole time. I couldn't

Enlightened

stop looking around the room, either. I sat there for a while, trying to figure out how anyone would get in or out of this odd place, and wondered how long I would be just sitting here. I did wonder to myself for a bit if I was experiencing some kind of odd blindness, or if my brain was broken. After a while I figured that I was either dreaming or had died. I did remember falling, but had no memory of hitting anything, or of any pain. I also recall feeling rather annoyed and very disappointed right before my memories came back. I was sitting there on the cot with my arms crossed, thinking that the pastor at my church was wrong, and if this was heaven it was far more boring than what he had been describing.

Once my memory returned, and I realized what had happened, I started calling out Luke's name right away.

"Luke!" I shouted into the empty space. "*Luke...*you can come in! I'm aware now!"

Luke appeared in my transition room right away. "Good," he said upon entering. "How are you doing?"

"I'm okay," I assured him.

"Kaleb is here too."

"What?" I was surprised at first, but then memories began to rise to the surface. All at once I remembered everything that happened my last day on Earth. We found each other all right. It was all flooding my mind now. Meeting Kaleb down on Earth as Jacob, the clumsiness, the cliff, and all that transpired between us immediately afterward. I shivered once I got to the memory of Kaleb's wide, panic-filled eyes as we started to fall.

Such mixed emotions were churning within me now. My method of concentrating beforehand on what I wanted to achieve on Earth *did* work for more than just helping me do better at school. It worked for finding people! Naturally, I was thrilled to learn this. The best part was that I'd just proved to my class that you really can pull what you want to through the barrier.

I was envisioning all of us striving for such great things together now, and setting the ultimate example for all the other classes to follow. But then there was this other part—a small part, really—that felt badly. In my quest to prove that my method worked, I may have caused an accidental death. Not just for myself, but for one of my classmates. I didn't know for sure if this was what had happened. There was no way I could have known that my method would do such a thing, if it did. Still, I couldn't help feeling a little bit guilty, and wondered how mad Kaleb might be at me.

I was already starting to cringe over the possible anger that could be awaiting me.

"Oh, Lukie…" I glanced up at him with a sheepish expression. "…Now I feel terrible."

He looked at me with his brows creased a little. "What for?"

Enlightened

"I'm thinking that it might be my fault that we are home already."

"Accidents happen, Harmony." He sounded reassuring, but I still felt bad.

"I just wanted to prove that my method works. I didn't mean for us to go home early."

"I'm sure he knows that," Luke said.

"Maybe." I wasn't feeling so sure.

"He did volunteer to help you prove whether or not your method works, remember? I've never known Kaleb to not be understanding or reasonable… I'm sure he's fine."

"*Well*," I said as I hopped down from the cot, "I guess there is only one way to find out."

I focused my eyes on the area across from my cot and imagined my weathered blue door with its lovely wrought-iron hinges, and slowly it appeared, boldly standing out against the bright white room. I opened the door, and stepped out into our classroom.

Kaleb was already leaning against his door when I walked in. Our classroom surroundings had changed to a meadow filled with white flowers, encircled by a forest in autumn. Leaves were falling gently all around us.

He looked like he was lost in thought. He was staring at the ground, with a soft smile on his face. I tiptoed carefully toward him. I felt relieved that he didn't look angry, but was still nervous that he might be. I figured it was smarter to check anyway, just to be sure.

"Are you okay?" I asked him, interrupting his deep thinking.

He looked up at me right away and smiled kindly, just a hint of nervousness in his eyes. "Yes." His brows creased a little. "…I'm sorry about the cliff."

I let out a sigh of relief. I was so thankful he wasn't mad, and wasn't blaming me or my method for our accidental deaths.

"It's okay." I smiled at him sympathetically. It sounded like he let out a sigh of relief too. "Accidents happen." I shrugged at him.

We both stood there quietly for a while. I didn't know what else to talk about, and watching him, I don't think he did either. He kept glancing down at his feet and then back up at me, always smiling, but not saying anything. As the silence continued, it started to become a little awkward, so I started searching my mind quickly for something to say. Like an idiot, I decided to stick with our present topic.

"As you can see now…my method does work." I smiled at him as innocently as I could, folding my hands together in front of me, trying not to appear smug. "We found each other."

He narrowed his eyes in a way that looked playful. "That could have been just luck," he said.

Having high expectations often leads to disappointment. His reply caught me by surprise. Now,

Enlightened

I don't know exactly what I was expecting his response to be, but it certainly wasn't what he ended up saying. I stood there for a moment, a bit speechless, not quite sure how I should proceed, as I processed what he said. I was filled with such disappointment, and just couldn't understand how he did not see that my method worked. When high expectations do turn into a disappointment, it often turns again, becoming anger.

"That wasn't luck…" I was trying to control my tone, but it ended up having a defensive edge to it, and it made me sound bossy. "That was you and me using my method, and it working," I replied.

"*Pffttt*…no…that was a coincidence," he said smoothly.

"That was not a coincidence," I huffed at him. "It worked."

"Do you really expect me to believe after one time that your method was the reason we found each other, over other, more logical possibilities?" he asked, now he was the one with the bossy tone.

"Enlighten me." I crossed my arms. "What other, more logical possibilities could there be?"

"*Well*…fate. We have no control over who we come into contact with down there—and you know this," he said, pointing his finger at me. "Yes, we used your method, but we have no way of knowing which one it was."

"Are you kidding me?" I couldn't believe it. Before I walked out here, I was so nervous about the possibility of him being mad at me. Now I was aggravated with him instead. I'd just proved that my method worked, and had died in that process. We both did. We found each other, like I said we would.

I sighed from the frustration. "Jaire, John, and Gwen were all standing on the cliff when we left. When they get back, we'll just ask them. If they are not convinced, then we'll try it again."

Just then, Jaire's door opened and he walked out. "Oh good…you guys are still here," he said as he closed the door behind him. As he walked toward us, he started chuckling. "*Man*…you two sailed off that cliff!" He made a motion with his hand, gliding it up, and then he whistled as he glided his hand down.

"Shut up, Jaire." I narrowed my eyes at him. "Why are you home already?"

"Snake bite." His brows were creased as he replied and then looked at Kaleb. "What's her problem?"

"She's just mad because I don't think she proved anything," Kaleb replied.

"Proved what?" Jaire asked. Though I could easily tell by his tone that he knew what Kaleb was talking about.

"Her *concentration* thing," he said, doing air quotes. He sounded so arrogant, and it was grating on my nerves. "She thinks it worked."

"It did work," I butted in.

"*Luck*," Kaleb said back.

Enlightened

"There is no such thing on Earth, and you know it," I barked at him.

"I'm gonna have to agree with Kaleb on this one," Jaire interrupted. "That was an awfully big claim you made last class, and one time simply isn't enough to prove you can pull what you want through the barrier," he said, shaking his head gently. "I'm gonna bet *anything* that the others will think so too."

As frustrated as I was with Kaleb, I could see Jaire's point. It was gonna take more than one time to convince all of them.

"Fine." I threw my hands up, and groaned. "We'll do it again."

"*That a girl*." Jaire smiled and gave me a firm pat on the back. "Way to go, making sacrifices for the good of your classmates."

"Is that your way of volunteering this time?" I asked Jaire.

"*Nope*…Kaleb can be the guinea pig again…I'm sure he doesn't mind." He patted Kaleb's shoulder. "Do ya, buddy?"

"Sure, why not." His shrug seemed indifferent. "It's not like it's gonna work *twice*," he challenged, holding up two fingers and staring me down with a smartass grin.

I felt like I was under attack. He was egging me on and I couldn't figure out why. My mind was swimming with questions and possible reasons for the insanity that was currently happening. Maybe he did feel like the rest of them? And maybe he was just doing this to prove that to the class? For what? Some kind of brownie points? As if that kind of stuff really happened here.

I stood there with my fists clenched, wishing that I had just kept my mouth shut when they had asked me why I was doing so well on Earth. Maybe they should all just fend for themselves down there, and I'll just keep doing my own thing like I always have, I thought to myself. I shouldn't have to go to such great lengths to prove myself to anyone. Why should I help any of them if this was the way they were gonna behave? Of course, I did realize that Jaire and Kaleb weren't the only ones in my class. They were just the ones that I was dealing with right now, and they were making me feel like I was backed into a corner. Maybe the others would feel differently and be a bit more open-minded to my idea. This thought made me realize that I was stuck proving myself this way whether I liked it or not. At least until enough of them saw that if they concentrated hard enough, they really could pull what they wanted through the barrier.

Chapter 6

THE NEXT FEW LIVES ON Earth were more of the same thing. Kaleb and I would concentrate on finding each other before we would leave here. Then, after some years would pass on Earth, we would. Not one time did we miss. Every first greeting was basically the same. The second we would get close enough to each other down there, that's when the acrobatics would start. We would slam right into each other, bump our heads together, tripping and flipping over one another every single time. Always somehow causing one of us—mainly me—if not both of us to die.

No matter how far apart they placed us on Earth, Kaleb and I would find each other. It was my theory that using my method made us like magnets—*accident magnets*, as Gwen so kindly put it. We were hurdling toward each other like comets at light speed, coming at each other so fast that we were literally crashing into each other. We gave new meaning to the phrase *bumping into each other*, because in actuality we really were.

It's a unique feeling, being on this end of this odd little situation. I got shoved out a second-story window, and then was lucky enough to snap my neck and be trampled by a horse I'd spooked when I hit the ground. In the next life, I was rolled onto a *very* highly active beehive and then stung to death (no, I am not kidding). Then imagine the surprise I felt in the life after that one, when a certain someone was running with a wallet he'd stolen, and then shoved us both off a train platform into the path of an oncoming train. I still don't know if that person ever got their wallet back.

I'm sure all of this must seem rather disturbing from where you're sitting. I know I would certainly feel that way if I were reading this from where you are. It's quite an interesting perspective for me, being here right now knowing all that I do, versus being on Earth and having the limited knowledge that we are allowed. It really turns things around and sheds a different light on it—don't you think?

With the knowledge of home blocked from our memory, life and death can seem so absolute from the human perspective. Death seems final, bringing with it fear of the unknown, and such anguish to the ones that are left behind.

You know what they say: *hindsight is always twenty/twenty*. Imagine what Earth would be like if this knowledge weren't blocked from our memory. It would certainly change the way we view our lives while we are there. Naturally, if some were armed with this knowledge,

Enlightened

they would be much more adventurous, never taking their life seriously enough to truly learn anything. Life on Earth would take on less meaning. Then again, perhaps knowing our lives do go on would help some to live their life with less fear and appreciate their time there. Maybe they would strive to be better because they know? Isn't having a little knowledge better than no knowledge at all? Something is better than nothing, isn't it? To be able to utilize this knowledge might help propel us forward and help us gain a sense of purpose. If only there were a way to leak some of this knowledge somehow…

Naturally, my classmates were extremely amused by all of this. I've been greeted with rounds of applause, teased about being the clumsiest soul in existence, and a couple of times they were all nice enough to hold up score signs like they were judging an Olympic competition.

They are all very lucky that I love them as much as I do, and have such an excellent sense of humor.

When I walked in after yet another accidental death, this one being an impalement that was quite…*gruesome* (you're welcome, for sparing you from *those* details), I was all done proving myself, and had enough.

My hands were already balled up into fists as I made a beeline straight for Kaleb. "This little competition is over!" I yelled at him in front of the whole class.

He stood up from the floor with a very amused expression on his face. "No, it's not," he replied simply.

"Oh, yes it is!" I pointed my finger angrily back and forth between me and Kaleb. "This is done!"

"Okay, okay, *fine*," he said, putting his hands up in an effort to calm me down. "I don't want you to be angry with me."

I sighed in relief and smiled at him. "Thank you."

"You're welcome." He smiled back.

✦ ✦ ✦

Rachel Ellis
March 1914, Somewhere Over the Atlantic Ocean

There hadn't been a hint of sunshine since we'd left London. A dense fog hovered over the ship from the moment we left. It clung to the boat as if it were following us, warning us all of impending doom.

It was incredibly cold up on the sundeck. I was wearing my good wool coat, my hat and gloves too, but none of this seemed to make any difference. I kept my arms crossed tightly against my chest, trying to keep the heat in, but the frigid air went right through me anyway. I was shivering uncontrollably at times, and my teeth were chattering so hard, I figured it was only a matter

Enlightened

of time before they shattered. As miserable as I was, I felt this was the lesser of two evils. The conditions below deck were far worse.

A lot of people on board were very sick, and had been taken below deck to be cared for. It smelled so horrible down there. The air was humid and thick with the aroma of vomit and waste. There was no real way to escape the smell completely, even being out here. The scent seemed to carry and hit you in the face every time someone opened the door.

Those like me who were not yet sick were waiting out their time up here. We all knew it was only a matter of time before we discovered which one of us was next. To say that this voyage was plagued with illness and depression would be an understatement. Several people had already died, and a few bodies had been tossed into the ocean. I had my doubts that the rest of us would make it to New York alive.

"Travel to America," my mother said to me with a smile before I got on board. "My sweet Rachel...*go get your share of the fortune to be had there!*"

She and my father had saved every penny to send me to America to live with my aunt and uncle. They felt that sending me on this boat alone would be a far better opportunity for their seventeen-year-old daughter than staying with them would be. They were both convinced that the streets there were lined with gold.

Billie Kowalewski

I leaned against the railing, chuckling to myself. My parents' beliefs about America and this trip were ridiculous to me. I shook my head just thinking about it. They told me taking this boat would be wonderful, and that I'd be in America before I knew it. I kept wondering how they would feel if they knew what this trip had turned out to be like for me. Or how they would feel if they knew that this ship seemed to have bigger problems than just a large amount of sick passengers. A lot of things were broken or falling apart. I'd seen boards fastened over broken windows, and ropes holding sections of railing together along some of the stairs. Would they still have sent me off like this if they'd known? Often there are questions without any answers.

I looked down when I felt something touch my ankle. I jumped back, and let out a startled scream when I saw a large rat trying to crawl up my leg. I gave it a good kick, sending it sliding across the deck, and then my body convulsed hard from the cold and revulsion.

Tears began welling up in my eyes as the mounting stress from this horrible trip finally started to take its toll. I turned back toward the water, trying hard to see through the thick fog, and I just let the tears fall. I was hoping that if I looked hard enough I would see the end of this awful journey. I was begging God for a small sign that this would all soon be over.

Enlightened

A couple that was walking past suddenly stopped, and then one of them began retching right behind me. I looked up angrily toward the heavens when I heard the slap of the vomit against the floor and felt its warmth as it sloshed across the back of my legs. I couldn't imagine how this voyage could possibly get any worse.

That was when I suddenly heard him. Between the sobs and the foul heaves of my fellow passengers… someone was singing.

"Row, row, row your boat…gently down the stream… Merrily, merrily, merrily, merrily… Life is but a dream."

My first thought was that he must be crazy. I found his song, and his cheerful tone, to be very offensive, considering the situation. His voice brought with it a strangely familiar irritation, too, that I couldn't quite place and seemed to be hitting every single one of my nerves.

I turned to look for the brave soul that would dare to strike such a match in a place that was vastly overflowing with so much fuel. Boasting such happiness like that amongst such misery seemed like a very foolish idea to me. Perhaps he's an idiot, I thought to myself.

I finally spotted him across the boat. He couldn't have been much older than me. He was strolling carelessly through the crowd as if he were on a pleasure cruise, untouched by the surrounding misery. His hands were stuffed into his pockets. A red scarf was wrapped around his neck and tucked neatly into the dark grey coat he was wearing. The frigid breeze coming off the water gave his cheeks a rosy glow and tousled his short brown hair. He moved as if he didn't have a care in the world, singing away with a smile on his face.

I quickly discovered that I was not the only passenger he was offending. People were starting to become angry and were shouting at him, as he continued to walk through, happily singing his song. I shook my head in disgust when his smile grew, and then he began to sing louder, and added a skip to his step. Clearly, madness was quickly sweeping through this ship.

"Row, row, row your boat! Gently down the stream! Merrily, merrily, merrily, merrily! Life is BUT a dream!"

He must have a death wish, I thought to myself.

A rather big and fiery-looking man with orange hair stepped forward. "Hey, *idiot!*" the man angrily shouted across the boat. "*You looking for a fight?!*" He stood up on a bench and pounded his fists against his chest before pointing his finger at him and shouting some more. "*Because you got one now, goop!*"

The fiery man charged right for him, and the singing man began to run. Chaos ensued, and fights started to break out amongst the other passengers all over the boat. I stood there frozen, not quite sure what to do or where to go hide.

In seconds, I was suddenly backed up against the railing. "Stop!" I started shouting, waving my arms out

Enlightened

in front of me. "*Stop!*" The singing man had turned, looking backward as he ran, and was now charging straight toward me.

He hit the puddle of vomit at full speed, and then he hit me, shoving me hard against the railing. The railing gave way upon impact. The singing man and I were sent flying off the boat into the air, then plummeted into the icy water below.

✦ ✦ ✦

ONCE MY MEMORIES RETURNED, I imagined and opened my door faster than I ever had in my entire existence. I charged into our classroom, and was angry to find that Kaleb wasn't in there yet. I marched right over to his door, crossed my arms, and waited there, fuming.

Kaleb finally opened his door. Panic swept across his face the moment he saw me, and then he quickly slammed the door shut.

"Kaleb, get your butt out here!" I yelled.

I could hear the sound of muffled voices behind his door. Most likely Kaleb's guide, Jack, talking to him. I could only really guess, though, at what they were discussing.

Kaleb's door slowly opened and he quietly walked out, looking down as he did, not making any eye contact. I sighed and rolled my eyes as he continued to stall. He took his time, casually shutting his door as well.

He finally brought his eyes up and looked at me with the most composed, blank expression I had ever seen. He knew he was in trouble.

"Are you kidding me?!" I blurted out angrily, not bothering to control my tone. As far as I was concerned, he'd earned it. I drummed my fingers against my arm and waited for his explanation.

"What?" he asked innocently.

"You know exactly what," I snapped at him. "We had agreed that our competition was over," I reminded him.

"I know." He kept his innocent tone.

"Then what was that?!" I quickly hurled back at him, growing impatient with his brief little answers. "I just got shoved off a boat *by you* in the middle of the Atlantic Ocean, and that's all you have to say?! You had better start talking!"

I watched him take in a breath. "I was doing my own kind of testing."

I gasped. "Excuse me?!"

"Did you really think that I wouldn't?" He said this as if it were something I just should have expected. I was shocked by his audacity.

"You didn't even ask me!" I yelled.

He shrugged. "I didn't think you would mind."

"You should have asked me, Kaleb!"

"I couldn't."

"Why not?!" I demanded.

Enlightened

"Because I wanted to see if it would still work if you didn't know."

"Of course it will work." I threw my hands up. "It always works!"

"It does appear that it worked, didn't it?" He made a funny face, like he was trying to keep himself from smirking. "Of course"—he shrugged nonchalantly—"it was probably just fate again."

"Cut it out!" I yelled at him.

"What?" He seemed very amused by my anger.

"Stop it! You know what! It works! Now, *let's move on*!"

"No," he said with a playful grin.

My eyes were wide. "No?!" I questioned, now more aggravated than ever.

"Not…gonna…happen," he said.

"Why? Why me?!" I demanded.

"Because testing it on someone else might not work as well."

"All the more reason to *pick…someone…else*!" I yelled at him.

He shook his head. "No."

"*Knock it off.*" I screamed with clenched fists.

He narrowed his eyes and leaned in. "How are you gonna stop me?" he challenged, pausing between each word for added emphasis.

My mouth dropped open and I stood there totally stunned. What has gotten into him? There had to be rules against this kind of thing somewhere, I thought to myself. But then I thought, perhaps two can play at this game. Compared to him, I had more experience with pulling the information I needed through the barrier. Maybe I could come up with a way to avoid him somehow, or prevent him from accidentally killing me again. I was already dreading our next encounter on Earth.

Chapter 7

I was at my wits' end with all of this. For whatever reason, Kaleb was fixated on continuing to test my method, while using me as his "guinea pig." And sadly, I was not so successful in trying to avoid him on Earth either. Twice so far I'd tried, and both times, not only did he find me, but I still ended up going home early. I was fortunate enough to be shoved by him out into a busy city street and then get struck by a bus in *two separate lives in a row*! I keep wondering what the odds are of dying the exact same way twice in a row like that is. There is a reason for everything. Perhaps this meant something? It's been very frustrating to say the least.

In the meantime, I was trying my very best to see the bright side in all of this. One of my classmates was using my method. Granted, at the moment it was not doing me any favors, but he was still using it, and learning that it worked. So I guessed that was all that should really matter.

There is way more to life here than just school, of course. Earth does play a very big part in our lives, but that's not *all* we do. Can you imagine if this was the only thing we did? It would be so boring! Some endless circle of going to Earth and just coming home, and then standing in some kind of line, like mindless drones, waiting to do it all over again… *Ahhh! No thanks!* Thankfully, our lives here are not like that at all.

Up until this very moment you have been living with a very limited viewpoint. You can thank the barrier that's hidden deep inside your mind for this. With this in place, you can only see what's right in front of you. You can only remember so much, as well. I, Harmony, am going to temporarily lift this barrier out of the way for you, and show you that there really is more to life than meets the eye.

Welcome home!

Imagine a world with unlimited possibilities, one you can change any time—at your will, whenever and however you choose—with just your mind. Our world is fueled solely by love and our imagination, and nothing else.

Every single thing that is on Earth is here. Of course, there are things here that have not made it to Earth yet. Eventually they will. In the same way everything else has gotten there: within the mind of one of you.

Our world is not only filled with unlimited possibilities, but is also never-ending. You could go a very long time, if you wanted to, travelling our world without ever seeing a single soul. Yes, there are those here who do.

Enlightened

As I touched upon briefly in the beginning, I live in a forest that I imagined. It's filled with everything that I love about being in the woods. It's bursting with a mixture of oak trees and pines. The scent of the pine trees and the earthy soil is amazing. A stream flows through it as well. It runs along the edge of a perfectly placed large, flat rock that is wedged up against a very fat oak tree. It's my favorite spot, and I sit there often.

Of course, there's much more to my forest. I have a path that is made of small light-colored pebbles and lined with bright green leafy ferns. At any time I can veer off the path to explore any parts of the forest that I wish, and I do this all the time. At the end of the path is my hammock bed, which swings from two perfectly placed pine trees.

Across from my bed is a freestanding light-blue door that is wedged between two small boulders, framed with more leafy ferns. This door leads to my washroom, which is fully equipped with a walk-in closet, and before you even ask, no, we don't need a toilet.

Our abilities here will always surpass anything and everything that is currently on Earth, and this will never change. Being able to travel by thought, as I mentioned briefly in the beginning, is an excellent example of this. Another shining example is our ability to communicate by thought as well, or in Earth terms, *telepathically*.

Billie Kowalewski

No one knows why these things are not a part of Earth. Perhaps someone in the universe thought that these abilities would get in the way of us learning what we need to? Or maybe it has more to do with the human fear factor? This I don't really know. Being the unusual thinker that I am, I have noticed one of these abilities does occasionally, from time to time, *leak* through the barrier. Can you guess which ability I am referring to?

If you guessed telepathy, you are the winner! There have been many times when I knew what someone else was thinking when I was on Earth. I've noticed that most of the time this happens with someone I talk to a lot telepathically here. Like Gwen, for example. I can always tell what she is thinking on Earth, no matter what. We often shrug these things off as just a coincidence while we are on Earth, but when we're home we know better. There are other leaks like this too, of course. Like when you travel to a place you've never been before and then you discover you are very familiar with it. Or meeting a complete stranger, and then, after talking with them for just a few minutes, you feel as though you've known them for years. There is a reason you feel this way. Most likely, you have been to that place, and you do already know that person. We carry so much of ourselves down to Earth that these kinds of *leaks* happen all the time. Try to remember, the barrier acts a lot like a coffee filter. It keeps the bulk on one side, while only allowing what is

Enlightened

important through. So just like coffee grounds will get through the filter occasionally, sometimes memories will unknowingly leak out in the same way. This probably has a lot to do with how I figured out so much about the barrier in the first place. I have a tendency to notice little things that most will miss, and I question everything.

Before I show you what you've been missing, I'd like to clarify a little something you have probably been wondering, and that we here tend to forget about. Here, age is defined by knowledge, not by years like on Earth. So to put it in a way you can understand, my classmates and I are the equivalent of someone on Earth who is in their late teens or early twenties. There are many classes here like ours, which are at all different stages of development. So the more we learn, the more we grow. Time is also something that is not measured here either. So no clocks or calendars ever, because our lives here are infinite.

These time and age differences are the reason I condensed our story in the way that I did. If I hadn't, I'm sure I would have lost you long ago. With our lives being infinite like they are here, we can go a very long time between events without anything going on. I do realize that time is of the essence for you. So now that you are *enlightened* about the way life is here, we can move on.

As far as I know, our home is bigger than anything else in existence. I often picture it like a spider web with strands that stretch out far to infinity. The thickest part of the web is always in the center. To me, the center is always the strongest part, because this is where all the strands meet. This is how I view us, and our world as well. Your heart is in the center of your body. It's where your veins meet, pumping life throughout your body, and it gives you strength. In the center of our world is where we are the strongest, and all of our paths will eventually meet. It is where our heart is, too, and we call it Artopia.

Pronounced *are-toe-pee-uh*, it is the only official city here. This is where we all go to find each other, and where we all go to have fun. It has everything you could ever possibly imagine to do here and more. Things like nightclubs, sports venues, concerts, amusement rides, restaurants, games, toys, you name it. If it's fun, and it exists, Artopia is where you will find it. The best part about Artopia is that none of it costs any money. Money is something that only exists on Earth and will never be here.

This is where our next relevant part takes place.

I was lying in my hammock bed, enjoying a well-deserved slumber, when I was awakened by a telepathic call from Gwen…

Harmony? Are you busy? Gwen's voice suddenly echoed through my mind, waking me up.

I was…but I'm not now. What's up? I replied back to her in thought.

Enlightened

I'm sorry I woke you, but Anna just called me. Everybody is going to Artopia to ride the bumper cars. Do you want to go?

Yeah, sure…sounds like fun, I said.

Awesome! She sounded excited now. *I'll meet you there. We're going to the toy store after, too!*

Okay.

I got up once I felt the connection fade, and headed into the washroom to get ready. No, it is not necessary for us to shower and brush our teeth here. Only human bodies need that kind of maintenance. We do not suffer from rotting teeth or other ailments that come from poor hygiene like people on Earth do. We never experience pain, either. However, it is my belief that since we carry so much with us, regularly practicing "Earth like" habits here will give me a better chance of developing them once I am down there. I've had a few bad experiences.

When I was done, I quickly checked myself over in the full-length mirror hanging on the back of my washroom door. I felt quite pleased with my outfit choice. I had picked a modest short-sleeved maroon T-shirt with a V-neck and a simple pair of blue jeans. A very comfortable choice for riding bumper cars. I couldn't complain about my hair either. I had decided to leave my hair alone and let my long, wild brown curls do their thing, spiraling down past my shoulders. I'm more about comfort than appearance, normally. I'm very happy no matter what I look like. Most of the souls here feel the same way I do. One of the many perks of being home. We always look good, and feel great all the time. Your soul is always beautiful.

I walked out of the washroom, shutting the door behind me. Where I was going suddenly sank in, bringing an excited smile to my face. I closed my eyes and inhaled deep, letting my mind go completely blank. I then pictured the grand entrance to the bumper cars in my mind. The entrance was tall, and framed all the way around with little pulsating light bulbs that flashed yellow and purple. At the top was a large arched sign with the words "Soul Collider" painted in purple and gold. I continued to smile and was filling with even more excitement as I held the image in my mind.

Then I heard the sound of a loud bell ringing.

"*Harmony's here*!" a familiar voice shouted. I didn't have to open my eyes to know it was Gwen. "C'mon, Harmony! Hurry up, and get your butt in here! We have to teach Maggie a lesson!"

"Aw…don't be such a sore loser!" Maggie teased.

"I'm not…I just can't get this car to go where I want it to! I'm trying a different one next round!" Gwen replied.

I opened my eyes, and happily ran over to the fence to watch the girls. Poor Gwen was stuck trying to get out of a jam she was in with a few other souls who were

Enlightened

riding, and Maggie was laughing and bumping her. Maggie was totally making it difficult.

"Don't worry! I'll be in the next round as soon as the bell rings!" I yelled to Gwen. I was watching and laughing at the girls when the familiar voices of the boys from my class were suddenly behind me.

"Hey *girls*...we're here, and we're ready to *ride!*" Jaire said as he entered.

"Lemme-at-em!" John exclaimed.

I turned around and was surprised by Kaleb, who suddenly wrapped me in an enormous bear hug, lifting me off the ground. "*Whoa!* Hi guys!" I said mid-squeeze, my eyes bugging out a little too. I did chuckle, though I'm afraid it probably sounded a little awkward. After my last encounter with Kaleb at school, I wasn't expecting any gestures like this at all. It was very confusing.

"Jaire has a surprise!" Kaleb announced happily as he placed me back on my feet.

"What's the surprise?" I asked, and then I started to chuckle. "Did you run out of jokes?" I teased Jaire.

"You wish!" Jaire snapped back, and then he smiled wide. "Hey, Harmony." He held out his arms like he was an airplane. "*Weee...*" He started rocking back and forth, and then quickly bent down. "*SPLASH!*"

"Brat!"

"*You know*...if you had added a somersault before you hit the water, you would've gotten the full ten-point score…instead of the nine and a half I gave you." He snickered. "You were penalized for lack of creativity."

I smacked his arm. "So what's the surprise? Did they discover you're the only soul in existence with a head full of sawdust?"

"Ha, ha, ha! No, smarty pants…I built my own house."

I was surprised, and at the same time impressed. He certainly did have such a way with wood. I should have seen this coming.

"Wow, that's awesome! How come you didn't tell us you were building a house?"

"Because I wasn't totally sure that I could do it. Plus, I wanted it to be a surprise. You should come and see it… It turned out really nice," Jaire replied.

"He's being way too modest," Kaleb butted in, giving Jaire a playful shove. "It's not just nice, it's *amazing*." He sounded more excited about it than Jaire did.

"Don't worry—I figured he was being modest. I do know Jaire. He may have a big mouth, but his creations are always beautiful," I replied.

Jaire blushed. "Kaleb helped me build it. I quickly discovered, building a house is *not* a one-man job."

I smiled at Kaleb. "That's great…I can't wait to see it," I told them both.

"We can all go there later if you want," Kaleb replied quickly.

"I'd love to."

Enlightened

The bell sounded, signaling that the ride was over, and souls were exiting the ride. Robin, Anna, and Maggie remained in their cars while Gwen got up and started walking over to another car.

"Maybe this one will be easier to turn?" she shouted over to me.

The boys and I walked in, and I picked a car next to Gwen. "So was Maggie being…*competitive*?"

"That's putting it mildly. She's just being herself, as usual." Gwen narrowed her eyes playfully toward Maggie. "That girl *needs* to get bumped!"

"You take the right side, I'll take the left!" I exclaimed.

"Let's get her!" Gwen looked all around with a playfully confused expression. "Why won't they ring that bell yet?!"

As I sat there waiting for the remaining souls to pick the cars they were riding in, I started wondering how many bumper cars were in here now. Last time I asked, there were two hundred and fifty cars.

Thank goodness the area they use for this ride is the size of a football field. There is plenty of room for dodging souls coming at you.

The bell rang, startling me, and I belted out a scream from the excitement. My car lurched forward as it came to life, and then it was game time!

I started turning the wheel hard left and hard right, trying to get out of the jam I was trapped in. *Jeez, these things are harder to control than I remembered*! I started to break free.

"Harmony, on your left! There's an opening!" Gwen shouted to me.

I looked over and quickly turned the wheel to make my escape. Gwen was making her way through on Maggie's right. I could see my target up ahead, and there was no way she was getting away from me.

"*I've got you now, Mags!*" I shouted as I closed in on Maggie's car. Maggie looked over her shoulder at me, smiled, and stuck out her tongue. By the time she looked back it was too late. Gwen smacked her car right into the front corner of Maggie's, making her jump. I screamed playfully, and smacked into Maggie's backside. Gwen, Maggie, and I burst into laughter.

Maggie started turning her wheel hard right. "You're going down, Harmony!" she exclaimed. I screamed, and quickly started turning my wheel as fast as I could, trying to escape, when I was suddenly struck in the side by Anna. I started turning my wheel the opposite direction when I noticed Robin just tooling around the rink, trying to avoid all the bumping action. I pointed toward Robin so the girls could all see.

"I think someone has escaped this excitement long enough!" I yelled.

All four of us took off, zeroing in on poor, unsuspecting Robin. Her eyes grew wide when she happened to look

Enlightened

over her shoulder and saw all of us coming. She quickly tried to make her getaway, trying to weave through a large crowd of bumper cars, but that ended up getting her bumped by Kaleb and John. Poor Robin was trapped with nowhere to go. One after another, the four of us bumped into Robin hard, me being the first! The boys were certainly laughing at us.

Suddenly, I saw an opportunity for a little revenge. I causally turned my wheel hard to the left to back out of the jam, turning the car around. Then I turned, bumping Kaleb's car on the side, and took off as fast as I could, laughing as I did.

I glanced back and Kaleb was fast on my tail. I let out a squeal, pushing the pedal to the floor. Out of what seemed like nowhere, Jaire came up alongside on my left, while Kaleb still followed. I turned hard right and Kaleb and Jaire had to dodge each other.

"She's hard to catch!" I heard Jaire yell to Kaleb behind me.

"She only thinks she is! I'll catch her!" Kaleb yelled back.

I looked over my shoulder and Kaleb was gaining on me. I could hear him laughing, and I was filling with such excitement as the chase went on. The closer he got, the bigger the thrill became, and the more I was yelling and squealing.

Without warning, a few unknown souls got in my way. I had to let off the pedal a little, and veer to the left to try and dodge them. That's when Kaleb suddenly slammed hard into the left side of my car. Kaleb threw his head back and laughed. I couldn't help laughing too.

The cars suddenly lost power, and the bell rang, signaling that the ride was over. Kaleb walked over and held out his hand to help me out of my car, and I let him. He was still giggling over his victory.

"I didn't think I was going to be able to catch you! You were so fast!" he said.

"If those souls had stayed out of my way, I'd be tasting sweet victory right now!" I replied between chuckles.

When I turned to start walking toward the exit, I saw Gwen, Maggie, and John standing in a semicircle chatting, and occasionally one or more of them would look in our direction. All of them had a peculiar expression.

I turned to Kaleb. "What's going on with them?"

"What do you mean?" he asked casually.

"They're looking at us funny," I replied, my brows narrowed slightly from the mystery.

"Hmmm…maybe they're wondering what else we're going to do while were here?" he suggested with a light shrug of his shoulders.

"Maybe." I was having my doubts. "Gwen did say something about all of us going to the toy store, though. Perhaps they are just discussing that?" When I looked at him, he just shrugged again. "I, however, was thinking

Enlightened

about going to the Sweet Shoppe to get some cotton candy while I'm here too…I do love that."

He smiled softly at me as we continued to walk. "That sounds like a good idea. You could always go to the Sweet Shoppe after the toy store, and then we can all meet up at Jaire's new house."

I smiled back at him. "That sounds like an excellent plan."

Gwen came up to us as Kaleb and I walked through the gate. "So what are we doing now?" she asked.

"I thought we were going to the toy store next?" I replied.

"Well, yeah." She paused awkwardly for a moment. Her eyes flickered toward Kaleb and then, in an instant, right back to me. "Just checking to make sure the plans didn't change," Gwen said.

"Why would they?" I asked her, not missing *that* brief exchange.

She shrugged. "Sometimes they just do."

"*Okay…*" She was obviously dodging, so I let it go. "After the toy store, I am going to the Sweet Shoppe, and then Kaleb suggested we all meet up at Jaire's."

"You and your cotton candy!" Gwen said.

"So what, *I like it!* It amazes me that they can make sugar do that, and it's tasty," I said happily.

She playfully shook her head, smiling at me. It couldn't be any clearer that she was totally keeping something from me, but what? Perhaps I would figure out what it was the longer we all hung out. The toy store could prove to be interesting…or maybe Jaire's house would be.

Chapter 8

When we arrived at the toy store, we were all spread out. For some reason, whenever we come here we never all visualize the same thing. As usual, I visualized the entrance, while the others pictured other parts of the store.

I love everything about this toy store, so for me, the outside is just as important as the inside, and always the best place to start. The building is shaped like an old stone castle, complete with two pointed towers, one on each side, with blue flags mounted on the peaks. It has lots of arch-shaped windows with the newest toys displayed in each one. Right above the entrance is a wooden sign shaped like a curved ribbon that has the name "Ti-Ko Creations" carved into it. My favorite part is the door. It's a large arch-shaped door made of heavy wood. When you step on a special pad that has the name of the store on it, the door cranks down with chains, and a portcullis rises up as you walk through. It's quite a store.

Once you walk through the entrance you become very mesmerized by all the different toys that are displayed everywhere. There are dozens of shelves, made of dark wood, stuffed with puzzles and games. Tables are filled with animals that dance and flip. There are small airplanes that hang everywhere above your head. Gigantic stuffed sea creatures like whales, dolphins, and sharks hang from the ceiling in places too. There's a huge balcony that wraps all the way around the back of the store with two grand staircases that meet on both sides of the main entrance. On the left and the right, just after the stairs, are two large doorways that lead to a huge room with aisles of the larger toys, dolls, and bicycles.

I started looking for the other souls I'd come here with once I entered. I didn't see anyone at first, so I went over to one of the glass cases to see what was new.

Tucked in between the dollhouse miniatures and the toy trains was a case full of little boxes. Each box was very unique. Most were rectangular, and each had different designs on them. A small oval-shaped silver box stood out from them all.

A very intricate raised vine pattern wound all the way around the outside of the box, connecting two roses in the front. Carved on the top were two small hearts linked together.

"Oooh…that's a pretty box," I said softly to myself.

"Would you like to see it?" asked the gentleman behind the counter. I was surprised because I didn't think I'd said that loud enough for him to hear. I'd seen this soul in here many times before. He was a very kind soul with light-brown hair and blue eyes. He had a warm smile, and his nametag said his name was Tim.

I paused and pressed my fingers to my lips. Of course I wanted to see the box up close, but lately I'd had many...*ham-fisted* moments, and wasn't feeling so sure of myself.

"Um...sure," I said with a little hesitation.

The quaint little box seemed so delicate and perfect. Like it should remain behind its protective case, away from clumsy hands like mine. The clerk opened the case and removed the silver box and placed it on top in front of me. I carefully traced the hearts on top with my fingertips.

"Wow, I've never seen anything like it," I said with a warm smile. It seemed unusual for a toy store though. I felt it would fit better in a jewelry store, or a museum. "Why would you have boxes like these in a toy store?"

Tim turned over the box and started to wind the key on the bottom. "A toy store is not just about the toys, you know—it's about creating magic and whimsy." He smiled as he placed the box back on the counter. "Besides, this is no ordinary box." Tim lifted the delicate lid. "It plays music."

The inside of the box was blanketed in a soft purple satin. A sweet melody poured from the box and hung heavy in the air all around me. I felt soothed by the peaceful little song, and I closed my eyes for a moment, just listening. "What song is that?" I asked.

"The song is called 'Que Sera, Sera,'" he replied. "It means *whatever will be, will be*."

I opened my eyes and smiled at him. "It's nice."

"Harmony?—*Harmony?*" a familiar voice called out to me. It sounded like Gwen. I turned to Tim. "Thank you for showing me this. It's beautiful."

"Anytime, dear. I hope you all enjoy the store. Do come and see me if you have any questions or need any help."

"Thank you."

Gwen came bouncing over. "Oh, hey, there you are. We were all in back checking out some of the bicycles… What are you still doing up here?"

"I was just looking at a very pretty music box."

"Oh, that sounds nice," she replied before glancing around. "Have you seen Kaleb at all? He was just with us a moment ago while we were playing with the bikes, but then he kind of disappeared."

"I haven't seen him," I replied, lightly shaking my head. "I'll bet he's around here somewhere. It's not like him to just leave and not say anything."

"True. I think I'll try calling him." Just as Gwen spoke, Kaleb came casually walking over. "*Oh*, there you are! Where did you go?" she asked.

"I was just looking around the store, and it occurred to me that I hadn't seen Harmony yet. So I came up front to see if she was up here. It seemed like she was taking a while."

Enlightened

"Sorry, I got caught up looking at one of the music boxes," I told him.

"Its fine, I just thought perhaps you changed your mind and went to the Sweet Shoppe already," he said.

"No, I didn't. But if you guys don't mind, I think I am gonna skip wandering the rest of the store, so I can go get my cotton candy. I'll meet up with you guys over at Jaire's."

"No, not at all." Kaleb smiled. "We'll see you there."

The Sweet Shoppe in Artopia does have all of the same characteristics of candy stores on Earth, but it's enormous in comparison. That's just the way it is here. Everything is made to accommodate the large number of souls that exist, and could possibly visit. Plus, you need all that space to house every single kind of candy, and for new sweets that are constantly being created. This is true for every single store here. New things are endlessly being designed, all the time. There's even a section of Artopia where you can go to watch things being invented as well.

Cotton candy is one of my favorite treats. I love watching the sugar being poured into the machine, and then seeing it spun out into colorful fluffy cotton. Naturally, I love eating it too.

Now, if I were you, bells and whistles would be going off in my head, and I'd be suddenly wondering: Didn't she just say they don't need a bathroom? How does that work? What happens after they eat something?

Our bodies here are vastly different than Earth bodies are. The easiest way I can convey this is to compare a human body to an automobile. It is a solid type of vessel for us, or a *vehicle* to use. Human bodies need "fuel," in the form of food and water, to create the energy we need for it to run, and to keep it running properly. The better the fuel, the longer your vehicle will last, and therefore the better it will run. Then, just like a car will release exhaust from the fuel that powers it, the human body will release the…*waste*. It's pretty much the same principal.

You have to admit, the human body is an amazing creation. Unlike a car, it will change over time, stretching and growing as time goes on. I always find this fascinating. Of course, just like a car, sometimes the human body you end up with is not so perfect, and you get stuck with a lemon.

Our bodies here are not solid, really. In Earth terms, we are spirit, or *energy*. Since we are already energy there is no reason to create any, and this is why we never feel hungry. There is also no need to go to the bathroom, because there is nothing to *release*. Unfortunately, our energy is not strong enough to power a human body alone, which is why we need to eat the extra fuel. We have food here for educational purposes, and will eat it simply for pleasure and our enjoyment. Here food is made up of the same type of energy that we are. So in

Enlightened

other words, *we are what we eat*. Did you really think that saying came from somewhere else?

The clerk in the Sweet Shoppe happily filled eight bags with cotton candy for me. I thought it would be nice to bring each one of my classmates a bag. They are, after all, my closest friends, and we've been through so much together. History that extends for eons exists between us all.

It didn't take me as long as I thought it would to get eight bags of cotton candy. I started to wonder if everyone was at Jaire's yet or not. Since I travel by thought, I need a specific soul or place to concentrate on in order to get to where I want to go. Otherwise, I run the risk of ending up somewhere unintended. Yes, it would be much funnier for you, but it would be totally embarrassing for me. So I decided to call Gwen first to see if they were still at the toy store, or if they were already at Jaire's. No need for an embarrassing mishap!

Standing outside of the Sweet Shoppe, I took in a deep breath and called out Gwen's name in my mind.

Gwen?

Hey…did you get your cotton candy?

Duh, of course I did. Are you all over at Jaire's yet?

Most of us, Robin isn't here yet. She stayed behind at the toy store to look at some of the porcelain dolls. She said she'll catch up with us when she's done…Kaleb is here, though.

Well, that's good…I'll be there soon, I replied in my mind, and then canceled my connection with Gwen.

Since I didn't know anything about Jaire's house, or what it looked like, I decided to concentrate on just finding Jaire. You can find anyone here using that method, unless of course they block it for privacy purposes. I love traveling using someone to concentrate on instead of a place because I never know where I might end up. Way more fun!

I closed my eyes and cleared my mind, starting to concentrate on Jaire, but then I suddenly recalled the last thing Gwen said, and was immediately distracted.

I opened my eyes and went to sit down on the bench in front of the Sweet Shoppe. I felt like I needed some time to myself before I went to hang out with everyone. I sat back against the bench and sighed.

There had certainly been a lot of strange things happening around me lately. All those accidental deaths in school. Then the odd behavior from my classmates at the bumper cars earlier. Especially Gwen. What was that? It was so not like her to behave like that with me. She was my best friend; she was not supposed to avoid telling me things. She'd never done that before. She normally tells me everything. I was searching my mind for a possible reason for her to be doing that. And why did she feel the need to tell me Kaleb was there? So what? After all those accidental deaths, she knew that I would prefer to

Enlightened

avoid him a little at the moment. It was probably better I did, to ensure we kept the peace in school. I sat there, weighing whether I should not bother going to Jaire's house and just go home instead.

Of course I realized doing that would hurt their feelings, especially Jaire's. He'd worked so hard on that house he built; Kaleb had, too. It would disappoint them both if I skipped going this time and didn't see all their hard work.

Ugh, fine! I'll, go! I thought to myself.

When I finally got to Jaire's house, I ended up landing on the front porch, where he and the others were already sitting and drinking iced tea.

Jaire got up to greet me. "It about time…*welcome*! C'mon, let me show you around," he said, excited, and he quickly took me by the arm. "You should start on the front walkway," he said as he whisked me down the steps.

He held on to me firmly, and casually patted my arm as we strolled down the front walk together. Then suddenly he spun me around. As soon as my eyes took in the whole picture, I gasped in awe.

The house was absolutely beautiful, just as I'd expected. Jaire's house was a log cabin of rich, deep browns. A row of three windows were on the top where the second floor should be, and two picture windows were on the bottom on both sides of the front door. The picture windows both had an intricate branch pattern sprawled across the glass. The house was wrapped all the way around by a porch that had the same branch-pattern theme in the railings. Jaire always saw the art and beauty in the way a tree grew and used it in everything that he built. He'd definitely done that here. His house was a unique work of art.

My mouth hung open. "Wow, Jaire." I gasped again and turned to him. "…*This* is incredible."

"Thank you." He smiled with such pride, and it was very evident in his tone too. "But you haven't seen the inside yet."

"Well then, let's go see it," I told him as I tugged on his arm.

Jaire and I walked up onto the porch, and he opened the front door to let me in. The inside was just as breathtaking as the outside. The living room, dining room, and kitchen flowed together in a wide-open floor plan. The staircase leading up to the second floor had the same branch pattern in the railings that was on the windows and in the porch railings. The staircase was placed perfectly in the center. Naturally, all his furniture was wood too, and most likely handmade originals by him as well.

"Wow, Jaire, did you make all the furniture too?" I asked.

"Yes. Anna sewed together the cushions for the chairs and the sofa for me. I'm not so sure I could have done as great of a job with the sewing as she did."

Enlightened

"Jaire, you have certainly outdone yourself… What's next on your list?"

"Not much at the moment. Maybe some shelves for in here, and I will be building a workshop on the side of the house for all my wood projects."

"Is that all?"

"I don't know. For now, I guess." He shrugged. "Would you like some iced tea?"

"Sure, I'd love some."

Robin had finally arrived and was showing everyone the new doll she'd gotten from the toy store. She loved collecting porcelain dolls.

"Hi, Robin, have you had a chance to look around here yet?" I asked her.

"Not too much. I've mostly seen the porch so far. I've been waiting for Jaire to give me the grand tour," she politely stated.

"Jaire, why are you making Robin wait like that? Get on it already," I said, nudging Jaire's arm.

He smiled at me. "Like I wasn't going to. Robin, please follow me," Jaire replied.

As beautiful as Jaire's log cabin was, I felt like there was something missing. After glancing around I realized what it was.

"You know, Jaire, I think you could use some plants around here. Like maybe some rose bushes in front of the railings, and some lilac bushes on the ends of the porch would be nice too." I said.

"Yeah, I've been thinking something along those lines. I'll get around to planting some eventually," he said.

"Hey, when you're ready, I'll help you with that," Kaleb added.

I sat with my friends for a long time on Jaire's front porch. We were chatting, and drinking iced tea, and of course snacking on a little cotton candy I had brought for them. Sitting all cozy on Jaire's porch, I found myself becoming sleepy, and thought maybe I should return home. I wasn't the only one thinking about this. John got up and started saying his goodbyes first. He felt tired, and wanted to go home too.

I stood up and stretched. "I think it's about time I went home as well," I said.

"Thanks for coming by to see my house, Harmony," Jaire said, and then he gave me a hug.

I leaned back a little to look at him. "No problem. Your house is incredible. Just like everything else you make," I told him with a smile.

"Thank you. That means so much to me, coming from you. You've always been such a great friend."

I smiled at Jaire's compliment.

"See you guys later," I said.

I closed my eyes, letting my forest home fill my mind to take me there. I opened my eyes once I heard the

Enlightened

sound of the stream. When I turned around, I jumped and gasped, surprised to see Kaleb standing next to me.

"I'm sorry, I didn't mean to scare you." He smiled as he held up my bag of cotton candy. "You left your cotton candy at Jaire's."

"I was so tired I didn't realize that I forgot it. Thank you," I replied.

Kaleb smiled. "Anytime, Harmony."

Chapter 9

WE WERE ALL SITTING IN our classroom once again, waiting to begin another life on Earth. Our classroom surroundings were of a desert island this time. In the center were two tall palm trees with coconuts swaying gently in a soft breeze. The ocean was lapping against the backs of the doors. I kept myself busy while I waited by happily squishing my toes in the sand.

I giggled when I looked up and saw Kaleb was squishing his toes in the sand too. It appeared he enjoyed it as much as I did. He looked up when he heard me laugh, and then smiled once he realized why I was.

He crawled through the sand and then sat down in front of me. "I'm sorry for all the trouble I've caused you lately." His voice was soft, and his eyes were sincere.

"It's okay, Kaleb." I smiled kindly at him. "Of course I forgive you."

"I just wanted to let you know, I'm all done testing your method. I see now that it really does work. Thank you for teaching me that. I'm sure it will greatly improve the lives I live on Earth in the future."

Enlightened

"You're welcome," I replied with a big smile. I was so happy that I was able to help him by teaching him my method. I felt like things between Kaleb and me would be better from now on. "I'm so happy that I was able to help you."

✦ ✦ ✦

Lucille Marshall
August 1940, Virginia, USA

"Well, don't you look nice," my father said as I walked past him in the living room. He was peeking at me over the top of his latest science-fiction novel. "Where are you off to this evening?"

"*Daddy*...I'm meeting the girls at the summer carnival...you already knew this," I replied with a smile. "Mom said you're both going, too."

"*Oh*...yes." He casually cleared his throat, repositioning his reading glasses. "The carnival...I had almost forgotten."

I looked at him with a raised brow, and chuckled. "How is that possible? Mom has two pies entered in the contest, and she's been going on about it for weeks."

"Perhaps I didn't hear her?" He casually shrugged while fighting the urge to smile. "I am going a little deaf in my old age."

I just shook my head at him. More like selective hearing, I thought to myself.

He shifted in his recliner, and then turned back to his book, pretending to read it. "You do look very nice for someone who is just going to the summer carnival… is there a particular reason?"

Did I overdo it? Maybe it was my hair? I ran to the foyer to check myself in the mirror. I had styled my light-brown hair into victory rolls, parted off to the side a little, with nice neat curls that went all the way around the back of my head. My outfit, though, was simple. It was just a white blouse with a pleated blue skirt that had little white flowers on it. I had put on a little makeup, but I didn't feel like I'd overdone it. I was hardly dressed up. I'd seen girls put on a bigger show than this for school.

I grabbed my purse. "I'm thinking you're just partial," I said to him.

"Maybe that's it," he replied with a smile and a wink. I went over and kissed his cheek before I left. He then turned his attention back toward his book.

I was halfway down the front walk before I let out my sigh of relief. It bothered me when my father got really inquisitive like that. Probably because he always saw right through me. I had put in a little extra effort

Enlightened

this time, for a reason I didn't feel comfortable enough to share with him. I was meeting my friends at the carnival, but a certain boy would be there with his friends as well. A boy that I'd had quite the crush on for a while now—and recently, I'd heard through the grapevine that he just might feel the same for me.

It was pleasantly warm, just right for mid-August. The sun was low on the horizon now, but wouldn't be setting for a few more hours. I had more than enough time to make it to the carnival before it would set for the night. I was taking this walk alone, and for once, it wasn't bothering me in the slightest. I had my dizzying thoughts about what might happen this evening keeping me company along the way. I skipped and bounced along the dirt road I lived on with a huge smile. I was happy, and I could feel it down to my soul that my whole life was about to change. Magic was certainly swirling in the air around me tonight. I was filled with hope that I wouldn't be taking this walk back home alone.

My best friend came running over as I approached the carnival gate. "Lucille!" she yelled, all excited.

"Geraldine!" I smiled and waved at her as I paid the man in the little booth for my ticket.

She practically jumped on me, hugging me tightly once I walked through. She squeezed me, and started to bounce as if she hadn't seen me in weeks, instead of just the mere hours it had actually been.

She let go and started towing me by the arm. "Come on! Shirley and Beatrice are waiting for us over by the tables."

The second we got to the tables, I started looking around anxiously for the boys. One boy in particular. Shirley and Geraldine exchanged a sideways glance with each other.

"None of them are here," Shirley commented casually. She knew full well exactly what I was doing. She smiled at me sympathetically once I finally looked at her. "We've been here for a little over an hour now, and haven't seen any sign of them yet."

"Did Dale say who is gonna be here?" I asked her.

"Dale said it's just gonna be him, Henry, and Vinny," she replied. Dale was her boyfriend at the moment. For how long, though, remained to be seen. She had a tendency to keep her relationships brief, and had somehow managed to turn dating into a sport.

"Vinny?" I groaned loudly. "—*Seriously?*"

"Luce, Vinny is Henry's best friend. Did you really think they wouldn't hang out together tonight? This is something you're gonna have to get used to if you end up going out with Henry."

"I know… It's just… Vinny can be mean sometimes, and he stares at me funny… It makes me a little uncomfortable."

Shirley looked at me with an odd expression. "Dale and I hang out with them all the time. Vinny is okay. A little weird at times, yes. Generally speaking, though,

Enlightened

you have nothing to worry about with Vinny. He's always had nothing but the nicest things to say about you."

"Really?" I was surprised that any of them talked about me at all.

"Yep, Vinny is always asking me how you are, too. Actually, it's very sweet."

I started to feel a little guilty for what I'd said. "I'll give him a chance. Especially if things work out between me and Henry. I don't want to cause any trouble."

Shirley smiled. "That's the spirit!"

"We should do something while we wait for the boys," Beatrice added, toying with a strand of her curly ginger hair. She was always trying hard to keep the peace.

"*Oooh*, I know! Let's go for a ride on the carousel!" Geraldine suggested. She could barely contain her excitement.

A distraction was probably just what the doctor would order, I thought to myself. "Let's go!"

After we purchased our ride tickets, the girls and I got in line for the carousel. We chatted casually as we waited, which turned out to not be very long at all. The ride operator let us in, and we quickly made our choices. I picked a very majestic black stallion with a gold saddle that was on the inside. Beatrice chose the pink horse in front of mine, and Shirley picked the white horse right next to hers. Geraldine picked the horse right next to me, of course, which was a shade of brown that reminded me of milk chocolate.

The music was loud and festive as the carousel turned. I tried to focus on just chatting with Geraldine, but it was difficult. I kept skimming over the faces we were passing by as we circled, my eyes failing to land on that certain one. My disappointment grew with each failed pass, as I feared that he may have changed his mind, deciding not to come out tonight after all.

Geraldine turned to me with a big smile, and leaned over a little. "*Luce*, they're here."

My eyes lit up and my heart skipped a beat. "Where?"

"Over by the popcorn."

I looked in the direction of the popcorn stand as the carousel came about, and there he was. He looked *so* good tonight! His brown hair was parted on the side, with a nice neat wave combed into the front. He was wearing his red zippered pullover over a white T-shirt, and a pair of blue jeans. He had his sleeves rolled up, and the cuffs on his pants were too. I was instantly starting to swoon.

He, Dale, and Vinny were standing in a close circle. It appeared that Henry and Dale were talking to Vinny about something. Their arms were crossed and they both had serious expressions. It was hard to tell what exactly was going on because Vinny's back was to me, and I couldn't see his face.

Enlightened

Geraldine leaned over again. She had noticed something was going on too. "I wonder what's going on with them tonight?"

I shrugged. "Good question." Maybe they are tired of Vinny's attitude problem, I thought to myself. I felt bad the second I thought this. Vinny was Henry's best friend, and I had promised to give him a chance. Henry was worth the trouble it might cause.

The ride came to a stop, and the girls and I exited the ride. Geraldine, Beatrice, and I followed Shirley as she walked toward the boys.

Dale's eyes lit up the second he saw her, and he came running over. "Hey, baby," he said, greeting her with a smile. He kissed her cheek, and put his arm around her shoulder.

Henry and Vinny were still talking very seriously as we approached. Henry glanced at us quickly when he noticed us walking up, and then turned his attention right back to Vinny. His expression was hard to read at first. He had his hand on Vinny's shoulder, and he looked upset, or worried. Angry, even. Henry finally looked up once we reached them, and then Vinny slowly turned around. It was then that I understood what was going on.

I gasped once I took in Vinny's appearance. He looked like hell. His clothes were dirty, his sandy blond hair was a disheveled mess, and he was sporting a very prominent black eye. His hands were stuffed into his pockets, and his shoulders were hunched forward. He was looking down at the ground like he was trying to hide. It was dark outside now, but the lighting from the concession stand turned his black eye into a true shiner. A knot started to form in the pit of my stomach at the sight of it. Who on earth would do such a thing?

I stepped forward reaching out to him. "Oh my god! Vinny, what happened?!"

He shrugged away from my attempt to touch him. "Nothing…I got smacked in the face with a piece of lumber at work today." It was very obvious from his tone and body language that he was lying.

"Are you okay?" I asked him. I was leaning down a little trying to look him in the face, but he kept trying to back away.

"I'm fine," he snapped, cutting me off. He put his hand up, trying to keep his distance. "It's no big deal."

I looked over at Henry and he just shrugged a little. He let out a sigh, then quickly composed his face into a smile. "Really, Luce—he's okay," Henry said, trying to reassure me. "Enough of this." He was looking at me and then turned to Vinny. "This is a carnival, and we're supposed to have fun. Let's forget about all of this for now, and just enjoy tonight."

"I second that," Dale added. He nudged Vinny. "Why don't we go find something to do."

Enlightened

"We could go on a ride. The girls and I still have some ride tickets," I suggested.

"I'm not really in the mood to go on any rides right now," Vinny said. Although he tried to control it, his tone had a sour pitch to it. "You guys go ahead… I'm gonna go check out some of the booths," he said before quickly walking away.

I just looked at Henry. I didn't know what to think or say, so I kept my mouth shut, fearing that I might say something stupid. It was not like I knew what to say in this kind of situation anyway.

Henry took in a breath and let it out. "How about you and me hit up the Ferris wheel?" he asked me with a smile.

I smiled back at him. "Sure."

After Henry bought his tickets, the both of us got in line for the Ferris wheel. The line was long and so was the wait, but neither of us noticed. We were quiet, and kept glancing over at each other and smiling. I don't think either of us really knew what to say just yet.

Out of the corner of my eye, I saw my parents walking past. My father stopped to look at Henry and me. He stood there holding his hotdog, smirking at us, and just shook his head. My mother took one look at us and then noticed him. She scowled at him, and quickly grabbed him by the arm, towing him off, muttering something to him as she did. I suddenly let out the sigh of relief I hadn't realized I was holding in.

The line moved up a little. Henry and I were now much closer to the front, and it was almost our turn. I was starting to twist into a bundle of nerves now. My heart was pounding, because I knew I'd be sitting right up against him in the seat, and we would be, for the most part, alone for the first time.

Suddenly, Henry reached over and took my hand. That nearly sent my heart leaping out of my chest. I started to worry because I could feel a small bit of sweat starting to pool in the nervous palm he was now holding. I was smiling, though, and I could see out of the corner of my eye that so was he. We stood there frozen, facing forward. Neither one of us was brave enough to look at the other.

The ride operator let off a couple and opened the gate to let us in. Henry held my hand, leading me to the seat. We both sat down, and the operator closed the lap bar around us. He pulled the lever and then we were off!

As we were rising up, I noticed Vinny in the crowd. He stood there watching us, and his eyes were filled with anger. His stare gave me chills.

Henry noticed me shiver. He put his arm around me and started rubbing my shoulder, playfully narrowing his eyes at me. "Are you actually cold?" he asked, chuckling a little. "It's August."

Enlightened

I turned to him. "No," I said softly. "I just saw Vinny. He was watching us, and his expression worries me." I paused for a moment, trying to better phrase the question that I was about to ask. I didn't want Henry to know how much Vinny scared me. "Do you think he is okay?"

"It's hard to say, Luce. He's been through a lot." He let out a sigh. "I'd be guessing either way." He looked away, down toward the crowd as he spoke. "He needs to get out of that house. He and I talk about getting our own place all the time. I've been saving for it, but I just can't get the money fast enough."

"Oh" was all I could think to say. All of this was information that I didn't know anything about.

Henry just smiled at me and took my hand. I could tell by the look in his eyes that he realized that I didn't know anything about Vinny's home life.

"He doesn't have it like you and I do, Lucille. His father is a belligerent, drunken asshole." He spat those words and started to sound angry. "He makes him work, and is nice enough to take all of his paychecks. He never gets a dime of what he earns, *ever*. He beats him all the time…and his siblings…his mother too."

"Oh my god…" Every encounter I ever had with Vinny started to make sense. I started to feel so guilty for thinking about him the way that I always had. "Is that what happened to him tonight? Did his father do that?"

He heaved a heavy sigh. "Yes."

"If there's anything I can ever do to help, please let me know. Maybe my parents would be okay with him camping out on our sofa or something."

"That's very kind of you," Henry replied.

The rest of our ride was short, but nice, and certainly less serious. We let go of talking about Vinny for a while. He told me a few jokes. Ones that I was way too embarrassed to ever repeat, but were very funny. We talked about our upcoming senior year at school, and our plans for after graduation. He planned on joining the service when he graduated, and I told him of my plans of going to college to become a teacher possibly. We talked about our families, and our mutual friends as well.

"Dale really likes her," he commented about Shirley.

"She seems to really like him as well. But that might not matter with her. She's so competitive all the time. Everything in her life has to be perfect…or better than what someone else has. Geraldine and I have noticed that this seems to include her relationships, too."

His eyes were narrowed in confusion. "Should I warn Dale?"

"No." I shook my head. "So far, he's lasted longer than the others have. So I'd say there's a good chance he'll last."

We ended up watching the pie judging after we got off the Ferris wheel. I had promised my mother that I wouldn't miss it. Henry was a good sport about it, and

Enlightened

he even clapped with me when my mother's lemon meringue pie won first place. She was beaming with pride when she went up to get her ribbon.

Both of my parents came up to meet Henry afterward. Henry shook both my mother's and my father's hands. If he was nervous at all, he didn't let it show.

"If it's okay with the both of you, I'd like to walk Lucille home this evening." I was screaming and excited on the inside, but I retained my calm composure. Please, for the love of God! Say yes, Dad! I kept praying on the inside.

My father was watching me closely with a smug "I knew it all along" expression on his face. He turned to Henry. "It's fine, but be sure to have her home at a reasonable hour."

"Of course…yes, sir. My curfew is ten thirty; she'll be home before ten the latest. My father would tan my hide if I missed mine."

"Very good," my father replied sternly, before looking at me with that embarrassing expression again. I hugged my mother, and then my father. He didn't let go of me right away and pressed his lips against my ear. "If he tries anything…I will bury him in the backyard," he whispered before letting me go.

I stepped back slowly, looking at my father as I did with a very composed and hopefully unreadable expression, and then smiled at him. I was trying very hard to pretend that I hadn't heard that. "Thanks..." I was at a loss for words. "I'll see you both in a little while."

Once Henry and I finally walked away I started to relax again. We played a few games, and he won me a little bear by shooting down a bunch of bottles with a BB gun. It was at this point that we ended up meeting up with the others, minus one.

Henry looked a little concerned. "Has anyone seen Vinny?"

Everyone shook their heads and exchanged glances with one another. Shirley sighed. "He probably left. He wasn't having a very good time tonight."

"Maybe," Henry replied. He sounded worried, and was distracted by his thoughts. "I'm gonna go look for him real quick." He looked up at me. "...Luce, I'll be right back."

"Okay."

Shirley went off with Dale, and I hung out with Beatrice and Geraldine while I waited for Henry to return. Naturally, our topic was Henry and me, and boy was I gushing!

"*He met my parents*! Oh my God, that was soooo *embarrassing*! My dad whispered in my ear about burying him in the backyard if he tries anything! Thank *God* he didn't hear that! I would have just died! He's walking me home tonight, too!" We all started bouncing and

Enlightened

squealing with excitement from my news, and then Beatrice suddenly changed the subject.

"Do you think Vinny is okay?" Beatrice asked.

"I don't know. Hopefully Henry finds him. I know he's very worried about him," I replied.

"I wonder what happened to him… Maybe he got into a fight with someone… I wonder if the fight is even over… Maybe he should call the police? Do you think we should?" Beatrice seemed very uncomfortable with the whole situation.

"I don't think this is anything for us to get involved with, and I seriously don't think we need to involve the police," I replied. I was being careful not to say too much. I wasn't sure if it was my place to.

"Bea, I'm sure he's fine… Don't worry, he probably just went home," Geraldine added. I shivered at the thought of that possibility being true.

We ended our discussion when we saw Henry walking up. Right away I was concerned, because he looked very upset.

It looked like he was forcing himself to smile. "*A-a-a*re you ready?" He struggled to speak, and he seemed very…distracted.

"Is everything okay?" I asked him. "Did you find Vinny?"

"Yes, I found him. Everything is fine," he replied. His tone was hardly convincing, and he appeared a little nervous. "Let's go."

I felt a little hesitant watching his body language, but I followed him. "Okay."

I said my goodbyes to Beatrice and Geraldine, hugging them both before we left.

Geraldine smiled at me. "You better call me in the morning!" Her statement came out like a happy demand.

"Don't worry, you know I will," I assured her, shaking my head and smiling.

Henry and I finally left, beginning our walk home. The light and the noise from the carnival gradually started to fade into the distance. The night sky slowly started to become more vivid as we walked, revealing the full moon and all of the stars. The only sounds were the toads in the trees and crickets in the grass.

I don't think either of us knew what to talk about. It was obvious that Henry was thinking about something. Most likely Vinny. He was very quiet and seemed very lost in thought, kicking little pebbles as we walked. I was very curious about what had happened when he found Vinny, but I decided not to pry. I figured he seemed upset enough. I didn't want to add to it and have him upset with me.

I heard him sigh suddenly, and then he stopped walking. "Luce?"

"Yes?"

"I'm sorry this isn't turning out to be such a pleasant walk."

Enlightened

"It's okay, it's understandable. A lot of stuff was going on tonight," I replied.

He started walking again, and I followed. "You don't even know the half of it."

"What happened? Enlighten me," I replied.

"I don't think Vinny wants to be my friend anymore. In fact, that's what he said."

I gasped. "He did?" I was surprised. "Did he say why?"

"He said he can't trust me, and that I've never really been his friend. He said that everyone likes me, and not him, and that he's tired of me never sticking up for him. He also said he's tired of living in my shadow." He stopped walking and took my hands. The moon was casting just enough light for me to see the seriousness on his face. "None of that is true. I've always treated him like he was my brother. I've always looked out for him. I've always been there… He's just not making any sense tonight."

"Whoa…" I didn't know what else to say. "I'm so sorry that happened to you," I replied.

He just squeezed my hand and held it, weaving his fingers with mine. We started walking again, turning down the long dirt road that led to my house.

I strolled happily down my road, looking up, playfully swinging our intertwined hands. I was simply appreciating the night sky, and the company I had with me. I was smiling, trying hard to salvage some of this evening by just being happy about my present circumstance. Even if it hadn't started off so great.

I heard him take in a deep breath and let it out. "What are you thinking about?" he asked me. It seemed like he was just trying to make conversation.

I glanced at him, smiling. "Nothing really. I'm happy, and I was just admiring the stars like I always do." I turned to look up at the sky and sighed happily. "I love the night sky. Have you ever seen anything more amazing?"

He paused for a moment, stopping us in the middle of the street. "You," he said on an exhale.

He slowly came in closer. My heart started to pound once I realized what was about to happen. He was leaning in now. His blue eyes, now a shimmering grey under the moonlight, burned with a fierce intensity. He reached up, and cupped my face gently in his hands. I closed my eyes, and pressed my lips to his. We stood there kissing in the middle of the street, his lips so tender against mine, under the stars and the light of the full moon. I was under his spell now, and was rejoicing on the inside. My magic had finally arrived.

We were interrupted when a branch suddenly snapped.

"*Well*…isn't this just *wonderful!*" Vinny said as he stepped out of the woods and into the moonlight. He sounded very angry. The moonlight made his glare look very sinister, and it sent chills down my spine.

Enlightened

"Vinny…" Henry started to speak, but then Vinny started to clap in a very loud, sarcastic way, cutting him off.

He was looking at us with a vindictive grin. "You two make such a great *couple*!" He practically spat those words at us, his tone oozing with sarcasm. "So it's safe to assume, then, that a congratulations to *you two* is in order?"

Both Henry and I just stood there frozen, staring at him. I don't know about Henry, but I sure as hell didn't know how to respond. He looked back and forth between Henry and me with a crazed look in his eyes. "*Right, guys?*"

"What has gotten into you?!" Henry said. "You knew I liked her!"

Vinny pursed his lips and brought his hands up into the prayer position, touching his fingertips to his lips, and then pointed at Henry. "And you knew that I did too." He started to slowly shake his head. He had a callous grin, and his chuckle had a dark edge to it. "But how I feel never matters to *you*."

"You didn't say a word, Vinny!" Henry barked at him. "*Not one single word*, until tonight!" he huffed. "What do you want me to do? Just step aside and let you have her? Not a chance!"

I just stood there in total shock at the turn of events unfolding right in front of me. Two guys were arguing in the middle of the street over me? My head was spinning. This couldn't be happening…

"You and I are no longer friends!" Vinny snapped angrily at Henry.

"You made that fact very clear at the carnival, Vin. From now on, *you* are on your own!"

"FINE!" Vinny yelled back. "I don't need *YOU*!"

"Come on, Luce." Henry put his arm around me. "We have to get you home before your parents start to worry."

Henry and I started to walk away. Vinny came charging at Henry, yelling, and shoved him to the ground. Vinny jumped on top of him and started punching Henry repeatedly, very hard.

"I HATE YOU! I HATE YOU!" Vinny kept shouting. They were both rolling on the ground, punching and shoving at each other.

Henry rolled over, pinning Vinny down to the ground, and punched him in the jaw so hard that I heard a crunching sound. Vinny rolled to his side and lay there in the street, crying in defeat. Blood was dripping from his mouth and nose. Henry got up, panting, and wiped the blood from his own mouth with the back of his hand, looking down at his now former friend.

"If I were you, I'd stay down!" he said, pointing at him. "And don't you come anywhere near me, or Lucille, ever again! From this day forward, we are not friends, and you no longer matter to me!" Then he spit on him.

"Come on, Luce." He put his arm around me. I let him lean against me as we started to walk away.

Enlightened

I was startled suddenly by footsteps rushing up fast behind us. Vinny swung a thick branch, knocking Henry hard face down into the dirt. Henry rolled over, putting his hands up. Vinny's eyes were wild, and he raised the branch high above his head. My survival instincts kicked in, and I lunged myself at Vinny, struggling hard to grab the branch. Vinny put his hand up, shoving me back hard by my chin. I was sent flying backward into the air, and hit the back of my head on a very large, sharp rock.

Chapter 10

We carry so much with us when we go to Earth. So much more than we ever really realize. Souls are famous for carrying their feelings about something or someone with them, and those feelings will manifest themselves on Earth. Sometimes in a not-so-pleasant way. Of course, while we are on Earth we can never figure out where those feeling stem from. It isn't until we get home that we remember, and then feel bad about what we did or how we behaved.

Once my memories came back, I never cried so hard in my entire existence. This was the first time anyone in my class had ever behaved like that. I had no idea what was going on, and didn't know what to think. Luke came in shortly after. He rushed to my side quickly, and put his arms around me.

"*Shhh*…it's okay. It's okay," he said, kindly rubbing my back. "Everything is okay, honey… You're home now."

He pulled back a little and held my head in his hands to make me look at him. He was inches away as the tears streamed down my face. "If it makes you feel any better…Kaleb is locked up in jail for the rest of that

Enlightened

life." He said this with a teasing tone, trying to make me laugh, but it failed miserably. I just continued to cry.

Luke pouted at first, and then he suddenly perked up. "You know what you need?" Enthusiasm was building in his tone. "I think you need to blow off a little steam… away from school and your classmates… You need to let things go for a little while… It'll make you feel better, and it will probably help." He nodded and smiled at me. "Since we're both done early, how about you join me at the club?"

What he said started to sink in, and I slowed down a little. "You want me to come to your club?" I asked between the sobs. I was a little surprised. This was the first time he had ever asked me.

Still smiling, he just nodded his head. "As my personal guest."

I sucked in a jagged breath. "Okay."

"Wait here," he said. He was excited, and then he disappeared before my eyes.

He returned a moment later with a black garment in his hands and held it open for me: a black T-shirt that had "The Legendary 7" printed across the front in shiny silver. All of the letters and the number were jagged like lightning bolts. I thought it was the coolest shirt I had ever seen.

"This is for you," he said.

I wiped under my eyes and took the T-shirt. "Thank you," I replied. It did make me smile a little.

"Let's go." He was very excited, and took my hand. "You can change at the club."

I was more than surprised when he led me to his motorcycle. My eyes were wide when I looked at him.

"You want me to ride on this?" I asked him. I'm sure I sounded shocked.

"Did you really expect to get there another way?" he asked. He opened up the seat, revealing a compartment. "You can put your robe in here."

I quickly took off my robe and stuffed it into the compartment, along with the T-shirt. Luke shook his head once he saw what I was wearing under my robe. I was wearing a brightly colored tie-dyed T-shirt with a sunburst pattern that Anna had made for me and a pair of black denim pants. The center of the tie-dye was a happy bright yellow, shaped like a large sun bursting out from the middle. The sun was framed by a mix of oranges and reds. It was and is one of my favorite things to wear.

"It's a good thing I gave you the shirt… You'd stick out like sore thumb wearing that at the club."

He straddled the bike and kicked the kickstand out of the way. He slammed his foot down on the kick-start, and the engine roared loudly when it came to life. He revved the engine. "Hop on!" he yelled to me with a smile.

Enlightened

Reluctantly, I climbed on the back.

"Hold on to the handle that's on the back of the seat!" he yelled to me over the engine.

I reached behind me and grabbed the handle with both hands. "Okay, got it!" I yelled back.

He twisted the handle, revving the engine, and we suddenly took off down the street, leaving the school and all of my troubles behind.

The wind was whipping against my face, throwing back my long, wild curls. We were winding down streets that I had never seen before until now. It occurred to me, while traveling on the back of Luke's motorcycle, how much of our world I had missed out on, traveling by thought all the time.

I think we are all a little guilty of that here. We all tend to take our world for granted when we're home. Perhaps this is the reason we cannot travel by thought on Earth? Maybe someone in the universe thought removing this ability from Earth would teach us to slow down and appreciate home more? I made the decision right there to change this about myself.

I quickly gained an understanding right away as to why Luke chose to travel this way. For the first time in a long time, I felt a strong sense of freedom. Riding on a motorcycle certainly does make you feel that way. I found myself melting as we moved, and I was starting to smile. I couldn't help thinking that Luke was right; this was probably exactly what I needed.

It didn't take us as long as I thought it would to reach Artopia. Yet another reason for me to adopt a slower method of travel here. It's not like any of us were punching a time clock here anyhow. Everything here truly took no time at all.

Traveling through Artopia like this was a whole new experience. I spent most of the time on the back of Luke's motorcycle looking around at the bustling city. I had been to certain parts before, but I am embarrassed to admit that up until that point I had seen very little.

I didn't realize it at first, but as we were making our way through Artopia, I started to notice that the scenery around us was reflecting particular time periods on Earth. It gradually and seamlessly changed as we moved, progressing and evolving like Earth had over time. It was almost like we were driving through history. Each time period was represented in the architecture of the buildings and the types of businesses in them. It was evident in the landscape, the styles souls walking along the sidewalks were wearing, and the vehicles we were passing by. I recognized quite a bit as we passed through. I couldn't help reminiscing a little, too, about certain lives I had lived in each one of those time periods. One thing that I found surprising about all of this was how

Enlightened

small each section was. Normally things here were on a much grander scale.

"Why are these sections so small?" I shouted to Luke over the rumbles of the motorcycle.

"They're not. It's an effect. It only seems small to us because we're driving through. If we stopped to visit one, the area would open up and expand."

Once we moved past the 1940s, time progressed, turning into the future. I gasped as I watched the progression in the architecture around us, and the various style changes that I had yet to see on Earth. It was fascinating. I became concerned, though, when I realized the changes stopped progressing.

"Luke, why did all the changes stop?!" I asked. I admit, I was worried right here that life on Earth might come to an end.

"Because no one has thought up anything new yet," he yelled back. "Don't worry. The next time we come through, you'll see something different. That's the nice thing about coming through here. It's a reminder that nothing is ever lost, and creativity will never stop."

I stopped looking around so much when I noticed the sky up ahead in the distance was starting to change. Then we passed by a sign that read: NOW LEAVING DAYTIME ARTOPIA. HOPE YOU ENJOYED YOUR STAY! The sky around us was growing dim as we continued down the street, making our way through the city. When we passed by the first streetlight, I became excited. This would be the first time I had ever visited the nighttime section.

Our world is vastly different than Earth is in regards to night and day. Unlike Earth, here in your home, you control when the sun goes down and when it will rise. Your home is your heaven, so you are in control, and free to do with it whatever you want.

We have a little less control in regards to Artopia. We can add to it all we want. Imagination and creativity are very important and never stop here. But what we add must be placed in the right sections. These rules make things in Artopia easier to find.

Then, not every activity is done in the daylight. There are some activities that require darkness. And since every business and activity is never closed, Artopia must have sections like this. So the sun will never set in daytime Artopia, nor will it rise in the nighttime section. Having a city like this is a necessity in a world that doesn't keep track of time. None of us are on the same schedule. Artopia is the original city that never sleeps.

With the exception of the streetlights, the sky was totally dark now. We were starting to pass by other nightclubs along the way. Ones that to me looked very strange, and had strange names to match them. One was called SoulBack Saloon. The building looked like something you would see in the Old West era on

Enlightened

Earth. Bright lights and loud piano music were pouring out of it as we passed by. The building itself was made of dark wood and had saloon doors. Horses were tied to the porch railing in the front. The souls that were standing outside it were wearing dusty-looking clothing and cowboy hats. Another one we passed by was called Boogie Heaven. This one was a more modern brick-style building, trimmed with little light bulbs around the doors and windows. The girls waiting outside that club had big poofy hair and were wearing lots of sparkly gold and platform shoes, while the men were wearing flared pants and butterfly collars.

We started to pass by a number of motorcycles that were parked along the street, so I knew we must be getting close. I finally saw it when we turned a corner.

The building was a very dark color. It looked like it was black, but, being in the nighttime section of Artopia, it was hard to tell what color it was exactly. The sign over the entrance was almost as dark as the building except for the lettering. The name of the nightclub, The Legendary 7, was all lit up and had a twinkle to it. It was very cool.

Motorcycles of all kinds were *everywhere*. I saw some with these huge handlebars that Luke called "ape hangers." Then there was one with a sidecar on it, and a few that Luke said were called choppers. They all had various designs on the gas tanks, and most of them were decked out with elaborate exhaust systems covered in shiny chrome. It was quite overwhelming.

Luke turned off the engine, and I could already hear a lot of noise coming from the club in between the rumbles from the other motorcycles.

He opened up the compartment on his motorcycle and handed me my shirt.

"Come on," he said, starting to lead the way. He pulled the elastic from his long dirty-blond hair and shook it out on the way in. My eyes were wide once souls with long hair like his started to greet him. He was high-fiving some, and gave one soul a high-ten. He called another soul, who was wearing a leather jacket with a lot of zippers on it, "dude," gave him a playful shove, and was bumping knuckles with others along the way. For the first time, I was seeing Luke in a whole new light.

Luke opened the door and the sound decibels soared to an enormous level. He motioned for me to go ahead of him, and with wide eyes, I walked inside The Legendary 7.

It was the biggest, craziest, wildest thing I had ever seen in my existence. Colored lights were pulsating all over the club. There was a band on stage playing a loud type of music that, until now, I had never heard before. It was energetic and very…*thunderous*. There was a male soul with long, curly brown hair thrashing away on a massive drum set, and other souls with long hair playing colorful guitars unlike any I had ever seen

Enlightened

in my existence. Souls with long hair, dressed similarly to Luke, were everywhere. They were jumping up and down, dancing, and swinging themselves and their hair to the music. Some were dancing on catwalks high above the main floor, and a few were hanging from the rafters. All of them were shouting, whistling, and pumping their fists in the air.

The crowd in the club cheered wildly when Luke and I walked in. Luke's face lit up and he threw his hands in the air. He put his fingers in his mouth and whistled loudly, and then the whole club went silent. He suddenly pointed to me. "Hey, everybody! This is Harmony! *LET'S SHOW HER HOW TO HAVE A GOOD TIME!*" he shouted, and threw his fists into the air.

The whole club cheered excitedly, yelling my name. I just smiled and waved back. The band went back to playing, and the crowd went back to dancing.

Luke turned to me. "Follow me," he yelled.

I followed Luke through the crowd to the other side of the bar and up a flight of stairs. He opened a door and motioned for me to go inside. I walked in, and he shut the door behind us. The music was muffled in the background.

Luke's office was simple-looking. The walls were covered in dark wood paneling with a large picture window that overlooked the entire club. Posters of souls with long hair and wild-looking clothes hung around the room.

He walked over and plopped himself down in a chair. He threw his feet up on his desk and leaned himself back.

"Have a seat," he said, pointing to the chair across from him. I sat down quickly. He placed his hands behind his head before starting to speak.

"Pride…Lust…Gluttony…Greed…Sloth…Wrath, and Envy. The seven deadly sins are the legendary seven, and what rock music is based on."

"Rock music?" I questioned. "What is rock music?"

He sat up and leaned forward, resting his arms on the desk, looking me square in the face. "Allow me to enlighten you," he said with a proud smile. He got up and pointed out the window toward the stage. "The kind of music that band is playing right now, my dear Harmony, is rock music. This particular style playing right now is a tad more aggressive and modern than what will be introduced on Earth in the next decade, but all of it will challenge the masses the same."

My eyes were wide. "Rock music?"

He nodded. "Yep… Bands have been practicing here to get themselves ready. Some of them have already departed for Earth. These guys here will be leaving soon as well, and they're gonna be hugely popular down there."

I got up and walked over to the window. "I don't understand," I said, as I watched the guitar player drop to his knees and pluck strings on his guitar really fast. "What is so challenging about this?"

Enlightened

"Well, as you know, Earth is changing, and is becoming more modernized. You'd be surprised at how unaffected people have become by the traditional challenges that are thrown at them because of it. Other types of music are in development right now, too, with the same intent."

"So rock music will challenge them?"

"Earth is *very*…conservative right now, and music is always influential." He crossed his arms. "This is gonna shake them *all* up!"

"Will I get to see this?"

"*Oh yeah!*—I've been looking forward to it!" He was beaming. "It's too bad, I can't join you down there at that point. That would be fun!"

I smiled at him. "It would be."

"Why don't you change your shirt, and then you can join me downstairs," he suggested.

"Okay."

Luke pulled a curtain shut over the window, and then walked out of the office, shutting the door behind him.

I couldn't resist glancing out of the window again, so I pulled back the curtain a little to peek through. I was fascinated by what I was witnessing. The dark-red walls, and the enormous speakers and lights hanging off of them. The huge stage. The wild long hair swinging around. I watched the guitar player take his guitar and then swing it around himself fast by the strap and catch it. He leaned back and started plucking away at the strings again, making the guitar squeal.

This must be one of those things that would only make sense to me if I were on Earth, I thought to myself. Sitting here on this side of the situation I just wasn't seeing how this would upset anyone.

Once I was done changing, I left my tie-dye on top of Luke's desk and walked out of the office, shutting the door behind me. It was much quieter than I was expecting as I walked out and started coming down the stairs. The band that was playing when we came in were packing up their things, and it looked like another band was getting ready to play.

Just as I started to look around the club for Luke, I spotted a heavy crowd gathering around the bar. They began pounding their fists on the wood bar like a drumroll. I started laughing when I saw Luke pop up from under the bar with a huge smirk on his face, shaking a large bottle. His hair hung loosely around his shoulders. His muscles were tense as he kept his thumbs over the opening and gripped the neck of the bottle, shaking it hard. He then threw his head back and laughed darkly when he released his thumbs, spraying the bottle's contents all over the demanding crowd.

I had an enormous smile on my face as I approached the bar. I was already feeling ten times better than I was before we left the school. Seeing Luke this way had been

Enlightened

very…*enlightening*, and had helped tremendously. I did worry, for a fleeting moment that my relief might only be temporary, but I quickly let that go. I decided that I would rather enjoy hanging out with Luke than to continue to wallow in any misery.

Luke had been my guide for a really long time, but that was all I'd really known of him up until that point. I felt like I was receiving a big gift in a way. He was allowing me into his world for the first time, and it made me feel like more than just his student. I felt like we were becoming more like family.

Luke motioned for souls to let me in. "What'll it be, darlin'?" he asked me with a big smile.

I didn't know what to order, so I shrugged at him. "I don't know… What do you recommend?"

"For you, I would recommend a soda. I don't need you carrying down any new habits."

I smiled at him. "A soda is fine. Even on Earth, I've never been much of a drinker."

"Let's keep it that way," Luke said with a wink and a smile.

One of the other bartenders, with long dark-brown hair, passed me a cola.

Luke patted the bartender on the back, then introduced us. "Harmony this is Tyler… Tyler, this is my student Harmony."

Tyler and I shook hands.

"It's nice to meet you," I said to him happily.

"Likewise," he replied with a big smile.

"Tyler's just paying his dues by working behind the bar before he leaves. His class is going down next. They are gonna be so big!" Luke said proudly.

Tyler was beaming. "I hope so... This place is the easy part... You never know what will happen once you get down there...everyone has free will."

Luke patted him on the back again. "No matter what happens, you're always welcome to play here when you get back."

"Awesome!" Tyler replied.

The new band started up and souls started rushing to the stage. Luke grabbed my soda off the bar and started motioning for me to go join them. "Get out there! *Go!*"

I did as I was told, making my way through the crowd of souls, getting as close as I could to the stage. The lead singer came rushing across the stage with a microphone in his hands. His long blond hair fanning behind him as he ran. He dropped to his knees, sliding across the stage, bringing the microphone to his mouth as he did, and took in a deep breath.

"*Ohhhhhh...YEAH!*" he yelled.

The crowd cheered, throwing their fists in the air, and the band started wailing. Souls around me were dancing, and I just stood there, still, watching the band. I wasn't too sure if I liked this yet or not. It didn't take me

Enlightened

long to figure it out, though, because soon I was dancing right along with everyone else. I was really liking rock music. It was energetic and made me happy. I couldn't wait for Gwen to get back, so I could tell her about this, too. Knowing her spunky, energetic nature, I thought she was probably gonna love this as much as I did.

How anyone on Earth would end up finding this upsetting at all was beyond me. It seemed pretty harmless to me. But what did I know, really?

Music was always a great way to take a break from the mundane, no matter what kind it was, and from where I was sitting, the mundane I'd been dealing with had been pretty insane, if you ask me. Luke was right in bringing me here. I let go. I laughed and danced, forgetting all about my problems with school and Kaleb for a while.

Chapter 11

It seemed like a decent-enough solution. I decided to just avoid Kaleb at any and all cost. I felt that this might be my only choice for the time being. At least until I found out what his problem was.

I procrastinated when it came to going to class this time. I knew everyone was already there and waiting on me, but I didn't care. I was dragging my feet, big time, for a good reason.

I think it's ridiculous the way they make us wait around in the classroom every time, staring at each other, anyway.

In my case, sitting in class right then would have only invited trouble, and let's face it, that's where all of it started! I would rather wait out my time at home, where there was less trouble and I was happier, and then I'd go to school.

Luke made several attempts to call me in, and I simply told him each time that I was not coming until everything was ready for me to go straight down to Earth. I was not fooling around anymore.

I was dressed and ready to go. I decided to wear the shirt Luke gave to me in hopes that it would bring

Enlightened

me a little luck, and I had on my school robe over it. I waited out my time on my rock, watching the water in the stream cascading by my feet. I was thinking about how best to handle things in regards to Kaleb on Earth. I was debating whether or not I should bother again with concentrating on avoiding him entirely—*which worked out oh-so-fantastically before!*—or if perhaps I should try a different method. Like maybe concentrating on being very cautious around him, so accidents were less likely to happen? Maybe? I wasn't sure what was gonna work.

Try to avoid him? Or just proceed with caution? Earth was a big-enough place. Maybe I'd get lucky this time and I wouldn't find him at all. I started chuckling to myself. *Fat chance of that happening!* I always found Kaleb! Suddenly, I recalled a little something that Kaleb said in the beginning of all of this.

"Because there have been countless times where we didn't always find each other."

I don't know why this hadn't caught my attention before, but it certainly had it now. His statement was true. There had been a bunch of times where my classmates and I didn't find each other. I could think of a bunch of lifetimes where someone from my class wasn't there. All except for one. I sat there really thinking hard about this, trying to come up with at least one lifetime on Earth where Kaleb wasn't there, and I couldn't. It was proving to be pretty much impossible.

Luke called me in the middle of this realization, putting an end to it. It was time to go.

When I arrived in my classroom, the doors were already open, and everyone was standing around waiting. Judging by the sour expressions on all of their faces, I figured it was safe to assume that they weren't all that happy about waiting for me. It still didn't bother me in the slightest.

Kaleb tried to approach me right away, and as he started to speak I quickly cut him off.

"*Harm—*"

"*NOPE!*" I announced to him sternly, with my hand in his face. "I don't want to hear it!" I barely looked at him, either. "You can save whatever this is for later!"

I turned to walk into my transition room, suddenly locking eyes with Jaire. We both smiled at each other briefly, then shivered noisily from the memory of us from that last life. We chuckled, and I was shaking my head. *Ahhhh…the things that only happen on Earth*! I thought to myself.

Luke was waiting for me, standing right by my cot when I entered. He had his hands tucked behind his back and a gentle smile on his face. The question I had about Kaleb before I left sprang to mind again, so I decided to ask him about it. He'd been there watching all of my lives, and would know the answer to this question.

Enlightened

I hopped up onto the cot, and looked up at Luke. "Do I have time to ask you a question before I go?"

"Yes, one. What is it?"

"Thinking back through all of the lifetimes I have lived, can you recall one where Kaleb wasn't there?"

Luke made a funny face before answering. "We can talk about that when you return," he replied.

"Well, that figures," I huffed. "Shoulda seen that coming!"

Luke chuckled. "Lie back, Harmony. It's time to go."

I lay down on the cot, starting to concentrate really hard. *I have to be careful around Kaleb... I have to be careful around Kaleb,* I repeated over and over in my mind. Luke smiled and waved his hand over me.

"Be well, Harmony... I'll be watching you."

✦ ✦ ✦

"So what do you have to say for yourself?!" I stood there on my rock, staring Luke down. "None of this is *my* fault!"

"How you conduct yourself while facing any problems is always your own fault," he snapped back.

"How I conducted myself is not the problem here, Luke, and you know it!" I was pointing at him as I continued to yell. "It is about Kaleb sending me home early every chance he gets! Not to mention *you* actually having the nerve to send him to wake me up! I have every right to be this upset!"

"You're too blinded by your own anger to see anything, or have any rational thoughts!"

"So what happened, huh?! Why was I home early again?! He must have had something to do with it! What did he do?!"

"*Nothing*," Luke yelled.

"Ugh!" I threw my hands up. "You're impossible!" I yelled at him.

"My job is not to make your existence easier. My job is to help you learn to become a better you, and right now you are *severely* off track! I will let you know when your classes start," he replied firmly.

"Fine!" I snapped at him. Luke disappeared, leaving me alone in my forest, and I plopped myself down on the rock, still fuming.

I sat there, grumbling to myself. "All of this is ridiculous! Kaleb started this whole mess, and now because of him, I'm stuck taking classes! This is just great!" I grabbed a pebble from the ground and chucked it into the water. "Watch, with my luck he'll be taking them too, and we'll be stuck sitting right next to each other! O*h, lucky me!*" I threw another pebble, and it plunked into the water. "Why can't I avoid this guy?!"

I got up and began stomping my way down the stony path toward my hammock bed and my washroom. I'm

Enlightened

just gonna change my clothes and then I'm going to bed, I decided. After everything that I had been through, all those accidental deaths, his possible involvement in this last one, plus Luke sending him to wake me up, I was extremely exhausted.

I was still cranky, but felt a little better once I finally crawled into bed. Sleeping here is the same as it is on Earth. Same feelings, and we dream here as well. It's one of the few reminders we have on Earth of home.

I willed it to be night, and sighed in relief when the sun in my forest finally set and the stars came out. I let out a yawn as I lay there watching the stars twinkling through the treetops. My hammock bed swayed gently, rocking me into a much-needed slumber.

Chapter 12

IT DOESN'T MATTER WHERE YOU are. Whether you are here or on Earth, the learning never stops. This is just an unavoidable part of who we are, and most of the time, we all embrace it.

One part about school here that I find wonderful, besides going to Earth, is that there's a class for everything. Do you want to learn to be a better cook? There's a class for it. Are you thinking about improving your carpentry skills? There's a class for that too. Or maybe you have trouble getting along with others on Earth? Maybe you would like to learn better ways to face your fears? Make scientific discoveries? Perhaps you want to become an engineer or a surgeon in your next life? Maybe animals fascinate you? You can learn about all of this, and so much more. Of course, all of this education is unlimited, and, unlike Earth, doesn't require any money. The only cost is your willingness to participate.

You are always free to take any classes that you wish, as often as you want. I've taken advantage of this many times. Of course, there are classes that guides will assign to you as well. Any classes assigned by them you have to

Enlightened

take, and you have no say in the matter. There is usually a good reason for why they assigned them, so, no, we cannot skip them.

The classes Luke assigned me—as frustrating as some of them were—were very informative. I have to say, though, I was extremely relieved when I was done with the anger management class. It was intimidating. I felt that there were souls in that class who were far angrier than me, and could probably benefit from a second round.

The Jumping to Conclusions class, to me, was boring. It was mostly roleplaying scenarios, and pointing out the two different sides of the conflicts that we don't always know or think about. How *assuming things is always a recipe for disaster.*

It Takes Two wasn't much different. More roleplaying, explaining "it takes two" to argue, and pointing out that the one who resists or walks away is typically the real winner. Oh, and did you know, you don't need two to argue? I argue with myself all the time! *Ha*! Yeah, I know, that was a corny joke. The instructor of the class wasn't so thrilled by it either.

After that class, I went up to the kiosk in the school foyer to get my next assignment from Abra. She's a sweet woman with long, curly blond hair and kind green eyes. She helps to keep track of class assignments and attendance for the guides. I find her amazing because even with so many souls in existence she somehow always remembers everyone's name. A gift I wish I shared with her.

"Hello, Harmony, how was your class?" she asked.

"It was fine." I sighed.

"Oh, that good, huh?" She chuckled lightly.

"It was good enough." I shrugged, indifferent. "I need to get my next assignment."

She handed me a slip of paper. "Here you go, dear."

I looked at the slip of paper, expecting Compassion and Understanding to be my next class. Instead, it was Going to Extremes. I was confused and looked up at Abra with narrowed eyes. "Is this right?" I asked her.

"Is what right?"

"This assignment…I thought I was taking Compassion and Understanding?"

"You were…but Luke came in and changed it while you were in your anger management class."

"Oh." I was surprised by the sudden change. "Am I signed up to take anything else after this Going to Extremes class?"

"I don't think so, but let me double-check." She looked at her computer and began typing, and then glanced back at me. "It doesn't look like it. It's just this one."

"Oh." I didn't know how else to respond, or what to expect. I was groaning on the inside a little now. It sounded an awful lot like he'd signed me up for another type of anger management class. *This is just great!*

Enlightened

She smiled at me. "You'll love Going to Extremes. It's a great class, and one of my favorites. More souls should take that one."

I was having my doubts. "I hope it's good. Thanks, Abra."

When I arrived in the classroom where Going to Extremes was being held, I was pleasantly surprised by the setting. There was a stream similar to mine, only much hillier. The water flowed down over rounded rocks like a small, gentle waterfall. Bright green moss dripped down from the trees that lined the stream, and blanketed the ground leading up to the rocks along the bank. Small pink flowers were growing between the small boulders. Rays from the sun shone through the trees, and small yellow butterflies were fluttering through. It was quite breathtaking.

I sat down on the moss with the other souls who were attending this class, facing the small waterfall. A female soul with delicate features and long dark-brown hair that flowed down to her waist appeared standing before us. She had on a long, white silk robe similar to the one I wear when I go to Earth. She smiled kindly at all of us before sitting on one of the small boulders along the edge of the water.

"Hello, and welcome to Going to Extremes. My name is Zipporah, and I am going to tell you a story." Her voice had a gentle and soothing tone as she spoke.

Billie Kowalewski

"There was only darkness in the beginning…and then imagination came in the form of light…

"Out of this light, creativity sparked, forming a union between the two. Now, there will never be one without the other. Out of this light is where we come from. Each one of us is imagined and then created like a work of art. We are made one by one. Bringing forth more light than there was before with each new creation. To be one of a kind, to stand out and fill a gap where there once was nothing, like no other.

"There are reasons we are created in the way we are. We like our traditions here, our patterns and synchronicities. Everything carved out into neat and tidy rows creates predictability and is easier to manage.

"Imagination and creativity can be taken in far-off directions. Sometimes it can be taken to *extremes*." She smiled kindly as she glanced over us all. It seemed as though she purposely saved me for last, her eyes resting briefly on me.

"This was the case in the beginning, when imagination and creativity were fresh and new. Extreme souls were being created. Charmeine and Zuriel were two of these far-off creations. What made them so different from the rest of us was that they were created at the same time.

"At first glance, they appeared to be just like the rest of us, and for the most part they were. Charmeine was kind and soft-spoken. She had long, wavy blond hair

Enlightened

and shimmering blue eyes. It is said that Charmeine had a love of the ocean, since she had a gift for understanding sea creatures. Zuriel was a ruggedly handsome man with brown eyes. His long brown hair was always tied back, curling neatly, centering between his broad shoulders. Zuriel had a connection to the sea as well, only his was nautical. He always found comfort on small boats and the grandest of ships.

"Because they were the first, no one understood what set them apart from the rest of us. But like us, they were given the same freewill, and the freedom to live their existence the way they chose to. Allowing them to discover what makes them special on their own. As you all know, self-discovery is the only way to learn here.

"Once they began traveling to Earth, it was discovered both shared a connection with the other in a way not yet seen until them. It never mattered how far apart they placed Charmeine and Zuriel; one would always find the other.

"The force of Charmeine and Zuriel's connection was incredibly strong. Once they were placed on Earth they became like blazing comets, hurtling toward each other at light speed, coming at each other so fast that they would crash into one another. Over and over this occurred. Every first greeting was like the last. They were slamming right into each other, knocking each other over, tripping and flipping over each other every time. It was only a matter of time before Charmeine and Zuriel ended up falling madly in love.

"It was on a ship crossing the Mediterranean Sea that Zuriel called Charmeine his *compañero del alma*, which means his soul mate. He knew that their intense love for each other wasn't ordinary. That it came from a different place or connection. It wasn't until he arrived home that he understood this further.

"We all learn at a different pace. The one and only rule we have about learning on Earth is that we must learn our lessons on our own. Because of this rule, Zuriel had to keep his discovery a secret until Charmeine discovered this for herself.

"The story of their romance spread throughout our world, told by the souls who witnessed their love firsthand. They talked about their clumsy greetings and how they could feel what the other was feeling. How they couldn't resist the other's alluring scent, and how they could barely breathe on Earth when they would part. Charmeine and Zuriel were the only souls that truly were made for each other.

"The time came once again for Charmeine and Zuriel's class to return to Earth. It was decided that one soul was not needed this time, so Zuriel volunteered to stay behind. Charmeine would travel to Earth along with the rest of the souls in their class.

Enlightened

"Zuriel stayed with Charmeine right up until the moment she had to go. Though the time they would be apart would be short, Earth would make the time feel much longer for Charmeine, a concern that never entered anyone's mind.

"Life on Earth began well for Charmeine. Her name was Elizabeth. She was born into a wealthy family in France during the sixteenth century. She had a happy childhood that was filled with love.

"As the years progressed, a depression slowly began to creep into Elizabeth's life. This depression became more pronounced in her teen years. She was plagued with dreams of a ruggedly handsome man with long brown hair, who was coming home on a ship after a long sea voyage.

"The dreams always drew Elizabeth to the ocean. She felt a small amount of relief visiting the village's rocky coastline. She would walk along the edge of the high cliffs that overlooked the choppy water. Breathing in the crisp salty air helped her breathe some, and dulled the ache in her body. Though this aid was always temporary.

"She would wander the streets of her village, appearing lost at times. She seemed to be always searching, expressing to others that something was missing. That she ached and could not breathe. That she felt empty and alone.

"As time went on, her depression became much darker. She spent many days and nights alone in her room with her curtains drawn, withdrawing from her life. Expressing to her family how she just wanted to be left to die.

"Her family did everything that they could to help Elizabeth. Her guide worked hard, trying to influence her in the way he normally would to get her back on track, but she just wouldn't respond. The harder they tried to help her, the deeper she sank. Her depression was so deep, swallowing her up like quicksand, dragging Elizabeth down faster and faster.

"Her family on Earth speculated that marriage might possibly help her break free of this depression. So her father arranged for her to marry a young baron by the name of Nicholas as quickly as possible.

"When Elizabeth received the news of her engagement, she became enraged, lashing out at her family members.

"*If I must marry Nicholas, that night will be my last!* She shouted angrily at her father.

"*You are my daughter, and I will not allow you to continue your life this way!* He cried to her. Her father shut Elizabeth up in her room, locking the door behind him. *Do not let Elizabeth out of this room! She will marry Nicholas tomorrow!* He shouted at the servants.

Enlightened

"Far too often we don't see the effects of our actions until it's too late. Setting events into motion that could have possibly been prevented.

"Elizabeth spent that evening crying in her room long into the night. She couldn't understand what was wrong with her. Much to her dismay, her life was spent in such misery. Each day for her was progressively worse than the last, with no known cause. Kneeling down alongside her bed, she prayed, *Why me?* She questioned over and over, *why won't somebody help me?*

"As the night dragged on, a plan began to take shape in Elizabeth's mind. A plan to free herself from her misery once and for all. Her family was unaware of what she had in mind, but her guide could hear her thoughts. He knew what she was going to do. So, while Elizabeth slept, he began plotting ways to deter her from being able to follow through with what she was thinking.

"The next day, preparations for Elizabeth's wedding went a lot smoother than anyone was expecting. The two female servants who were sent to help Elizabeth get ready breathed a sigh of relief when they unlocked the door. They found a smiling, happy woman who was more than accommodating, and strangely eager to put on her wedding gown.

"When Elizabeth was done getting ready, the servants walked her down to the front entrance, where her father stood waiting.

"She greeted him with a warm smile, and a gentle kiss on his cheek. Her father smiled back at her, seeming pleased at his daughter's change in attitude. He admired her smile and the glow in her eyes, feeling confident in his decision to arrange this marriage for her to Nicholas. He took her hand and the servants lifted the train to her dress, helping her as she stepped up into the carriage.

"Both Elizabeth and her father remained quiet during their ride to the church. The weather was beautiful. The sky was a deep cloudless blue, and a warm, gentle breeze flowed through the carriage windows. Birds were singing cheerfully off in the distance, while butterflies were fluttering about the wildflowers that lined the road.

"As they neared the intersection that veered off to the village's coastline, Elizabeth casually slipped off her heeled shoes under her dress, and reached for the door handle without looking. She was surprised by a small spider that was crawling across it at the same moment she reached for the handle. Elizabeth jumped back, letting out a startled scream, scaring her father and the carriage driver, who pulled the carriage to a stop.

"The moment the carriage stopped, Elizabeth immediately opened the door, leaping from the carriage. Her dress caught on a nail that was on the step, ripping a section of her train off as she took off running down the road that led to the shore. Her father and the driver jumped out of the carriage, quickly trailing after her.

Enlightened

"Her guide knew of her fear of spiders, and was frustrated that it didn't help deter her. He was even more frustrated that this actually aided her plan by causing the driver to stop the carriage. Her guide got to work quickly, setting up other derailments.

"Elizabeth held her dress up as she ran. Her long strides kept her father and the carriage driver from being able to catch up. Faster and faster she ran while conscious thoughts were running heavily through her mind. They were screaming that what she was about to do was wrong. That she should not do this, and that this solution was not the answer. But Elizabeth kept running, ignoring them, determined to end her misery.

"The weather started to change as Elizabeth ran. The wind began to pick up speed. Heavy gusts were flowing strongly in her direction. Her dress acted like a sail, catching the wind as she struggled to run against it, kicking up sand and debris into her face. A large tree limb broke under the force of a strong gust of wind, blocking Elizabeth's path. Her guide was expecting her to slow down or stop when he dropped the limb, but she didn't. Instead she ran harder, leaping over the limb, and continued on running. Frustrated that he had not received the outcome he was expecting, Elizabeth's guide brought on stronger deterrents.

"The sky grew dark as dark grey clouds began to creep in, blanketing the once-blue sky. Loud claps of thunder rolled in, echoing angrily off the surrounding mountains. She was pelted with hailstones the size of small pebbles. Lightning struck a nearby tree as she passed it, but Elizabeth forged on.

"The sky opened up and a heavy downpour soaked her and her dress in a matter of seconds. Her father and the carriage driver were beginning to close in on Elizabeth as she neared the rocky cliff's edge.

"Heavy thunder and lightning surrounded Elizabeth when she reached the edge of the cliff. She began crying as she looked down at the dark, choppy water. The waves below were crashing down hard, spraying and swallowing up the jagged rocks.

"Her guide pelted her again with hail, shouting in her conscious thoughts. *Don't do this!* He urged. *Taking your life will not end your misery!*

"With tears flowing steadily down her cheeks, Elizabeth inhaled the salty air. The image of the ruggedly handsome man from her dreams filled her mind, and unexpected calm began washing over Elizabeth, allowing her to breathe, and she finally felt at peace."

"Her father and the carriage driver finally reached Elizabeth. Worry was present on both of their faces as they approached her. *Elizabeth, please, come back to the carriage,* her father urged. *You don't have to marry Nicholas. I just want you to be happy.*

Enlightened

"Elizabeth turned and faced her father. With tears in her eyes, she forced a weak smile. *That's just it. I've never been happy. I don't think I'm capable of ever being happy, no matter what I do.* Elizabeth sighed and hung her head down. *This is the only place that I have ever found any peace.*

"She gathered her gown up into her hands and turned away from her father. Without warning, Elizabeth leaped off the cliff, disappearing into the cold, dark water.

"No one was expecting what ended up happening after Elizabeth jumped from the cliff. The moment she leaped, Zuriel fell to his knees, screaming in pain. Pain is something that only occurs on Earth and is not a normal bodily function for any of us. His cry could be heard throughout our world, stunning all who heard him. He rolled on the ground, too, clutching his throat as he struggled to breathe. The divine became alarmed by Charmeine's actions, along with Zuriel's cries and his suffering.

"Charmeine and Zuriel disappeared from our world shortly after this life. Some say they were erased. Some speculate that they are still undergoing the divine's intervention from Charmeine's suicide. While others now wonder if they ever truly existed at all, or if perhaps they were just souls like us with no real special connection, and this is all just a story. Proving to all that extreme souls like soul mates do not exist."

When Zipporah finished, everyone was so quiet you could have heard a pin drop. Souls gradually started to clap, all except for me. I was in such shock that I couldn't move. I sat there frozen while the puzzle pieces began falling into place one by one in my mind. I didn't want to even think it was possible, but it was too strong of a coincidence to think another way. This was just a story, wasn't it? Or was this what the problem had been all along?

Chapter 13

Everyone got up and left the classroom. Except for me. I didn't move. I couldn't. I just continued to sit there on the mossy ground in stunned silence. The story she told sounded way too similar to what went on between me and a certain someone. I suddenly had way too much I was thinking about. I didn't think it could ever be possible here, but I felt like my brain was gonna explode.

Zipporah noticed me frozen on the ground. Once the last soul was gone, she came over and knelt down in front of me. A look of concern was in her eyes.

"Are you all right, Harmony?" she asked.

I was surprised that she knew who I was, and that made me look up at her. "How do you know my name?"

"I know who you are." She smiled warmly. "And I've been waiting for you."

I narrowed my eyes at her response. I was expecting her to say something along the lines of Luke telling her, or, more logically, about knowing who was signed up for her class. She knew who I was, and had been waiting for me?... *What?*

"You've been waiting for me?" I was totally dumbfounded.

"Yes… It was inevitable that one of you, if not both, would wind up here."

"It was?"

"Yes," she simply replied.

I was having an incredible time digesting what she was saying. My thoughts kept scrambling here and there as new information continued to come in. I didn't know how to respond, and my thoughts were so loud I just ended up sitting there staring at her. I found myself mesmerized by her eyelashes for a bit. They were very long, and I just sat there watching her blink them occasionally. It was as if they were waving to me in a way. Then what she said suddenly registered.

"You must have so many questions," she said.

"I'm sorry… Did you say one of us?"

"Yes."

"Who?"

She didn't reply. She just sat there staring at me with her delicate smile, waiting for me to catch on to what I already knew, but hadn't admitted to myself yet.

"Me…and Kaleb," I said softly.

She just nodded.

"For how long?" I asked her.

She smiled. "Since you were both created."

Enlightened

I didn't know how to respond. I had heard of soul mates before, but up until this point I believed it was a term that was drudged up from Earth fantasies and stories. I didn't think that any of us shared any kind of special connection to anyone. I just thought that love was something that blossomed over time through friendships, like the kind I had experienced before on Earth. This is the way most of us here feel. There are tons of love relationships here that have existed for eons, but none of them have ever said anything about being extreme souls or *soul mates*.

She looked me over, examining my face closely. I'm pretty sure she could tell how I was feeling, because her expression was sympathetic. She took both of my hands into hers, and smiled kindly.

"The time of the extreme souls affected everyone, especially anyone who was on Earth at that time. An extreme soul is one that has certain characteristics or traits that are far stronger in one direction than the average soul. Most of them were just tremendously smart. Geniuses to an enormous degree. Once they were on Earth, many of them became wildly out of control, and were doing *very* heinous things. The worst ones had to be erased. Thankfully, all of that was a very long time ago.

"In the middle of all of that chaos is when Charmeine and Zuriel began. Of course, they were vastly different compared to the other extreme souls that existed at that time. Their only"—she paused for a moment as she searched for the right word—"...*flaw*...if you can even call it that, was that they shared a very strong connection to each other.

"What happened to Charmeine and Zuriel truly left a mark on our world. Out of all that chaos had come such beauty, and then in an instant it was gone. There was such a long period of sorrow after that. When they disappeared, many of us thought the time of extreme creations was over.

"However, recently we've been proved wrong." She smiled proudly at me at first, but then her expression changed. She narrowed her eyes and pursed her lips. "There was an extreme soul that was discovered very recently who was wreaking havoc on Earth." She shook her head with a look of disgust on her face. "Thankfully, that one has been erased."

"Is that what happened to Charmeine and Zuriel?" I asked. I had to admit, I was panicking a little right there. "Did they get erased?"

"I can't say for certain what happened to Charmeine and Zuriel." Her expression became very serious, and she looked me square in the eyes before she continued. "You have to do something *very* catastrophic on Earth to get erased," she said, trying to assure me. "The story, and this class, was passed down to me a long time ago. What I do

Enlightened

know is that after them, it was a very long time before our world saw another pair of extreme soul mates created."

She just smiled and stared at me.

"Really…who?"

She just sat there smiling at me, patiently waiting for me to catch on again.

It took me a moment but I eventually caught on, gasping once I did. "Us?" She couldn't be serious.

She just nodded. "I've been keeping an eye on your development, with Luke's help, of course, and Kaleb's guide, Jack's. Part of my job is to keep an eye on the extreme souls. Not all extreme souls go out of control. There are still quite a few in existence that are quite wonderful."

I had a ton of questions now, but one stuck out more than any of the others.

"Why weren't Charmeine and Zuriel dying?"

"Huh?" Zipporah looked at me with a puzzled expression.

"Kaleb keeps sending me home early, and that didn't happen to Charmeine and Zuriel in the story."

"That hasn't always been the way with the two of you…" She appeared to be searching her mind for her own possible conclusion. "You two have always lived full lives before." It seemed like she was questioning this more to herself, but then she looked at me. "It must be from something else."

That was when it all started to make sense. "We were having a competition," I began, and then I proceeded to tell Zipporah the whole story of what was going on in class. "I never really paid any attention before to what was happening when I met Kaleb on Earth. Not until the accidental deaths started. Honestly, I never even noticed. I just knew he was always there."

She laughed, with a tone as sweet as cotton candy. "It sounds to me like you both were intensifying something that already comes naturally for the two of you."

I let out a sigh of relief. It felt good knowing what the problem was, and it wasn't as bad as I thought. My method does work for achieving what you want, and for finding people on Earth. So I was happy to know those things at the very least. But then I had another question for Zipporah.

"Are we the only ones like this?"

"No…you and Kaleb are just the first pair of extreme soul mates that were created since Charmeine and Zuriel. There have been other extreme soul mates like you both created since…and we're all cut from the same cloth. Each one of us has a soul-mate connection out there somewhere, and it's only a matter of time before we find them. What makes souls like you and Kaleb unique is that your ability to find each other is much stronger than the average soul's. You and Kaleb have never and will never miss."

Enlightened

I nodded as I processed her answer, but then I had another question.

"So does this mean that I don't have a choice?"

Zipporah looked at me with a puzzled expression. "A choice about what?"

"Well, about me and Kaleb. Does this mean I have to be with him? Can I choose to love someone else if I want to?"

"Why wouldn't you be able to?" she questioned back.

I shrugged. "I was just making sure that was still the way."

"That will always be the way. You may love anyone that you want to."

"Good."

"Harmony, you are free to choose whom you love, and live your existence any way that you want. You've always been such a strong-minded, independent soul. I'm sure you will find, though, it'll be hard to resist the level of love and friendship that comes so naturally to you both. You and Kaleb were meant to be that way. You will be drawn to each other because you were made to be. It is your strongest trait. It is always a matter of time before we succumb to who we truly are, no matter how hard we try to fight it." She was grinning. "…And it sounds to me like someone else already has."

I just nodded at her again. I was thinking about a lot of things now. I was thinking about all of those accidental deaths, and all of the drama that went along with it. I felt bad now, because love was furthest thing from my mind this whole time. See? Hindsight really is always twenty/twenty. I could see it all clearly now, and I felt like an idiot. How did I miss it?

I was thinking about that last life I had shared with him, too. We were our naturally clumsy selves when we met in that life. We had bumped right into each other and fallen on the floor, but I didn't die then. Instead, I lived. I sighed in relief and started smiling at the realization. I didn't die accidentally this time! I did live for as long as I was meant to! I was so thrilled that this really was finally the case.

I looked up and smiled at Zipporah. "I didn't die accidentally in the last life."

"Well, that's good," she replied happily.

"Kaleb and I are extreme soul mates?" My question came out more like a statement.

She was beaming. "Yes."

I was sitting there thinking about that last life again, and about how much I loved him that whole time. My happiness darkened once I suddenly recalled what I did to him when I got home, and I felt horrible.

"I have to talk to Kaleb." I stated this out loud, mostly to myself, slightly forgetting about Zipporah's presence.

"Before you go, I need to warn you. You know what you both are, and although he is well on his way to discovering it, Kaleb has yet to learn about being an

Enlightened

extreme soul. Please be mindful that he needs to learn this on his own, in the same way you have."

I nodded at her. "I will."

"I should also warn you about one other thing… Do not go to Earth without each other. I hope you learned from Charmeine and Zuriel that doing that will not end well. History always has a way of repeating itself."

"I won't," I assured her.

"Good."

She and I both got up from the ground, and she gave me a big hug.

"Give me a call if you need me or have any questions," she said.

"Thank you, I will."

Chapter 14

It always amazes me how fast everything can change, and it always happens in the blink of an eye. It's even faster if it occurs on Earth.

I spent a great deal of time so angry with Kaleb, and now that anger was suddenly gone. I almost didn't know what to do with myself. I sat down on the steps of the school after that class, thinking about everything that happened, and about what I wanted. I had so much new knowledge that I didn't have before, and I didn't want to go talk to Kaleb until I knew exactly what I wanted for my life, regardless of what connected us. So much happens on Earth all the time. We have all kinds of relationships with each other down there. We tend to not read into those once we are here, unless we already know differently. Relationships on Earth just come with the territory.

A relationship formed here will change everything, I thought to myself. It will affect any relationships I have down there for the rest of the time I am in school. I then realized Kaleb's feelings for me already had with that one lifetime where I was Lucille. I shook my head and chuckled to myself. No wonder he behaved that way in that life.

Luke appeared, standing in front of me. He smiled at me when I looked up at him. His hair was fanned out, hanging over his shoulders, and he had on a typical tight black T-shirt. His thumbs were resting in the belt loops on a pair of blue jeans that were torn at the knees.

"Did you learn anything new?" he asked. His tone had a teasing edge to it.

I smirked at him. "A wise person learns something new every day."

He wandered over and sat down beside me. "That's a rather intelligent answer… Who's the handsome genius that taught you that?" he asked, continuing with his teasing tone.

I rolled my eyes and chuckled at him. "*You.*"

"That's who I thought." He chuckled and playfully nudged my shoulder. "So, what did you learn?"

I let out a sigh. "Kaleb and I are soul mates of the *extreme variety.*"

"You don't seem very happy about it," he commented.

"It's not that I'm not happy about it. It is interesting. I just haven't had a chance to think about any of it yet. All of this information kind of came at me all at once."

He nodded. "Yeah, it did. That tends to be what happens when we're distracted by our anger. It often makes what is really happening harder to see."

I smirked at him again. "Lesson learned."

"That's always what I want to hear." He smiled proudly.

"I am sorry I was being such a brat. I can't guarantee that it will never happen again, but I will make more of an effort to try to behave myself."

He patted my back, looking at me with a sideways grin. "I wouldn't want you to be any other way," he replied with a playful tone.

"So do you know what you're gonna do yet?" he asked me.

"Not totally. I do know that I owe Kaleb an apology at the very least."

"True… That you do," he agreed. "But do you love him?"

"That's what I am trying to figure out. I know how I felt in the last life I spent with him, but that was Earth… We're not on Earth anymore."

"So?" Luke shrugged. "That doesn't mean anything. Many of the relationships that exist here have begun there; been that way for thousands of years."

I nodded as I thought about what Luke said.

"Isn't it interesting the lengths the universe will go to teach us things? When two souls are right for each other, and they get close enough to each other on Earth, the universe will take those two individuals and knock them together in some way. It's as if the universe is shouting in that moment: Hey, look! You have found something special!"

I just nodded again in response.

Enlightened

He looked at me with a warm, sympathetic expression. "Don't base your decision on anything other than what is in your heart," he said, placing his hand on his chest. "If you always do that, you will never be wrong."

"I won't," I assured him.

I ended up going home after my discussion with Luke. I felt like I needed more time to think about everything that I'd learned. I had seen the error in my ways one too many times after jumping headfirst into things without thinking them through. I didn't want to make any more mistakes that way.

I decided to take a shower when I got home. I always found that doing dumb trivial things helped me think better. When I was done with the shower, I wrapped myself in a towel and went over to my walk-in closet to pick out something to wear.

I went through my clothes a few times, and I found myself being rather picky, for a change. Having a hard time trying to decide on what I wanted to wear, is something I don't ordinarily do.

I finally just settled on a blue stretch-cotton top and a pair of blue jeans. I put them on even though I still wasn't feeling all that thrilled about my choice.

I went over to the mirror that hung over the sink and started to brush my hair. As I was pulling the brush through my curls I finally started to think about Kaleb.

Before this whole accidental death mess, I had always thought of Kaleb as being warm and kind. He had always been very helpful to me in school, and was a good friend. I chuckled once I realized that before this whole mess, he was always the first one I went to whenever I was having any kind of trouble in class. Not once did I ever really notice that I did this, or think much about it.

I walked out of the washroom, shutting the door behind me, and wandered over to my hammock bed. I sat down and then leaned myself back, swaying the bed gently, wondering about this extreme soul mate thing. I started to wonder, since we have the freedom to live and love any way that we choose to, and knowing we have this extreme soul-mate connection, whether I was capable of loving someone else. Could I resist this connection that Kaleb and I shared? I was surprised when I found myself shuddering at just the thought of trying.

I then started to think about this last life that he and I had shared together. He was Seth, and I was Veronica. I loved him very deeply in that life, more than any other person I had ever had a relationship with on Earth before. None of them had ever been as intense or as united as this one was. Even the way he smelled was better. This was something that dominated my attention all the time in that life. A sweet honey-like scent rolled off of him all the time that I could never get enough of. I began wondering if it was our soul-mate connection that was the catalyst behind things like this, and why our love for each other on Earth was so deep and strong. I suddenly clapped my hand against my forehead and started chuckling as it all started to come together in my mind.

How even here I'd always felt more comfortable around him, too, like I was at home when I was near him. I'd always been able to count on Kaleb no matter what. This was especially true in that last life. He was the one I could always count on for anything in that life, and I would do anything for him in return. There was never any doubt. I was smiling and felt tingles going through me as I started to realize where my heart was already. Then a memory surfaced from the last life I lived on Earth, as Veronica Edwards.

We were sitting in his car, a black Ford Mustang convertible, and I was tucked under his arm…

"Do you know what I think?" I asked him.

"What's that?" he asked in reply as he casually rubbed my shoulder.

"I think we're soul mates," I told him.

"Really?" He sounded intrigued. "Why do you think that?"

"I get this feeling when I'm with you…that you belong to me, and I belong to you."

I glanced up out of the corner of my eye when he didn't reply. "Crap…I hope I didn't just freak you out."

He smiled. "No." He laced our fingers together. "I think the same thing."

"So, if you think that, then..." I got to my knees and climbed up into his lap, facing him. I took his hand and placed it on my chest, right over my heart. "You must know, then, how hard you make this throb every time I see you?" I started kissing his neck down by his collarbone and I heard him exhale noisily.

"How it aches for you every time you simply leave the room?" I added. I moved my lips to the other side of his neck, gliding them up to just under his earlobe.

"Mmmm..." I heard him say.

"So you can feel it then...how desperately in love with you I am?" I whispered in his ear.

I heard him exhale, "Yes."

I kissed his lips. "Good."

"Do you know why else I think we're so special and that we're soul mates?" I asked him. I was wide-eyed, and an inch away from his face.

"Why?"

"You know how some couples have that one song that's theirs?" I asked him.

"Yeah."

I smiled. "You and I have a whole band."

I shook my head and started to laugh. I was beginning to realize that even Veronica knew it before I did. The more I thought about everything, the more I realized how I felt. A part of me thought that I had

Enlightened

always known; I just didn't realize it until now. I found myself suddenly very eager to be with Kaleb.

I stood from my hammock bed, running my fingers through my curls quickly, feeling a little nervous. I felt horrible. He was still hurting and it was totally my fault. I owed him a big apology. But more than that, I wanted to tell him that I loved him too.

I took in a deep breath and closed my eyes, bringing Kaleb's handsome face to my mind to help me find him.

I became confused when the scent of earthy soil and pine became infused with the scent of sweet honey. I didn't feel the same shift in the atmosphere like I usually did when I traveled by thought, and none of the sounds changed either. I could still hear the stream—actually it sounded like I was closer to it than I was before.

I opened my eyes and was surprised that I was standing in a forest that was quite similar to mine. It was almost exactly the same. There was a stream like mine that flowed by a large flat rock, and the oak tree was the same. Now there was a log lying on the ground across from it near the bank as well. Bright, leafy ferns were growing out from around some of the rocks along the edge of the stream now, too. Another major difference was the soul sitting alone on the rock, hugging his knees to his chest with his head down.

Once I saw him, it all became real. I knew that I'd hurt him, and felt even worse seeing him this way. I ached for him, and worried for a moment that he might not accept my apology. It was what I deserved.

Kaleb slowly raised his head with a very guarded expression on his face. It was one of confusion and caution as he looked in my direction.

I felt a little tongue-tied at first. Seeing him outside of school was definitely different. He looked the same, but different at the same time. His sandy-blond hair was wispy along the sides and feathered just above his deep blue eyes. Instead of the same old school robe I usually saw, he was dressed casually in an open tan button-up shirt over a white T-shirt, and a pair of blue jeans.

His guarded stare made me feel like I was up on a stage ready to give a big speech in my underwear. I knew I should be the one to speak first but no words were coming to my mind yet, so I kept it simple. "Hi." A basic greeting, but I felt like it worked. I clasped my hands together behind my back, and rubbed a line in the dirt with my toe.

"Hi," he replied shyly. "Why are you here?" His guarded tone confirmed what I was witnessing on his face.

I relaxed my stance some and smiled softly at him. "I'm sorry for yelling at you when you came in to wake me up."

"It's okay." He shrugged. "I should have remembered you weren't a morning person on Earth. Why would you be any different here?"

Enlightened

I glanced down at my feet, feeling ashamed of myself. "I'm only like that when I first wake up from Earth. I experience a lot of confusion." I looked up at him. "I'm fine the rest of the time I'm home."

"Oh."

The awkward silence lingered. I quickly searched my mind for something to say to interrupt it. "Is anyone else back yet? Or are we the only ones?"

"Jaire and John should be here soon. We still have to wait a while longer for Robin, Gwen, and Maggie."

"Oh," I replied.

I knew how he had died in that last life, because I was there. But I didn't know if he had come home early, or if he had lived as long as he was meant to. I decided to ask, continuing with the small talk. "Did you finish? Or was your life…cut short?"

"No, I didn't," he replied. "But I don't have to repeat any lessons from that life." He let out a sigh, sounding relieved. "Did you finish?"

"Yes," I replied.

A proud, satisfied smile crossed his face the moment I answered. "Good." His tone confirmed his satisfaction. He then turned his head, staring into the depths of the cascading water.

His body language piqued my curiosity. "Why are you saying that?"

He looked up at me and his blue eyes spoke volumes before he did. "I was so determined to not let anything happen to you this time so that you could finish, I carried that down with me."

I started to walk toward him. His sweet honey-like scent became stronger with every step that I took. It was so irresistible that when I sat down beside him, I was almost overcome.

"Don't you ever do that again," I told him sternly.

He sat back a little, seeming defensive. "Why not?"

"Because that was horrible! I was so miserable after you left."

"I'm sorry. That was never my intention. I just wanted you to do well, and to not send you home early again."

Both of us sat there quietly for a while, watching the stream, not saying anything. I started to wonder why he'd never said anything in the beginning of that whole mess about being in love with me.

"Why didn't you tell me that you were in love with me before?"

He looked up at me. Rose colored his cheeks and he glanced down at the ground before he answered. "I've been trying to find a way to tell you for a long time, but I was too scared. It was especially bad once we started testing out your method. I admit now it was a bad way to go about trying to tell you. Then I didn't know how

Enlightened

to handle any of it, because I thought you were very mad at me."

"I did tell you many times that I had forgiven you." I nudged his shoulder with mine and smiled at him. "I can never stay mad at you."

I reached over and took his hand, weaving my fingers with his. I saw a gentle spark of hope in his eyes the moment they finally met mine. "I love you too," I admitted.

He was glowing. "Really?"

I nodded. "Yes." I smiled back.

He reached for me quickly, twisting his fingers into my hair, pulling me in, kissing my lips softly, and with such passion. My heart was bursting, and I was kissing him back just as eagerly.

He slowly sat back and when I opened my eyes he was smiling inches away from my face.

"Don't move," he said, right before he suddenly vanished.

I sat there on the rock chuckling. I was glancing all around me, trying to figure out what he was doing.

He appeared, standing in front of me holding a very familiar oval-shaped silver music box. I was looking at it when we had all visited the toy store together in Artopia.

"This is for you," he said as he knelt down in front of me, holding out the music box.

I gasped as I took the music box and smiled at him. "You got this for me?" I was so surprised.

"Yes, I had gotten this for you right before we left for this last life. I saw you admiring it when we all went to the toy store, and thought it was quite fitting for you." He shook his head in disbelief. "I never imagined it would follow you on Earth the way that it did."

I recalled it as soon as he said it. I had received the same style music box as a gift from my father in this last life. I was just as surprised at the recollection. Although with the way the universe works, teaching us about ourselves the way it does, I shouldn't have been surprised by this at all.

My heart was overflowing with so much joy. I was smiling, and placed my hand on his cheek. "Wow, thank you."

He was smiling warmly. "Open it," he encouraged.

I lifted the lid and gasped loudly when I saw what was inside. Nestled inside the box, resting against the purple satin, was a necklace he had made and given to me when we were on Earth last.

I pulled the necklace out of the box and held it up. It was just as beautiful now as it was when he gave it to me on Earth. The pendant was two hearts connected together like a linked chain would be. The first heart was upright and secured to a silver chain. The second heart rested on its side inside the V of the first heart. Both hearts were covered on one side with shimmering diamonds.

Enlightened

I was happily watching it sparkle. "I can't believe you remembered this," I said to him.

"I actually made that for you a while ago. I carried the design down to Earth with me. Your method is amazing for things like that."

"You made this?" I was astounded. "I didn't know you could do this."

"Yes, I have a gift for metals and stones… I'm surprised you didn't know that."

"Wow…I loved this when you gave it to me on Earth, and I love it here even more." I kissed his lips. "Thank you."

"You're welcome." He was beaming.

I was excited as I handed him the necklace. "Please help me put it on."

Kaleb crawled on his knees and got behind me. I held my hair up and he secured my necklace in place. "I promise to love and care for you. I made this necklace to symbolize that my heart is yours for all eternity," he said.

My heart was melting as he spoke, and once he was finished I turned to face him. "I promise to love you and care for you for all of eternity as well. My heart will always be yours. I love you, Kaleb."

A single tear trickled down his cheek. "I love you too."

Kaleb sat back against the tree and I tucked myself under his arm. I felt him tighten his arms around me as I snuggled up against him. He pressed his face into my hair and I heard him inhale, and then sigh in relief. I could feel that I finally was truly home.

"What was the music like after I left?" he asked out of the blue.

I chuckled. I felt like we were back on Earth sitting in his car. "You missed a lot of really good stuff."

"How was our band?"

"Kaleb, I wasn't really able to listen to Aerosmith after you left. It just wasn't the same without you… But I was starting to worry a little right before I left. Joe Perry had left the band. What if they broke up?"

"Really?" he sounded surprised. "When I first got home, I went to Artopia and looked them up, and found a ton of music left that they hadn't released on Earth yet."

I glanced up at him. "Really?"

"Yep, I believe Joe Perry returns because there's a lot left with his name on it."

"Oooh! You need to take me to hear that!" I urged.

"Don't worry, I will." He kissed my head. "We always have plenty of time."

"True, and we always have the option of seeing them when they make their return to The Legendary 7."

"*Exactly*," he agreed.

We were quietly sitting against the tree for a while, and then Kaleb suddenly started to chuckle.

"What's so funny?" I asked him.

Enlightened

"So are you gonna tell me now what I-95 is?" I glanced up at him. He had one brow raised and was smiling through pursed lips.

I narrowed my eyes at him at first. I sat there searching my mind, trying to recall what he was talking about.

"You said you were taking it to the grave, and we're a little past *that*," he said, with a teasing tone.

Once he said that, I recalled what he was asking about and flushed with embarrassment from the memory. It was something that had happened in that last life that I swore I would keep secret. I smirked back at him, feeling way too embarrassed to say what it was out loud. I reached up, cupping my hand over his ear, and whispered the answer to him. When I sat back and looked at him his eyes were wide.

"Did you do that too?" he asked, sounding surprised but at the same time impressed.

I playfully smacked his arm. "*No!*" I shouted feeling embarrassed. "I was just the one driving the car," I replied laughing.

Kaleb was laughing too. "That has to be Gwen. I can't imagine anyone else in that life brave enough to do *that*."

Still continuing to chuckle, Kaleb placed his fingers under my chin, and gently turned my head to look at him. He tenderly kissed my lips. "I love you, Harmony."

"I love you too."

Chapter 15

Have you ever woken from a dream that felt so real that you could have sworn it was? One that left you disoriented and confused for hours, that had you questioning what is real versus what is not? This is a common side effect we suffer here from going to Earth.

It makes sense to feel this way. Even though the situations are real, life on Earth is the dream, and this is our real life. Such a fine line exists between the two realities. Certain lives we live on Earth will cause changes within us as well. They affect us in a profound way, and always leave some kind of mark.

Even though I knew I wasn't Veronica Edwards, I was kind of feeling like her. The lines between reality and fantasy were blurring for me big time. I was doing the one thing I truly enjoyed about being her, just being with him. In a way, it was like no time had passed, really. We picked up right where we had left off back on Earth. But for me, time did pass while I was there. Five years had gone by between his death and mine. For him this time felt like nothing. It was like seconds—*a blink of an eye for him*. For me, that time had felt like forever.

Enlightened

You would think that, staring into Kaleb's blue eyes instead of Seth's green, I would have an easy time accepting the difference. The extreme change in his hair color and style should be ringing large bells for me as well. But it just wasn't. Even with his short, feathered sandy-blond hair and his fringe bangs, replacing Seth's chin-length jet black, he was still him. The man I fell head over heels in love with.

*Oh...*and then there's his voice! Kaleb's tone had always been deep and masculine like any other male's. But as Seth it was so much deeper, almost dark at times. I was chuckling to myself on the inside, recalling the discomfort his deep tone would cause people on Earth who didn't know him the way that I did.

I was just so extremely conflicted! There were moments sitting here with him where I just couldn't wrap my head around the simple fact that I was Harmony, and not Veronica. That I really was sitting here with him. Instead of being back on Earth, alone, miserable, and missing him.

I couldn't dare peel my eyes away from the most handsome soul that I have ever seen. I was fighting this feeling that this was all some sort of crazy dream, and that any moment I would wake up and this would all be gone. Looking into his eyes and seeing not just Kaleb's face, but Seth's. Knowing they were the same person, and knowing I now had the honor of spending eternity with him, was a lot for me to take in. I had to live with the loss of him for so long on Earth. Now, I knew that he and I would be together forever, and that nothing would ever separate us again. I was thrilled that this was true. But what I knew as Harmony and what I didn't know from being Veronica on Earth were at serious odds with each other.

As Harmony, I knew that I had lived many lives. I also knew that I'd had many relationships as a result. Not one of those other relationships had ever captivated me in the same way that Kaleb had as Seth. A part of me couldn't help but wonder if it was because I'd known him for so long, or if this soul-mate connection that he and I shared really was the driving force behind this spellbinding desire I felt for him.

I can be quite the inquisitive soul at times, and this soul-mate connection that he and I shared had me so intrigued. I was fascinated by the fact that he and I were created to only appeal to the other. Hence, the mesmerizing draw we both felt to always want to be near the other. The dull ache that was always tormenting me back on Earth whenever he wasn't with me and then plagued me once he was gone. Then there was that odd struggle-to-breathe thing. It was not so much that I couldn't breathe when he wasn't near me. It was more like I couldn't breathe right. Like the natural thoughtless flow of it became nonexistent. It was uncomfortable, and

Enlightened

I had to constantly think about and remind myself to breathe in and out.

And then there was his sweet honey-like scent. No matter how much I breathed him in, I could never seem to get enough of it. It became like aromatherapy the way it radiated through my body, traveling to each limb, helping to relax me and make me feel at peace. This sweet scent was strong in his hair, just slightly above his collarbone, lined his breath, and coated his lips. Just the thought of tasting this incredible sweetness made my mouth water, and sent my heart into an enthusiastic frenzy.

Going on what I had experienced, I could only imagine what it must have been like for Kaleb. I never missed it when he pressed his face into my hair and then took in a deep breath. Then to feel his body relax and rejoice at the same time as mine brought me this soothing sense of being home. There really is no other way to describe it.

Learning that he and I were extreme soul mates like Charmeine and Zuriel was making our time together here feel even more unreal. It was difficult knowing that I must keep this knowledge to myself until Kaleb discovered this too. I felt as though I was bursting at the seams in a way, and I could hardly contain myself. I wanted nothing more than to be able to share in this joyous news with him.

Billie Kowalewski

With the exception of the hair and eye color being different, he still looked like the same man that I was in love with. Even though I knew that what I was experiencing was real, the Veronica part of me wasn't allowing me to take any chances or to take any of this for granted. I couldn't help but marvel over everything about him. A part of me felt like I hadn't seen him in so long, and I couldn't stop studying every single feature, trying hard to commit them to memory. An insurance policy, I guess, just in case the tables somehow did turn and *this* life turned out to be the crazy dream.

My eyes were tracing along the curves in his lips. They were following the way his top lip arched, just slightly unevenly, which you would only notice upon very close examination. Even though they were not plump and full, they were firm and outlined softly. Still enticing and alluring, with a unique honey-infused sweetness.

It was almost impossible for me to keep from staring into his eyes either. As Seth, his green eyes were always deep and intense. They lured me in, calling me forward in a way that I never could resist. As Kaleb his blue eyes were just as inviting. They were hypnotic, causing me to become unhinged the longer I stared into them. His stare made me feel extraordinary, and with it came this sense tugging in the back of my mind, and I could swear I knew exactly what he was thinking. Just one of the many possible characteristics of our soul-mate connection, no doubt.

Enlightened

"Oh, I missed you so much!" I told him while I was hugging him, for probably the hundredth time, at the very least, since I'd been with him. We were doing what we always did back on Earth, sitting alongside each other, talking casually. Only instead of sitting in his sleek black Ford Mustang convertible, we were sitting together on a huge flat rock that was wedged up against a large oak tree.

He raised our tightly laced fingers to his lips and gently kissed the back of my hand. "Harmony, I missed you too," he replied, with a sympathetic smile. "We weren't really apart for that long."

"I know, but it felt like it!" I told him, throwing my free hand up. "It may as well have been an eternity considering the misery it caused me!"

He used his free hand to pull me closer and lovingly stroked my head in an effort to soothe me. "It's over, and we're together now," he replied. I felt him press his face into my hair, just like he always did back on Earth. His sweet honey-like scent wrapped right around me like a warm familiar hug, helping me to feel better. I heard him inhale as he kissed the top of my head. "For eternity, remember?"

"Thank God!" I exclaimed loudly. I reached over with my free arm, placing my hand on his cheek. I pressed my lips to his, kissing him wildly, running my fingers up and twisting them into his silky sandy-blond hair. Showing him just how relieved I was for that to be true.

When I finally let go, Kaleb chuckled. "Never mind what I said… You can miss me as much as you want," he replied with a large grin.

I smiled back, nudging him playfully with my shoulder. "I'm just so relieved that I'm with you again," I told him. I leaned my head back against the bark of the oak tree, letting out a happy, exaggerated "*ahhh*!"

"Being without you was one of the worst things I've ever had to live through. That experience is one that I never want to repeat again." I'd never sounded more serious.

I turned to face him, playfully rolling my head against the oak tree. I smiled joyfully as I stared into his eyes, allowing the happiness I was feeling to radiate through me from head to toe. This was something I'd fought with back on Earth after he was gone. It was such a struggle to carry on with my life after he died. I carried such sadness and guilt about his death for so long. It felt good to have that misery finally dissolve and to finally be at peace with it.

"A part of me wishes things could have been different for us back on Earth. It would have been such a joy to spend the rest of that life with you. Just being with you was all that I wanted. I'm so glad to finally have that," I told him.

"That's all that I ever wanted in that life too," he replied. "You were so amazing to me in that life… impressive is a better word for it. The things that you

Enlightened

faced…" He clenched his eyes closed and I felt his body shudder a little. He opened his eyes and looked into mine. "…To overcome those things the way that you did." His eyes burned with such affection and pride. "It was because of you." He smiled and gently caressed my cheek. "*You* made me want to be a better man."

I joyfully kissed his sweet lips, thanking him for that compliment. My heart was overflowing with such love and affection for him. He had always made me feel so incredible about myself back on Earth. It was comforting to know that this still held true here. My only hope was that I made him feel the same way.

I gently grazed my lips against his. "There isn't a need to improve upon such perfection," I replied, just barely above a whisper. I could taste his sweet breath on my tongue, and my body began to quiver. My heart began pounding when I noticed Kaleb was quivering too.

Our lips finally touched in what can only be described as desperation. As if true desperation can really be experienced here to any degree. The need for each other he and I felt in that moment was powerful and overwhelming. It felt electric as the sparks between us ignited, keeping that familiar fire of desire burning strongly within us.

I always felt extraordinary back on Earth whenever I kissed him. My thoughts would scramble every time, allowing any worry I had to escape my mind. He was my elixir at times, a way to cope with whatever dilemma I was facing. Making any tension I was feeling about anything simply disappear.

Kissing him here, however, was far better than I ever could have imagined. We were set free from all of the normal mundane worries and frustrations that we were accustomed to when we were on Earth. All of the feelings and emotions that we were used to become less intense here. A lot of them became nonexistent because they are not necessary anymore. This gives us the freedom to love each other unconditionally, in our natural way. Being able to love him this way made my soul feel as though it were soaring high whenever I kissed him. I felt truly free.

Knowing he and I were soul mates and could spend the rest of our existence together, and that I would never lose him, brought me such a true sense of peace. As Seth, he became my best friend, and I was filled to the brim with elation knowing our friendship had gone far beyond Earth and would continue on forever. I should tell him all of the things I wanted to after his death but never could, I thought to myself as I snuggled up against him. Besides, if I really am Veronica Edwards still, and this really is some sort of crazy dream, I should take full advantage of this before I wake up!

Clutching tightly to his hand, I took in a deep breath and exhaled sharply. "After you died," I began, staring intensely at our interwoven fingers. "I was…destroyed."

Enlightened

For a long time I carried such guilt about his death. I began to shudder as the painful memory of his accident filled my mind. It stirred up all of the feelings that I had fought so hard to get past but never could.

I took in another deep, cleansing breath and exhaled hard, trying to expel those feelings so that I could speak. "There really is no other way to explain it. It was like a piece of me left with you. I spent a lot of time analyzing your death, thinking of ways that I could have prevented it. How I didn't tell you often enough just how much you truly meant to me and how much I loved you. How I would have given anything to have saved you. You were and are my best friend. I was so very lost without you in my life."

Kaleb sat there in silence. He casually stroked the back of the hand he was holding, continuing to listen as I poured my heart out to him.

"At night, I would lie in bed fantasizing about what things could have been like for us had you lived. I would imagine the wedding we should have had, and us raising a family. But then reality would set in and then I would spend days and days after in tears. My body ached all the time and it was a conscious effort every day just to breathe. After a while, a part of me became numb and hollow, but the ache lingered. It was such an unusual feeling. I could no longer feel anything anymore except emptiness." I sighed. "It was as if I had just shut down."

"As time went on, I ended up doing things just to occupy my mind. Things to just keep me busy so I didn't have time to think anymore. Because I knew if I had time to think, I would think of you, and then I wouldn't be able to function. A part of me always felt guilty for carrying on with my life when you couldn't carry on with yours."

Kaleb ran his fingers down my cheek, stopping at my chin. He gently turned my head so he could look at me. He smiled sympathetically. "Thanks to the barrier, little did you know, our lives do go on. I did carry on with my life. I tried to send you messages letting you know that I was all right. Didn't you get them?"

I sat back a little, touching my fingers to my lips. My eyes were narrowed in frustration as I tried to recall if I'd ever had any sort of feelings or messages about him being okay, but I couldn't remember. "I don't know, I don't remember," I replied.

Kaleb sighed and then chuckled lightly. "I promise, next time, I will try harder."

I chuckled back at him. "You had better."

I smiled and then kissed his cheek. "You were the best part of that life. You made living it bearable and then you were gone. I was so miserable without you. I never want to live another life on Earth where you are not there. Promise me we'll be always be together there."

Enlightened

Zipporah's warning about how he and I should not go to Earth without each other was suddenly tugging at the back of my mind.

Kaleb smiled at me warmly. "Harmony, I wish I could promise that. We can't control when we'll go home…you know that."

I sighed. "True, but you can promise you'll stay with me there."

"I can't recall a single life where we weren't. I'm sure we will be."

I let out another audible sigh. "I guess just that will have to be enough."

I leaned in, pressing my lips to his. I kissed him tenderly. I took my time, lingering there, taking full advantage of the fact that he was here with me again at last. That he belonged to me and I belonged to him. That there would never be a doubt, and that nothing could ever take him from me again. I had both my hands gripping his shirt collar tightly. There was no way I was letting him go until I was ready to release him. I didn't want him to just hear the words of how I felt, but to feel them as well.

Kaleb's expression was comical once I finally let go. It was one of disappointment. His brows were narrowed, but his eyes were tender and wide. I ran my fingers through his silky sandy-blond hair and then down his left cheek, where he used to have his scar when he was

Seth. I then gently caressed his tender lips with my fingertips. "I love you so much," I told him, just slightly above a whisper.

"I love you too," he replied.

He took my hand in his and kissed the back of it. "Now it's my turn," Kaleb said with a soft smile. Kaleb placed his hands on the sides of my neck, gently cradling my face. He let out a carefree, happy sigh. "I have loved every single life that I ever had the honor of spending with you," he began.

His sweet honey-like scent was captivating, and his gaze was intense as he looked directly into my eyes. He tenderly kissed my lips, making my body come alive, awakening those familiar butterflies in my stomach that had been lying dormant since his death. They swarmed upward through my chest, swirling and dancing throughout as they rejuvenated my soul.

Continuing to hold my eyes with his, Kaleb smiled. "…But this last life," he said, on an exhale. He kissed my right cheek. "…Miss Veronica…" And then the left. He stopped to gaze affectionately into my eyes. "…Will always be my favorite."

He began running his fingers through my hair, playing affectionately with my curls. "I was in love with you from the moment we met in that life." He smiled kindly, narrowing his eyes playfully and bowing his head a little. "Actually, it's been just a tad longer." He winked.

Enlightened

"I spent a good chunk of my childhood in that life in such misery. That was, until you walked into my life. I knew there was something special about you the moment I saw you. I remember the excitement I felt when you and I spoke for the first time. Then the excitement I felt every single time you sat next to me, or shared something with me, or just hugged me. You were so amazing to me that I often found myself confused as to how I ever got so lucky to be blessed with such a wonderful friend as you. I recall worrying at times that somehow I would lose you. But no matter what I did you stayed with me, helping to dissolve that worry over time." He smiled kindly, and tenderly kissed my cheek.

His eyes seemed to smolder as he stared into mine. They were wide, and full of innocence. He seemed to be in awe. "You were my best friend in that life, and will always be my best friend for the rest of my existence," he assured me. His tone was saturated with sincerity.

Kaleb continued running his fingers through my hair, affectionately playing with my long brown curls. He seemed to be taking in more than just my eyes, the way he sat there glancing around at my face and my hair. He held his soft, happy smile. He would pause every once in a while, seeming to be losing his train of thought at times.

"I always thought your brown eyes and your light-brown curls were beautiful in that last life. But this…"

He combed his fingers through my curls, fanning them out in front of my face so that I could see them. "…Is absolutely breathtaking."

"Your natural colors are exquisite. Your Earth colors were so drab in comparison. I've never known dark-brown hair could shine the way yours does." He sighed in contentment. "…And then your eyes," he said on an exhale. "The glow they give off lights up your beautiful face, and they are exquisitely outlined by your long thick lashes. It's as if someone flipped on a switch when you came home, bringing you to life."

I could feel my cheeks flushing red. He wasn't a man of many words back on Earth. He did have his moments. But it was always what he did, and never what he said, that assured me of how he felt. Honestly, that had always been the best way. People have the capability of saying anything, and do so all the time. But showing someone by your actions instead helps them to feel it. If they can feel it, there is never any doubt.

I felt giddy and I couldn't help but giggle. "Our Earth bodies just don't do us any justice, do they?"

"No, they certainly don't. I've always thought you were the most beautiful girl in every other life. But I will always prefer the true you. I will always prefer this," he replied, combing his fingers through my hair.

"I love you too," I assured him.

Enlightened

His expression became serious. "I will always be grateful for what you did for me in that life, too." His words were spoken with utmost sincerity.

"It was extremely hard, and if it weren't for you, I would have had to live another life like that one. Thank you so much for helping me through that. I know I couldn't have done that without you."

I placed my hand on one of his, holding it against my cheek. "I didn't do anything. You did all of that work on your own. I was just there for you," I replied kindly.

Kaleb held his kind smile. "Don't be so modest. If it weren't for you, I know I would have had to repeat that horrible type of life. I know I couldn't have done that alone."

He was staring directly into my eyes, still cupping my face in his gentle hands. He leaned in and began skimming his nose down along my collarbone. I closed my eyes, as the feel of his sweet breath against my skin was causing me to melt. I felt him inhale as he skimmed his nose up my neck, stopping to kiss me just under my right ear. "My baby..." he whispered. He turned and began skimming his nose along the other side of my neck. He took his time, starting at my collarbone, going up, and again stopping to kiss me just below my ear. "I will cherish that life for the rest of my existence," he whispered again.

"Loving you was the easiest, most natural thing I have ever experienced on Earth. I struggled with so many things in that life and the only thing that ever made sense there was when it was just you and me." He chuckled. "I recall struggling with this ache there when we were apart, and how it would dissolve the second you were with me. It's funny, I remember thinking that this must be what heaven is like, whenever I had you in my arms."

I opened my eyes, and my breath caught when I discovered he was an inch away from my face. "You were my reason for living in that life. Nothing could ever change what you mean to me and nothing will ever change how I feel about you. My love for you knows no bounds.

"To be blessed with a beautiful soul like you is far beyond what I could ever have imagined for myself. I feel like the real me finally came to life after you told me that you loved me."

I smiled happily. "That's funny, that's how I feel about you, too."

Chapter 16

I COULD BARELY MAKE HIM out through the dense clouds that were billowing around him. He had his back to me as he stood far away and alone amidst the stark, never-ending white.

He turned around slowly and his lips turned upward into that glorious carefree smile the moment my eyes met his. I watched the clouds in front of him begin to roll up and out as he parted them with the stretch of his hand. He held his hand out to me, beckoning me forward through the dissipating soft white clouds. I smiled back at him as I happily began to make my way through the clouds toward him.

Standing tall and confident, he drew me in with his tantalizing, playful smirk. Continuing to call me forward, motioning me with his hand. The clouds around him continued to slowly disperse with every step that I took. They followed his lead as if they were one with him, mirroring his every move.

With a cool, quick flick of his hands, the clouds rapidly began tumbling downward. They rolled and swirled around him, dropping to his feet, revealing the sharp white tuxedo that he was dressed in.

I gasped when I saw how handsome he looked, causing me to pause for a moment. His all-white tuxedo was pristine and tailored perfectly, fitting his well-built physique. He looked even more glorious than ever, and I was reveling in the astonishing fact that he was mine.

He winked and smiled, nodding his head slightly, motioning for me to glance downward. I couldn't help gasping again, because to my surprise, I was wearing a beautiful white gown. The gown was made of smooth white satin that overlapped at the waist, creating a plunging V neckline. The overlapping waistline twisted together so elegantly, flowing gracefully into the dress itself.

The dress was gorgeous and I felt so amazing in it. But more importantly, he made me feel amazing. I eagerly began making my way toward him once again, more excited now than ever. I was overflowing with anticipation of just the mere possibility of what surprise he might have in store for me.

The clouds continued to swirl and dance at his feet hovering above the ground, covering the path in front of him. As I made my way toward him, I started to notice that the closer I moved, the farther away he appeared to be. I began trying to move faster, taking longer strides to reach him, but it was hard to get closer. The clouds began to pick up speed, rolling across the ground, imitating

Enlightened

my pace. Faster and faster they rolled, all while Kaleb seemed to be moving farther away.

A booming clap of thunder roared loudly, stopping me in my tracks, and the stark, never-ending white started to darken. Lightning crashed down hard, striking the path between us, tainting the once-white surroundings a deep dark red.

The clouds began suctioning downward rapidly where the lightning crashed, revealing a large canyon between us. A howling wind was whipping through now, pushing against me and causing my dress to thrash violently. I struggled to hold myself upright, fighting the force of the brute-strength winds. My pulse raced and my chest heaved as I desperately struggled to figure out what was happening and how I would reach him.

The canyon seemed to stretch on infinitely in both directions. I looked down over the edge and became horrified by its depth. The canyon was far deeper than I was expecting. I glanced back up at Kaleb, concerned with what must be going through his mind about our horrifying turn of events, and became confused. He continued to stand there, smiling, seeming oblivious to the danger we were currently in.

The wind continued violently, whipping through my hair as I fought against it, holding myself upright. Lightning flashed and thunder roared around us as I stood there, frantically weighing my options.

Desperate to get to Kaleb, I decided the only possible solution was to leap across. I took a few steps back to get a running start, and began running as fast as I could toward the canyon, fighting against the elements.

I could feel the ground under my feet begin to rumble as I started to run. As I neared the edge of the cliff I saw the ground at Kaleb's feet starting to break off, crumbling into the unknown. I pushed myself harder now, determined to save him. When I reached the edge of the canyon, I pushed off as hard as I could, leaping into the air. A large section of the cliff on the other side broke off midflight, and I just barely caught the edge of what was left. The impact knocked the wind out of my chest when I slammed my body into the hard rock. The canyon wall continued to crumble under my hands as I struggled to hang on and climb up. My feet flailed frantically as I struggled to try to find just a small piece to step up on, but it seemed to be no use. The wall was continuing to crumble away, and there was no way to stop it.

I glanced up, looking for Kaleb, to get his help, but I couldn't see him. I started calling out his name as I struggled to hang on, worried about what might have happened to him.

"*Kaleb*!" I shouted frantically at the top of my lungs. "Kaleb, where are you!"

Enlightened

"I'm right here," he replied. He sounded so calm, cool, and collected.

I swung my leg up as hard as I could, finally finding a lip to step on, and began pulling myself up. I was almost breathing a sigh of relief when I pulled myself up onto the ledge, but it quickly faded once I saw him. Somehow, still too far away for me to help him, he held on tightly to his confident smile, continuing to call me forward, oblivious to his demise. I could feel the blood draining from my face when my eyes took in the giant tsunami-sized wave behind him.

The wave began to curl and I started to run. I was quickly becoming frustrated that I seemed to be running in slow motion now. No matter how hard I tried, my feet could not gain purchase against the perpetually crumbling rock. The wave began to curl in more, falling right above his head. "*MOVE…KALEB!*" I screamed at the top of my lungs. My arms stretched out in front of me, ready to grab him, as I continued to push myself as hard as I could to run faster, stuck in slow motion. My eyes were wide, and I let out a blood-curdling scream as I watched in horror; the wave crashed down, crushing him…

"Kaleb!"

I woke up abruptly out of a sound sleep. The disturbing image of my love being crushed by a giant tsunami wave was still foremost on my mind. A dream that felt so real it was still causing me to shudder. If this were Earth, I would surely be drenched in sweat by such a nightmare.

What bothered me most about the dream (besides the meteorological events that were constantly trying to take out my only love!) was the part where I didn't even realize that I'd fallen asleep! This haphazard kind of thing usually only happens to me, and only happens when I'm home.

I got a little annoyed with this occasionally. Especially when I didn't make it to my bed and I fell asleep on the rock. I did have to admit though, falling asleep in the arms of my love wasn't so bad. This was something I'd truly missed after he was gone. Still, I would probably appreciate that fact just a tad more if I'd had a good dream instead of a nightmare!

He tightened his arms around me protectively, out of instinct. "Are you all right?" he asked urgently, as he rubbed my shoulder. He sounded half asleep himself, but his tone was saturated with worry. "What's wrong?"

I was so thankful that it really was all a dream. Out of all the things I could dream of, why in all of heaven did it have to be that? The love of my existence in constant peril and then crushed by a giant wave? I was extremely relieved to find that this was not the case, and that I was where my existence made the most sense. I was curled up with him, comfortably tucked under his arm on our rock, our bodies still resting up against the oak tree. I was surrounded by his sweet honey-like scent, with my hand still resting comfortably upon his chest.

Still shaken from the dream that quickly turned into my worst nightmare, I glanced up, peering affectionately into Kaleb's handsome blue eyes. I quickly combed my fingers into his silky sandy-blond hair, pulling him closer, pressing my lips to his, desperate to feel the relief that only his sweet lips could provide.

He eagerly complied, molding his lips to mine, groaning loudly in contentment. I could feel him melting and losing himself in the kiss right along with me.

He carefully pulled away to look at me. His expression was a sympathetic one. "Bad dream?" he asked simply.

"You have no idea!" I sighed loudly. "I'm so thankful it was just a dream."

He chuckled lightly. "Too bad that's the one thing we get to experience both here and on Earth."

"I don't mind so much when they're good dreams," I replied.

"Do you want to talk about it?" he asked. "I'm not sure who really says this, but *they* say it helps."

"No," I quickly replied, shaking my head. I was all too eager to forget about that one.

Kaleb chuckled. "Well, if you do change your mind, I will listen."

"I know, thank you." I smiled at him.

"You're welcome," he replied, and then smirked at me. "Perhaps I can do something to distract you from it then?"

I smirked back at him. My brow raised slightly in curiosity. "Hmmm…what do you have in mind?"

He sat up quickly, getting to his knees to face me, holding his kind smile. He began casually combing his fingers through my hair, playing affectionately with my long brown curls. He leaned in slowly, taking his time, all while taking a deep, drawn-out breath in. He gently kissed my neck down by my collarbone, causing me to intuitively lean my head back just slightly, allowing him to draw his lips up my neck, stopping at his usual spot just under my ear.

I could feel his lips gently brush against my ear and I started to tremble. "Does this help?" he whispered.

The butterflies were beginning to flutter about my body, causing my brain to malfunction just slightly. It took me a moment to put together rational thoughts to be able to answer that.

"A li-t-t-t-le," I stammered.

I heard him chuckle. He gently tilted my head to the other side and pressed his sweet lips to my neck. Running them up slowly, stopping just under my ear. "What about now?" he whispered again.

"W-w-wow," was all I could manage to get out.

Enlightened

Kaleb gently pressed his lips to mine. I eagerly began kissing him back, breathing him in. His sweet honey-like scent washed through me like a powerful elixir, helping me to feel better. I was losing myself once again, instinctively gripping his shirt up by his collar. I was pulling him closer now, compelled by the sweet taste of his lips.

He gently pulled away, grazing his lips against mine. I was trembling from the feel of his sweet breath against them. He started to chuckle. "All better?" he asked just above a whisper.

I held my eyes closed. "Uh-huh."

"Good," he replied. "I'll bet, though, that I can make you feel even better."

I leaned back, opening my eyes and narrowing them playfully, and crossed my arms. "Oh, really," I replied in a sarcastic tone. "And how do you plan to accomplish this?"

Kaleb laughed. "That wasn't what I had in mind at all!"

"Uh-huh," I replied, waiting very patiently for him to continue. When he didn't, I prompted, "Enlighten me."

He kissed my lips quickly with a warm, playful peck. "I realized that you and I had the honor of falling in love with each other twice. Once down on Earth and then again here when we got home."

I smiled at his realization. "Hmm…this is true." I nodded. "That did happen."

He took my hand in his and kissed the back of it. He looked into my eyes and smiled.

"Now the next time you and I go back down to Earth together we can fall in love with each other all over again."

"That is true too…we can do that," I replied, continuing to smile.

"Think of how fortunate you and I are that we can do that as many times as we want. It's not too often we hear about souls who get to do that."

I sighed audibly in utter amazement. How could anyone ever argue against that logic? Wow, he was astonishing and obviously incredibly smart! He and I got the honor of falling in love with each other over and over. It was a unique case. It would blow his mind, though, if he knew just how unique he and I really were in comparison to the other souls. That he and I would always be able to find each other on Earth, no matter the distance, every single time. We were drawn to each other because we were created to.

Oh, what I would give for him to understand this now! To come to the same conclusion that I had just a short while ago. I know, I know! Patience is a virtue!

I can be patient to a degree at times. But it can be hard when it's something I really want! I know, though, that I must be when it comes to learning. Everyone learns at a different pace, and each lesson can be easy for some, while at times harder for others.

Enlightened

I'd learned what we were before he had, and it was okay that he had not yet. With realizations like that one, it really was only a matter of time before he did. I just knew he would soon; I could feel it!

I leaned in and gently kissed his cheek. "Thank you, that did make me feel better."

Rose colored his cheeks and then he smiled. "I knew that it would."

I couldn't help the wide smile that spread across my face now. He really did make me feel so much better, helping me to let go of that crazy nightmare.

"Do you know what I think?" he asked suddenly.

"Not unless you allow me," I replied casually.

He playfully narrowed his eyes at me. "Smartass…I was thinking that perhaps you and I should imagine our own place."

I sat there frozen for a moment. I wasn't too sure how I should proceed. I glanced around at our surroundings, armed with the knowledge that he and I had imagined pretty much the same home. How did I tell him this without revealing too much? Perhaps admitting this part, though, would help guide him to understand what made us different? There were so many parts to this and so many ways that this could go. I knew I must be careful how much I revealed, though, so he would learn what we were on his own; it was the only way.

Kaleb sat there carefully studying my face, and then his expression changed, practically mimicking my own. "Is there something wrong?" he asked suddenly.

"I would tell you if there was," I replied.

"Well, I asked you about imagining our own place and then you became so quiet." He smirked at me and chuckled. "That's so unlike you."

I gave him a playful shove. "You're so funny," I replied sarcastically. I then took in a deep breath and exhaled before continuing to speak. "I didn't want to make you nervous before, but it appears that you and I may have imagined the same home for ourselves."

He sat back a little. His eyes narrowed at me in disbelief. "How can that be?"

I shrugged. "I don't know," I replied. I glanced around quickly and then I looked into his eyes. "There are some tiny differences, but it sure does look that way."

"That is impossible. I know that our homes can have similarities, but no two souls are alike enough to be able to do that."

I shrugged again. "Sure looks like we did."

Kaleb quickly got to his feet with a noticeable bounce. He had a sly look on his face and held his hand out to me. "Let's test this theory, shall we?"

I laughed at him and took his hand, allowing him to help me up. Kaleb and his tests! I thought to myself. I could only imagine what this test of his would entail. At least I didn't have to worry about dying accidentally here.

"Fine by me," I replied, my tone reeking with obvious confidence. "...I will take that challenge."

He casually led me to the beginning of the stony path that in my home led to my washroom and hammock bed. He raised his hand, pointing down the path. "What's down there?" he asked.

I smirked at him and then dramatically pressed my fingers to my lips, pretending to be deep in thought. "Hmmm...your bed and your washroom."

He narrowed his eyes at me. "Good guess, but anyone using the process of elimination could have guessed that." He leaned in a little, bowing his head, and winked at me. "Care to be a little more specific?"

My smirk quickly turned into a wide grin. I was having a hard time holding in my need to laugh, too. He always knew exactly which buttons to push to get me going, knowing full well that I loved a challenge. Only this time he didn't realize that I had the advantage over him. "Okay...your bed is a hammock, strung between two pine trees," I stated confidently.

I watched as he flinched back, a little surprised by my answer. "Not bad, not bad," he replied, waving his hand coolly and nodding his head, appearing to be impressed. He then narrowed his eyes at me and crossed his arms. "...What color are the sheets?" he challenged.

Again, I couldn't help laughing at him. "I don't know what you picked, but mine are green," I replied mid-chuckle. I took in a breath, trying to compose myself so I could continue. "…And your washroom door is a light-blue color and is wedged between two boulders."

I have to admit, it was funny watching the expression on his face change as quickly as it did. He went from self-assured right down to "holy crap" in an instant. His eyes were wide from the shock. He just stood there, frozen and totally speechless, stunned by my accuracy.

"Just so you know, I am only going by the fact that the rock by the stream is exactly the same as what I had imagined, too. So I am just simply stating what's in my home," I told him.

"Whoa" was all that he said, speaking just above a whisper.

I suddenly recalled that he had come to my home that one time when I had left my cotton candy at Jaire's. I was surprised that he hadn't noticed any similarities then.

"Kaleb, you've been to my home before. Remember? You came to bring me my cotton candy after I left it at Jaire's. Didn't you notice the similarities then?"

Kaleb's expression turned, and he now looked a little embarrassed.

"I'm sorry, but I was experiencing a bit of jealousy at that moment, and I wasn't paying enough attention to notice much else."

Enlightened

I quickly wrapped my arms around him, giving him a big hug. "It's okay. I forgive you," I told him.

Kaleb and I began walking down the winding stony path. We were strolling hand in hand through the trees, happily, of course. Neither of us was in any real rush. There was never a need for that here.

Being in the woods had always brought me such a true sense of peace. I glanced over at Kaleb as we walked and could easily see that he felt the same. He had a soft smile across his face and a carefree bounce in his step. He playfully swung our arms, lifting the hand he was holding to his lips occasionally to kiss the back of it as we walked. It was uplifting to know that he felt the same way about being in a forest as I did.

He had such radiance to his demeanor as we continued to walk. He was glowing and happy, as only a passionate soul like him could be. He reached up as we passed by an oak, picking a leaf off of a low-hanging branch. He handed me the leaf and smiled. "I'm sorry I doubted you. I just can't get over the fact that we imagined the same home," he said casually.

I took the leaf, twirling it between my fingers as we continued to walk, and smiled at him sympathetically. "Kaleb, it's okay. I would have reacted the same way. Even I think this is weird."

"Why do you think this happened?" he asked.

"I don't know. Perhaps you and I just have a lot more in common than we thought?" I suggested. I figured this was the safest answer to give, continuing to be careful to not reveal too much.

"Maybe." He nodded. "We have known each other such a long time. It is only natural that we would have some things in common."

"That's true," I agreed. Wow, he is close! I couldn't help thinking. He was waltzing right around the answer like a talented dancer. If only he would see it already!

We reached the area where the hammock bed and the washroom would be. To my surprise there was a desk, which looked like it was carved out of an old tree stump, with a nice little chair near the foot of the hammock bed. With the exception of this, everything else appeared to be the same. The hammock bed was to the left of the path, across from the washroom door. It was suspended between two very tall pines. The ground underneath was carpeted by their needles. The bed was covered with a soft dark-green comforter. The sheets were the same shade of green and were folded neatly over the top of the comforter, which bordered the two matching pillows.

I walked over to the washroom door and turned the handle. I tugged on Kaleb's hand, pulling him into the washroom with me.

Everything appeared to be the same. The sink was still across from the shower. The oval mirror was in place above the sink where it belonged. I closed the washroom door, checking to see if the full-length mirror was still there, and it was. The walls were still a golden wood tone, too. The only thing left to check was the walk-in closet at the far end of the washroom.

I opened the door to the walk-in closet and went in, pulling Kaleb with me. We both gasped when we entered. Across from the rack that Kaleb's clothes hung on was another rack, filled with my clothes.

"Wow," Kaleb said on an exhale as he looked around. He gently caressed the rack where my clothes were hanging. "There was always just a bare wall here before. Is this where your clothes have always been in your closet?"

"Yes." I smiled at him. "So it's safe to assume, then, your clothes have always been here?" I asked, running my hand across one of his hung-up shirts.

"Yeah," he replied.

"I'm guessing that perhaps our homes must have just merged together," I told him, shrugging my shoulders. I couldn't help wondering if our soul-mate connection was responsible for this too? Just like it had been for so much more. I was in awe.

"It does appear that way. Are you all right with our home being like this? We can change things if you would like."

I took a step toward Kaleb and put my arms around him. I glanced up, looking into his eyes, and smiled.

"I'm fine with this as long as you are. I've always loved living here, and now I love it even more because I get to share it with you."

With a glow in his eyes and a warm smile, Kaleb placed his fingers under my chin. He pulled me in closer, pressing his sweet lips to mine. He tightened his arms around my waist, holding me closely, giving me a warm hug. His sweet, honey-like scent was floating delicately in the air. I could feel without question in this moment that I truly was home.

Chapter 17

IT WAS PEACEFUL AS USUAL by the stream today—as it is every day here. I was tucked comfortably in my usual spot under his left arm. I was very relaxed, and my thoughts were adrift. Like the water cascading by at our feet, they flowed freely.

It was a nice change, sitting with him for reflection. Reflection is something we do to help us understand the lessons that we were taught in the life we just came from. Taking time to think about what we've done in the past helps shape us for the future. We all know we cannot undo things that we have done. But we do know we can learn from them. So whenever you take time to reflect about your past, take your time. It's better to have learned from your mistakes instead of continuing to make them.

Snuggling against him, my thoughts flowed freer than they ever had before. They wandered in and out in a random pattern, allowing the lessons from Earth to bubble to the surface.

Mindlessly, I played with the little white buttons on his green button-down shirt. I casually traced around the smooth plastic edge and the crisscross threads. My fingers, as if they had a mind of their own, continued on down along the hem, feeling the fabric of the blue cotton tee his open button-down shirt revealed.

The best place for reflection for me had always been on the rock by the stream. Kaleb had made this time even more enjoyable. His strong arms held me close and I fit perfectly in them, as if they were made for holding me. The most comforting part was I now knew that they actually were.

I'd never felt more at home in my entire existence. I closed my eyes, listening to the gentle hum of the stream. I was enjoying the simple feeling of being wrapped in his arms. His sweet honey-like scent swirled about as if caressing and soothing me. My entire being was rejoicing with each intake of breath, sending feelings of contentment tingling throughout my body.

I let out a relaxed sigh, enjoying everything about this moment. I was enjoying the coolness coming off the rock that I could feel through my white cotton socks. I loved the way the gentle breeze caressed my cheeks, and the way the perfume of the forest mingled with my love's sweet scent as it traveled to my nose.

Kaleb tightened his arms around me, pulling me closer, and I felt him press his face into my hair. He inhaled deeply, letting out an exaggerated "ahhh!" and he kissed the top of my head.

Enlightened

"Have you always smelled like this?" he asked, interrupting my random thoughts.

I giggled at his question, feeling a little embarrassed. "Um…I don't know… What do I smell like?"

"You smell like a sweet flower. Like a rose or a carnation. It bears a striking resemblance." He leaned in, inhaling again, letting out another exaggerated "ahhh!… I love the way you smell."

I chuckled. "Thanks. I love the way you smell too."

"Have you always smelled this sweet?" he asked.

I chuckled again, turning my head to smirk at him. "I don't know. No one has ever told me that I smelled like a sweet flower before," I replied, continuing to laugh.

He leaned in, skimming his nose down along my collarbone. As I felt him take in a slow, deep breath, I couldn't help closing my eyes. His touch was causing me to lose my train of thought.

"It's stronger here." He spoke as if making a mental note. "Definitely closer to rose than a carnation…"

I felt him take my hand in his. He brought it to his lips, kissing my palm, and then skimmed his nose along my wrist, breathing in, following the length of my forearm down to my elbow.

"Why aren't roses called Harmony?" he wondered to himself aloud.

I opened my eyes to look at him. "That which we call a rose by any other name would smell as sweet."

Kaleb chuckled and suddenly rose to his feet. He turned to face me, bending down on one knee, and took my hand in his.

He peered into my eyes and smiled, sending my heart into its typical frenzy. "I take thee at thy word: Call me but love, and I'll be new baptized; Henceforth, I never will be Romeo." He kissed the back of my hand. "Do you remember any more?"

I smiled at him. "A little." I got to my knees, grabbing his hand, and smirked at him. I dramatically placed the back of my other hand against my forehead. "O Romeo, *Romeo*! Wherefore art thou *Romeo*!" I clenched my fist, placing it against my chest dramatically. "Deny thy father and refuse thy name; or, if thou wilt not, be but sworn my love, and I'll no longer be a Capulet." I sat back, clasping my hands, placing them gently in my lap. I glanced up, grinning widely at him.

Kaleb stood up and laughed. He wandered over to a tree limb that had fallen down across from the rock that was lying in the grass. He hopped up and began playfully balancing on it. "Do you remember seeing that play in London?"

"Was that the life where you and I were servants?" I asked in reply.

He smiled "Yeah."

"I wouldn't say that we saw that, *really*."

He narrowed his eyes at me and then glanced around in confusion. "I recall watching that play with you."

Enlightened

I sighed. "Kaleb, we stood on wood crates and peered in through a window in the alley, while our bosses watched comfortably in the theater."

"So?"

"Do you recall the part where we were freezing our butts off?"

He shrugged. "Yeah, so it wasn't perfect. But we still watched it."

I laughed at him. "That life was horrible. I'm so glad we are past that one. I had a strong aversion to old bread for many lives after that."

"Oh, I know, me too! They could have fed the servants better. They had the money."

"Sleeping in the barn next to the horses wasn't much fun either," I added.

"I know, but we survived." He hopped down from the tree limb and walked toward me with a carefree bounce. He reached his hand out to me and smiled. I smiled back at him, taking it without question.

Kaleb pulled me up off the rock, taking me into his arms. He held one of my hands against his chest while holding on to me tightly. He tenderly kissed my lips and then placed his cheek against mine.

He began swaying me softly back and forth. His muscles were tight as he held me firmly up against him. I closed my eyes, breathing in his sweet honey-like scent, recalling all of the times he would do this with me on Earth.

He held me tightly in his arms as we swayed to no music. The only sound was our stream and the rhythm of our breath. I heard him chuckle right before he spun me out gracefully. I smiled at him as I followed his lead. He pulled me back, curling me in so my back was against his chest.

He rocked me gently in his arms. His eyes burned with a fierce intensity while he gazed into mine. He spun me back around, gently taking me securely in his arms. He kept our pace, and I moved with him, allowing him to sway us casually around our rock.

I chuckled when Kaleb playfully dipped me ever so gently. His blue eyes continued to smolder as he effortlessly pulled me back up toward him. "Do you remember living in Wales?" he asked softly, making casual conversation with me as we continued to waltz.

I chuckled. "How could I forget that one? I was constantly cleaning up vomit from you and my father."

"He had to pay me in some way for building that wall. His way was with shelter, food, and lots of alcohol." We were both laughing.

Curiosity got the better of me. "Why did you bring that life up?"

Rose colored his cheeks and he smiled kindly. "That was the life where I realized that I was in love with you."

I felt my cheeks flush as red as his did. "Oh," I replied softly, continuing to gush.

Enlightened

"Why didn't you say anything in that life?" I couldn't help but wonder.

Kaleb let out an audible sigh. "Well, your father in that life intimidated me for one. He was a big man. He had warned me from the start that you were off limits. Then, you kinda intimidated me. You were just so amazingly beautiful to me, and still are." He lovingly pinched my chin and smiled. "You're funny and smart…so compassionate and sweet. It was very hard working there. I always found myself so distracted while I was working and you were around. I was filled with such fear that you wouldn't feel the same way for me as I did for you." He shook his head. "That life ended with so many regrets."

A smile tugged at the corners of my pursed lips as I continued to blush. I was filled with such happiness learning about when he first fell in love with me. Though I couldn't say I was in love with him then. I could say that I did notice him. I couldn't help but wonder what would have happened between us if he had acted on this then.

"I wish you had tried then. I do recall finding you very attractive." I smiled at him. "Why do you think I always came out to where you both were working? It certainly wasn't to see my father."

Kaleb chuckled humbly. "Well, that life has passed, like so many others. We are together now and that's all that really matters."

"I agree," I replied, nodding my head casually. When he brought up the life we lived in Wales, I couldn't help recalling how we had met. Our greetings had always been accident-prone. But this one was distinctive and had such flair to it. Making it stand out so much more than our other greetings. I began thinking that if I brought it up, perhaps this would help guide Kaleb to understand what made us so special without actually telling him.

"Do you recall how you and I met in that life?" I asked him.

Kaleb stopped swaying with me as he started to think about my question. He then glanced down at our feet. He ran his fingers through his hair and then across the back of his neck before glancing back up at me with a sheepish expression. "I'm afraid that life is kind of a blur." He chuckled nervously. "Enlighten me."

I sat down on the rock and smiled up at him. I then patted the spot next to me. He took the hint and wandered over to sit by me. "My father had you sitting at the table in our kitchen. My arms were full from the garden when I walked in. I tripped over something, spun on my heels, and fell into your lap." I couldn't help laughing at the memory.

"Oh, yeah! How could I have forgotten that?" Kaleb chuckled. "Boy, we certainly are graceful, aren't we?"

I continued chuckling along with him. "I know. We do have our clumsy moments." If you only knew the reason behind this, I added mentally, hoping he'd come to the same realization that I had, but quickly realizing that probably there would be no such luck just yet.

"The life we lived in Georgia was better," he pointed out casually.

"That life was better. I did enjoy that one."

"I'm sorry about the end. I didn't mean to pull you off that cliff."

I placed my hand on his cheek. "I forgive you. I know you didn't mean to do that." I shrugged. "...You slipped."

"I felt worst about the life right before this last one." He hung his head down. "You know...the one in Virginia, when I was Vinny."

"Kaleb, it's all right." I leaned back, placing my back against the tree, and held my arms open to him. He crawled over, placing his head on my chest, and I closed my arms around him. "We all know how Earth gets. You were angry and weren't thinking clearly enough to control your actions. I know you would never act that way normally."

"But I pushed you," I heard him say just above a whisper. "I never thought I would be capable of doing something so horrible."

I gave him a squeeze and kissed the top of his head. "I love you, and you know I forgive you. How could I not? I know what kind of soul you are."

"I love you so much. Just the thought of losing you in any way upsets me," he confessed.

"You know losing me would be impossible. I promised to spend eternity with you and I will keep that promise. I could never love anyone else the way I love you."

I loosened my grip on him and glanced down when I felt Kaleb move his arm. I saw him wipe his cheek, possibly wiping away a tear.

I felt him tighten his arms around me, snuggling against my chest. "I know, and I love you too," he reminded me.

I pressed my face into his hair, inhaling his sweet honey-like scent. I closed my eyes, savoring the soothing feeling I got whenever I breathed him in. I always loved the way I felt on Earth whenever I did this. Breathing in his delicious scent here made me feel even better than it ever did on Earth.

I began running my fingers through his hair, comforting him, and became fascinated by its color. There was no rhyme or reason to the way the colored strands mixed together. The more I combed my fingers through, the more I found myself intrigued by it. It was mostly blond with strands of brown flecked in, making it look like beach sand.

I kissed the top of his head. There were never words good enough when we were on Earth to describe how in love with him I was. I knew it then—I would give up

Enlightened

my life for him. This still holds true now. Not that there would ever be any need to, but I would give up my entire existence for him.

"What are you thinking about?" he asked, just above a whisper.

"Hmmm..." I began, casually running my fingers along his shoulders, tracing along the curves of his muscles. "I was thinking about how much I loved you when we were on Earth."

He sat up to look at me with his brows narrowed playfully. He smiled kindly. "Really?" He sounded intrigued. He leaned in, grazing his lips against mine. "...And what about here?"

I couldn't help feeling drawn in by his sweet lips. "Umm... here, I love you even more."

"Really..." he teased. "Is this a fact?"

"Yes." I couldn't help exhaling in contentment as I spoke.

He pressed his lips to mine and they molded together perfectly. Kissing Kaleb here was far better than kissing him on Earth ever was. It paled in comparison. His kiss was tender and filled with the kind of strong passion that could only come from him. I reached up, combing my fingers through his sandy-blond hair, running them down the back of his neck, tracing along the curves in his shoulders and down his back.

I felt Kaleb tighten the hold he had around my waist, pulling me closer to him. He ever so gently laid me down on the rock. His sandy-blond hair hung down around his eyes, feathering and framing his gorgeous face. My heart pounded as I looked into his eyes as he hovered above me. His eyes burned with that intense desire that I was all too familiar with from him on Earth. He leaned in, kissing my lips fervently, pressing his body firmly against mine. He paused from kissing me for a moment, grazing his lips against mine to speak. "I love you," he reminded me.

"I love you, too."

Chapter 18

On Earth, trusting in another is one of life's hardest lessons. Relationships play a large role in helping us to learn about ourselves. Falling in love there can be so easy, but we are never truly sure about our other half at times. Because we all have free will, relationships can become messy and complicated. Doubts will creep into our minds, causing fear, helping to distort our opinions and judgments of that other person. This creates the perfect recipe for us to learn something important.

Relationships here are much different. We hardly ever feel any fear here, mostly happiness and peace. No matter what has happened between us on Earth, we all still love each other. We form true, everlasting friendships that are filled with trust and love.

When two souls fall in love with each other, the way Kaleb and I have, it is truly special. It is absolute. There is no jealousy or ever any doubt about how the other soul feels because here we only speak the absolute truth. We know no other way. Once this bond is created between two souls, it is unbreakable. These souls will spend eternity with each other.

It's a shame that Charmeine and Zuriel never got that chance, and that their existence may have been cut short. No one really knew what ever happened to them. Thankfully, I knew I would not go down to Earth without Kaleb, so this wouldn't ever be an issue for us.

I felt him press his face into my hair, planting a gentle kiss on my head. He started chuckling lightheartedly. "Is your mind always this busy?"

I couldn't stop my soft smile from spreading, becoming wider. "Only when I know we have class soon… Can't you feel it? I think everyone is home now," I replied.

I heard him sigh. "Yes, I was just thinking that as well."

He rolled to his side, leaning up on his elbow to look at me with a soft, gentle smile. His stare spoke volumes about how he felt without him having to say a single word. He casually moved hair away from my face and leaned in. He began tenderly kissing my lips, stirring those butterflies in my stomach into their familiar happy frenzy.

He pulled back some and I instinctively opened my eyes. He smiled at me, so naturally I smiled back.

"I'm surprised we haven't heard from any of them yet," he said.

I narrowed my eyes at his statement. That hadn't occurred to me yet, but he had a point. We usually heard from one of our classmates by now. "Yeah, that is odd. Gwen usually calls me right after she gets home."

Enlightened

No sooner had we spoken than Kaleb's expression changed, and he was staring off into the trees. His eyes were glossing over and he seemed to be distracted. I began wondering if one of our classmates had called him, most likely Jaire, Kaleb's closest friend.

As I waited patiently for Kaleb to finish his call, my mind continued to wander. I lay there on the rock, swooning about how handsome I thought he was. I began tracing the plains of his bare chest with my fingers, thinking about how lucky I was that he loved me the way that he did. I was enjoying the feel of his smooth skin against my fingertips, relishing my time with him there. It filled me with joy when I saw his expression change, going from his blank stare into a happy smile. I found myself smiling because he was. I was euphoric, which caused me to giggle a little.

He chuckled lightly, shaking his head gently before glancing down at me. When his eyes met mine, I felt my heart thump a little.

"Everyone is going to Anna's, would you like to go?" he asked.

I was overflowing with euphoria still. I'd go anywhere as long as he was there, I thought to myself. "Sure, that sounds like fun."

✦ ✦ ✦

Billie Kowalewski

"Heads up!" Jaire shouted. "Four serving … *zeeero*!" he teased, and snickered.

"Oh sure, keep rubbing it in!" Maggie shouted back. "Just serve the ball!"

Full of confidence, Jaire held on tightly to the ball and his smug smile. He ran his fingers coolly through his wavy brown hair. He stood there, playfully looking for our weakest link to punt the ball at. His eyes shifted from one side to the other as he carefully scrutinized the feminine opponents he and his teammates were facing. We'd all known each other for a very long time, so we knew which one of us was the least athletic. We all have our strengths, and, of course, our weaknesses. So he already knew which one of us would duck from the ball long before diving for it.

It was the girls against the boys in what was supposed to be a playful game of volleyball. You would think that our side would have the advantage. There were five girls and only three boys. So knowing that they were winning, you would think that they would play nice and just serve the ball. But since Maggie—the one with the tight blond ponytail and the red two-piece bathing suit—tended to be on the competitive side, Jaire loved to get her going.

I watched carefully on the other side of the net in a very cute yellow two-piece bathing suit. I stood there ready, rocking back and forth on my heels, waiting for Jaire to finally make his move. I didn't miss when his eyes rested the longest on our least athletic player, Robin. She was standing there in her modest green one-piece bathing suit, quietly playing with her curly ginger hair. He took a few quick steps forward, kicking up a little sand in his stride. He stretched his long arm out, holding the ball high out in front of him. He swung his arm hard with a closed fist and punted the ball high over the net. I followed the ball with my eyes, watching as it went up and over the net, making its descent on our side. Anna, with her straight black hair and black two-piece bathing suit, was closest to Robin. She dove for the ball, causing Robin to flinch out of the way. She pelted the ball hard with double fists, landing elbows first into the sand.

The ball ended up going sideways in my direction. I hit the ball with open palms over the net. The ball was then quickly served right back to us by John. Gwen in turn hit the ball, sending it backward to Maggie, who was standing behind her. Maggie hit the ball as hard as she could with open palms, sending the ball soaring over the net right back to the boys. Kaleb, who was right up against the net, jumped up quickly and spiked the ball, earning the boys yet another point…

Much like a family on Earth would be, we are a very tightknit group. We have faced so many crazy challenges on Earth together. Some of them turned out good, while others, of course, went badly. Facing such tough challenges together strengthens the bond we have with each other. While we are there, we laugh, we cry, fight, and say things we later regret, we hold grudges, and love each other. Then when we finally go home, all of those things are laid to rest and forgotten. Because here is where we become enlightened.

The volleyball game came to an end, and, unsurprisingly, we lost. Kaleb and I wandered over to sit on a blanket that was spread out under a palm tree. When he sat down he curled his legs in and opened his arms up to me. I sat down, placing my back against his chest, and he closed his arms around me. His delicious scent greeted me like a warm hug, welcoming me home. I smiled and closed my eyes as I inhaled his sweet honey-like scent. Like I did every single time that I breathed him in. I felt him press his face into my hair and take in a deep breath. Unconsciously, he and I let out a soft "ahhh…" at the same time. When we glanced up, there were six sets of eyes fixated on us. They were all frozen and staring at us as if we'd suddenly grown two heads. It occurred to me at that moment that we hadn't told any them yet that we were a couple.

Kaleb ended up being the one to speak for us. "Harmony and I are together now," he announced proudly.

The expressions on their faces began to thaw, and each one of them smiled. Gwen came running over to us and knelt down in front of me. "I knew this was gonna

Enlightened

happen!" she shouted excitedly with clenched fists. She then quickly grabbed me out of Kaleb's arms, wrapping me up in one of her tight hugs. "I'm so happy for the both of you!" she practically shouted in my ear.

I was laughing. "Thank you," I replied mid-squeeze.

She let go of me and then quickly grabbed Kaleb, hugging him in the same way. Kaleb was chuckling too. "Thanks, Gwen," he replied.

Gwen always says exactly what she is thinking the moment she thinks it. She does things this way too. This can be overwhelming, and this behavior does occasionally get her into trouble when we're on Earth. But she is good to the core, and because she is like this, she is always a blast to hang out with.

Gwen sat back, kneeling on the blanket, grinning ear to ear. Strands of her blond hair had fallen from her French braid. The ones that were framing her face looked dark against the deep blue sky behind her, while the other strands on the top were glowing as they caught the bright light from the sun.

"This is why I didn't call you right away like I normally would when I got home. I had this feeling that you guys were together now. It was so obvious that this was gonna happen."

Her statement caused me to sit back a little. I know that I think a part of me knew this too. But I didn't think this really was that obvious, at least not to the others. Kaleb must have been thinking something similar because he was the one who ended up replying. "Really?" he questioned. "How was Harmony and I getting together so obvious?"

Gwen held her glowing, happy smile and chuckled. She narrowed her eyes at us in disbelief. "Did you not see yourselves in that last life? I got to witness that right up close!" Her eyes were wide and her brows were high. "You two were on fire for each other down there!" she said, and then started fanning herself. "The way you two lit each other up was unlike anything I had ever seen! There wasn't a moment where you two weren't looking into each other's eyes or touching in some way… Then, hearing some of your conversations! There were times where you two would be talking and then the words would stop. But then you could almost swear the conversation was continuing, judging by the way you both would be staring at each other still." She waved her hand dismissively at us. "This was all inevitable, really. Even before this last life. You were always sitting next to each other. Always talking, laughing, and the *fighting*!" She shook her head. "How the two of you didn't get together before now is beyond me."

All I could do was laugh. It's interesting how we can see something someone else doesn't long before they do. When you're in the middle of a situation it is easy to misjudge things. I think it's simply because we're just up

Enlightened

too close, and I think this can obscure our view of things. Some of life's challenges are similar to objects if you think about it. If you take any object and hold it up close to your face, your view of that object becomes limited and you can only see part of it. Then take that same object and move it farther away; you start to see it much better. The lines and/or shape of the object become clear, allowing us to see so much more of it. Our perspective changes once we can see the whole thing. The same holds true for situations we face on Earth. If you find yourself in the middle of a tough situation, try to see it from different perspectives. Take a step back and look at the grander scale of the problem instead of maintaining that narrow view.

Hand in hand, Kaleb and I happily strolled along the shore of Anna's island. Just like Kaleb and I lived in a forest here and that was our home, each one of our classmates had a home that was unique to them that they enjoyed. Our homes truly were our hearts' desires. It was where we felt most like ourselves.

All of us had things in common, but for the most part we were unique individuals. So it did stand to reason that every single soul would have a distinctly different home. Even in cases where souls had a lot in common or they both chose the same type of home, their homes were still quite different. The fact that Kaleb and I had imagined the same home for ourselves the way we had was still mindboggling to me. Even while knowing that he and I shared such a special connection.

The others were off doing their own things as well. Robin was sitting on the blanket under the palm tree playing a violin. John was lying on his stomach on the blanket, happily engrossed in one of the science-fiction books he'd brought with him. Gwen and Maggie were off happily playing in the waves. They were jumping as the waves rolled, catching them and riding them in.

My attention for the most part was focused more on Jaire and Anna. Jaire happened to be a very talented carpenter. He had gone back home briefly to retrieve a wood chair that he had made for her. It was an Adirondack-style lounging chair, perfect for relaxing on an island like this. She was ecstatic to receive such a beautiful gift.

They started playing a friendly game of Frisbee. They were happily tossing the Frisbee back and forth to each other. But then I saw Jaire suddenly run at Anna, who had the Frisbee, grabbing her by the waist. They were both laughing as Jaire was trying to wrestle Anna for the toy. I began wondering if perhaps there was something between them. Perhaps it was a spark of something that had yet to become obvious to them. I then chuckled to myself on the inside when I realized the shoe was now on the other foot. The lesson had come around full circle.

Enlightened

I couldn't be happier for the both of them—if this turned out to be true. With Jaire's gift for carpentry and Anna's gift for sewing and painting, the possibilities for them were endless on Earth.

Anna's island couldn't be more beautiful, and we were all relishing our time here. The wide, open sky with its small white puffy clouds was breathtaking. Then the sand with its white and golden tones was just as gorgeous. It was very fine and powder-soft under my bare feet. The ocean water, which seemed to stretch on forever, shimmered brightly in the sun. Then the sound it made as the wave crashed down along the shore was so peaceful and serene, especially accompanied by Robin's violin.

Being able to share in each other's home like this was something we all greatly enjoyed. The best part was being able to take along a very treasured piece of my home to share all of this with.

Kaleb stopped walking and turned to face me. He combed his fingers into my long brown wild curls and smiled. He leaned in, pressing his lips to mine, sighing softly in contentment. He pulled back some to look at me. He had a glow in his eyes and a soft smile on his face. He reached down, winding his arm snugly around my waist while taking my hand into his free one. Casually, he began swaying with me along the edge of the shore. The water was lapping at our feet as we continued to dance. He then leaned in and rested his cheek against mine. His sweet honey-like scent surrounded me and I couldn't help closing my eyes.

Chapter 19

H̲a̲r̲m̲o̲n̲y̲, a familiar booming voice called out to me in my mind, waking me up out of a sound sleep.

Yes, Luke? I said in my mind. Not bothering to open my eyes just yet.

It's time for school.

Okay, I'll be there soon, I replied, and then I felt our connection fade.

I felt the hammock sway as Kaleb rolled to his side. I heard him groan a little. "Baby?"

Lying on my stomach, I turned my head to look at him. "I know...Luke called me."

Kaleb reached his hand over, brushing strands of hair from my face. "Are you ready to face everyone?" he asked.

I sighed. "As ready as I'll ever be." I went searching under the covers until I found his hand. I laced our fingers together, holding his hand firmly. "...How about you?"

"The same as you." I could feel him caressing my hand with his thumb. "This part can be so overwhelming sometimes."

"True, but at least neither of us has to face this part alone anymore."

Kaleb smiled. "Leave it to you to always find the positive."

A soft smile spread slowly across my face. "You're welcome." I quickly kissed his lips and got up. "Dibs on the shower," I announced, heading toward the washroom door.

Kaleb chuckled. "Go right ahead."

I opened the door and turned to look at him before going in. "What are you going to do while I'm in the shower?"

He turned over, burying his face into the pillows. "Finish my nap," he replied, with a yawn.

I chuckled at him and shook my head as I walked in.

As I was finishing up in the shower, I heard the washroom door open.

"It's only me," Kaleb announced as he entered.

I peeked out at him from behind the curtain and smirked at him. "I know. Who else would it be?"

He chuckled. "Good point," he replied on his way into the walk-in closet.

"I'm almost done," I called out to him.

"I figured you were," he called back.

I turned off the water and pulled back the curtain. "Would you mind handing me a towel?"

"Sure." Kaleb came strolling out of the closet wearing only a plain white towel. As he walked through the washroom, going over to the shelf, a memory from my life as Veronica sprang to the surface. Seeing him this

Enlightened

way caused my mind to blur for a moment. Distorting that line between my real life as Harmony and my momentary life as Veronica. It felt like an odd backward version of déjà vu in a way. Because this time, I knew I'd seen it before.

He turned and handed me the towel. "Here you go."

I wrapped myself snugly in the towel, tucking the corner in along the top. When I glanced up to step out of the tub I noticed that Kaleb was just standing there. He was smiling, and he had an odd look on his face as he continued to watch me. I started to wonder if perhaps lines were blurring for him as well. Causing him to think something along the lines of what I had been before.

He held his hand out to me. I smiled as I placed my hand in his, letting him help me out of the tub.

"Thank you." I waved my hand toward the bathtub. "It's all yours."

He kissed my cheek. "Thanks." He removed his towel, hanging it up on the hook, and then stepped into the tub.

I heard Kaleb turn on the water for the shower. An awkward feeling started to move in, making itself known in the washroom. It tainted the atmosphere in a peculiar way and seemed to be hovering between us. We'd known each other for so long, you would think we'd be past any awkwardness by now. I stood there for a moment trying to figure out what might be causing it. Perhaps it was the intimacy of the small room? It was certainly quite different than our usual wide-open forest.

I turned around to face the mirror over the sink. I grabbed my hairbrush and began pulling it through my curls. The awkward feeling could be stemming from the memories that were coming to the surface before. I could easily see how a memory like that one would cause this kind of tension. I chuckled to myself at the thought.

It also could have been because neither of us were saying too much. We were both busily getting ready for school, and this was the first time he and I were doing it together. I'm sure that was probably part of it. We were just not used to it yet.

Kaleb began humming a familiar song as he continued to shower. I put my hairbrush away when I was finished, and grabbed my toothbrush. I squirted on a little toothpaste and started to brush my teeth. I was listening to Kaleb and began humming along with him as I brushed.

I was having trouble remembering what the song was that Kaleb was humming. All I could hear in my mind was the melody; the words were a blur. The last time I had heard this song was through my human ears on Earth.

I rinsed off my toothbrush and placed it back up in the holder. Kaleb began singing the first few lines of the song, instantly helping me remember that he was singing an Aerosmith song called "Dream On."

Enlightened

Kaleb's voice flowed out from the shower and carried throughout the washroom. I sang along as I went into the closet and got myself dressed. I always loved that song, so I couldn't help singing along with him.

As I was pulling up my socks, a few lines from the song caught my attention. It occurred to me then that what he and I were about to face could be what was contributing to our awkward atmosphere.

No one likes to find out what they've done wrong.

I decided to fix my hair for a change, so I went back over to the mirror. I grabbed my hairbrush and an elastic from the jar that sat on the corner of the sink. I began thinking about my life as Veronica as I started to pull my sides up into the elastic, creating a half ponytail. I was trying to recall any of the wrongs I may have done to people while I was there. Some of my memories from that life had become a little hazy in the time I'd been home. I find it can be easier to recall the wrongs others have done than it is to remember the ones we've done ourselves. I would have to wait until class to find out.

I walked out of the washroom when I was done and wandered over to my bed. I sat down on the hammock bed and lay down across it. I swayed happily while I waited for Kaleb to finish getting ready.

This part of school isn't just about discovering what we've done wrong, of course, I thought to myself. We did find out the things we'd done right, too. Getting things right was what we all strove for when we departed for Earth. We all knew this.

No one can expect to get every lesson right on the first try. Getting things wrong is how we learn to eventually get them right. Life is about discovering what makes each one of us special. It's about what defines us. It tests us, helping us to learn who we really are, and how we truly want to be.

I did tend to enjoy this part of school at times. This part of school did not require us to wear our school robe. Casual attire was permitted. We only wore our robe when we traveled to Earth out of tradition. Plus, this was the part where we got to mix and mingle with the majority of souls we'd come into contact with while on Earth.

Besides our classmates, we come into contact with lots of other souls, and we impact each other's lives. These souls are the ones we've interacted with in some way, either good or bad. It's our chance to make amends, and make peace with regrets if we have any. Of course, there are occasions where a few of the souls we've come into contact with are not there because they are still on Earth. There is always time for those souls later, if need be.

I pushed the hammock back when I heard the door of the washroom open, so I could be upright to be able to look at him. Kaleb came out, clutching his jacket in one hand, closing the door behind him. His cheeks were still a little rosy from the hot shower. He

Enlightened

had his gorgeous sandy-blond hair combed, tapering the sides back. I watched him as he casually slipped on his camouflage jacket over his blue cotton tee, adjusting the collar downward.

I felt my heart thump when he glanced up at me finally. "Are you ready to go?" he asked. The blue in his tee made his blue eyes even deeper. I didn't think it was possible, but he was even more handsome than ever.

"Yep." I stood up from the hammock, practically leaping toward him. I couldn't help feeling a little excited. Kaleb and I had been together at school before a ton of times, and we had been in the same class since he and I started school. But not since we'd become a couple, and this would be the first time we would travel there together.

Kaleb took a step back and chuckled at me. "I guess so," he replied, taking my hands. Staring deep into my eyes, he lifted both of my hands to his lips and kissed each palm once. Then he tenderly lowered my arms, placing them around his waist. He wrapped his arms securely around me, while I snuggled happily against his chest.

Kaleb placed his lips against my ear. "Are you ready?" he whispered.

I smiled and closed my eyes. "Yes," I whispered back.

"Hold tight, and clear your mind," he whispered again.

I took in a deep breath, releasing it fully before tightening the hold I had around his waist, clearing my mind of all my thoughts. A moment later, I could no longer hear the sound of our stream, so I knew we were at school.

I let go, opening my eyes when I felt Kaleb release his arms. I stood up on my tippy-toes and kissed his lips. "Being in your arms is the best way to travel," I told him with a smile.

We were standing in front of the school's main entrance. The building was very massive as is the entrance, just like everything else here. The doorway is an immensely tall arch held closed by an arched double door. Though I've seen this entrance way more times than I can count, it still grabs hold of my attention every single time with its intricate detailed artwork.

The building is a modest crème color. Carved around the frame of the door are many uniquely different faces. All of which are different shapes and colors, have unusual expressions, and so on. This is to symbolize the diverse personalities that join together here who travel to Earth. There are so many that no one can ever stand here long enough to ever be able to see them all.

Then the doors themselves are a whole other matter. Carved into the wood doors are very detailed feathers from top to bottom that point inward toward the center. Each feather overlaps each other in the center where the doors separate. As you walk up the stairs the doors part,

Enlightened

like an angel greeting you with open wings. I have never seen its equal.

Together we began walking up the stairs. The doors opened as we approached. I felt such a sense of pride walking into school with him by my side. Kaleb glanced over at me and smiled warmly, taking my hand. It was apparent to me from the look in Kaleb's eyes that he felt the same. Hand in hand, we walked proudly together into the school.

Passing through the school's doorway with Kaleb by my side was like announcing to all that we were a couple. Though this did not happen, I felt like trumpets were playing somewhere in our honor. I'd like to think that perhaps they were, and we just couldn't hear them.

We stopped alongside the large flowing fountain that sat in the center of our school's vestibule. Though I'd seen this fountain many times, I felt as though I were seeing it through new eyes.

As I looked up at the cherubs in the fountain I couldn't help thinking about how they reminded me of us. How we had been with each other since our creation and how we were meant for each other. I then started to wonder if this fountain was just one out of the many clues that he and I had missed that were trying to tell us both all along that we were meant to be together.

Kaleb was silent as he brought the hand he was holding up to his lips and kissed the back of it. I glanced over at him and he smiled warmly. He then lifted my hand up high, gently twirling me. He pulled me in close, taking me in his arms. His sweet honey-like scent surrounded me like a warm fuzzy blanket, comforting and secure. He gently kissed my cheek and then placed his cheek against mine. He began swaying with me, waltzing us joyfully around the fountain. The water flowed steadily from the fountain, souls were bustling through the vestibule off to their various classes, but neither of us noticed. All either of us noticed was each other.

"I don't know how we've missed it," I told him, as we continued to dance. "More to the point, how I missed it." I shook my head. "Looking back over all of those lives we've shared. There have been so many clues in our past that have been showing us that we belong together. So many lives…so many…that you and I have shared together, pointing us in our natural direction." I chuckled. "I think in a way I've always known that you and I would end up spending the rest of our existence together."

I kissed his lips. "I love you," I reminded him. "The best thing I discovered about myself in that last life is how wonderful you make me feel. You were all that I ever thought about then, and this still holds true now. How did I say it then?" I paused for a moment, trying to recall what I had said to him on Earth. "…Oh yeah."

Enlightened

I chuckled lightly once I remembered. "I'm insanely in love with you."

Kaleb responded in the only way he knew how, his natural passionate way. He smiled at me warmly. His eyes burned with affection, releasing that one tear that slowly trickled down his cheek.

"I'm insanely in love with you too."

Chapter 20

Learning.

It's an unavoidable part of life. Both here and, of course, on Earth. There is always something to learn, no matter which way you turn. Lessons come at us in so many different ways, and take on many different forms. Like a wise person once told me, "There is a lesson in everything."

It is all meant to be this way. This is the way it was all set up. There isn't a single situation on Earth we cannot learn from. Each lesson we learn is stored indefinitely in the back of our minds, waiting for us to acknowledge it at some other time. For the eight of us, that time has come.

We sat cross-legged in a wide circle in our classroom. Kaleb's guide Jack was leading the class. He tends to be a tad different than the other guides. While my guide is super laid back, boasts confidence, has long dirty-blond hair, and dresses like a biker…Jack is the exact opposite.

Jack is tall and slender, with short dark-brown hair and hazel eyes. His pristine appearance can make him seem a bit stiff at times. He wears perfectly tailored pinstripe suits, and his shoes are buffed to a mirror shine. Never is a single thread or hair out of place.

Enlightened

Every one of us is very unique, after all, and it would stand to reason that our guides would be too. While we can stretch our imaginations here to our outermost limits, and most of us do, Jack doesn't normally. Like a blank canvas, his surroundings are stark, never-ending white in all directions. Not that there's anything wrong with it. It's just, well, not as pretty in my opinion.

Jack stood in front of the doorway to the courtyard. Even though he had a gentle smile across his face, his hands were clasped behind his back and his composure was very rigid. He glanced from one side to the other, taking in the faces of the eight souls that were sitting patiently, waiting for him to begin.

"I see all of you made it back in one piece," Jack said with a light chuckle. The eight of us started exchanging awkward glances. He cleared his throat when his attempt at humor failed to make the impression he was after.

"Well then…we should begin." He gently nodded.

"Does anyone here have anything they would like to talk with each other about before entering the courtyard?" Again, Jack was scanning the faces of the class.

I sat there for a moment, thinking about Jack's question while glancing around at my classmates. This was the time where we would discuss any lingering issues from Earth we might have had with each other. More often than not, we really didn't have that much to talk about at this point. A lot of times we didn't remember anything we should discuss either. I—along with the rest of my class—was coming up empty-handed.

"No one has anything to discuss?" he asked the class again, waiting patiently for one of us to reply. The eight of us were glancing around at each other, but no one said a word.

Jack brought his hands to the front and lightly clapped them together. "Well then, if no one has anything to declare now, the time has come." He held his hands out and motioned for us to rise. "...You may enter the courtyard."

The eight of us were quiet as we rose to our feet. We started to move slowly, one by one, toward the entrance. I watched quietly as my classmates started to make their way through the doorway. First John and Gwen, with Maggie trailing behind them. Anna's expression was empathetic as she reached out and took Jaire's hand, and they walked through together.

I turned to look at Kaleb, who was standing by my side. He removed his jacket and held it open for me. "For luck in the courtyard," he said.

I smiled at him. "Thank you."

I pushed my arms through the sleeves and pulled the jacket up over my shoulders. I ran my hands along the back of my neck, pulling my hair out from under the collar. I wrapped my arms around his waist, hugging him tightly, and placed my head against his chest. I couldn't

Enlightened

help taking a deep breath in, inhaling his soothing sweet honey-like scent.

"I wish I had something to give to you," I said.

He held me tightly in his arms, pressing his face into my hair, inhaling deeply. He kissed the top of my head and then turned, resting his cheek against it. "You gave me you." He was caressing my back, comforting me with his gentle touch. "I don't need anything else," he replied.

I lifted my head up and kissed his cheek. "I love you too." I smiled at him.

We let go of each other and he took my hand into his, lacing our fingers together. "Are you ready?" he asked.

I took in a deep breath and let it out sharply. "Yep." I lifted his hand to my lips and kissed the back of it. I looked deep into his blue eyes; my expression was one of concern. "Remember, you don't have to face all of it alone."

"I remember." He smiled. "…And neither do you."

Kaleb and I started walking toward the doorway hand in hand. I could feel the tension mounting with each step that we took. His grip on my hand tightened as we met the threshold. I paused for a moment and looked back when I realized one of our classmates was dragging her feet. She stood alone just a few feet from the entrance, playing anxiously with her curly ginger hair.

"Come on, Robin," I called to her.

Jack placed his hand on her shoulder. "Go, child… It will be all right," he told her.

She let go of her hair, and started walking toward us. Kaleb and I walked through the doorway first, and then Robin followed us in.

"Harmony?"

I stopped dead in my tracks and let go of Kaleb's hand. I turned on my heels and crossed my arms. The sound of that voice brought with it a familiar irritation that was suddenly boiling under my skin.

"*Oh*...and what do you want?!" I snapped at her.

My reply caused Robin to flinch like I had just slapped her. "I'm sorry, for not always being there for you."

"That's it?!" I huffed. "What about you always going along with everything that woman said, huh?!" I shook my finger at her. "I grew up in that life alone living with you and *HER*!"

Tears were welling up in Robin's eyes. "I'm so sorry, Harmony. I shouldn't have done that. I should have found the courage to stand up to her more." The tears were streaming down her face now.

"You did find a small amount that night I got kicked out," I reminded her. Memories from my life as Veronica Edwards were continuing to emerge. I relaxed my stance some. "If it wasn't for you, that night could have been a lot worse."

"At least I did something right." Robin smiled. "I did apologize that night for some of my behavior, too. Don't you recall?"

Enlightened

Every memory from that lifetime was continuing to fill my mind more and more. "I do." I nodded. With tears in my eyes, I held my arms open to Robin and embraced her with a warm hug. "...And I forgive you."

So, I'm sure you're probably wondering what just happened, right? When we first arrive home, we are relieved of the burdens we have faced on Earth. We are given ample time to adjust to the natural environment of our true home. This gives us time to rest, which allows us to fully appreciate the honesty, trust, and unconditional love that we are all given.

None of this ever leaves us here. In the courtyard, however, it does become a bit altered. Once we cross the threshold of the courtyard door, we become more like our Earth selves, with an added twist...

The moment we walk through, our minds begin to flood with every single memory from our time there. Add to that the fact that we only speak the absolute truth here, and I bet you now understand what just happened between me and Robin. So when we face each other here, there is never any denial about what we have done, because we cannot lie. There is no "I don't knows" or "I don't remembers" either, because we do. This is our chance to right the wrongs we have done to each other, and to discover all of the things we have gotten right.

There certainly could be some individuals out there who get things right on the first try. I am not one of them. In my past I have made tons of mistakes. What is most important is that I have learned from them. It doesn't mean trouble for me here if it takes me a while to understand something. Everyone learns at their own pace. This is always okay; we are supposed to.

Let's face it, though—there are times where we didn't know that we did something wrong. Sometimes that person we hurt never said anything. Then there are the times where we are so ashamed of what we did, we cannot seem to find the courage to face that person. So we avoid them, instead of admitting what we have done. These things are okay too, and here is where we can set those burdens free and finally lay them to rest. This is our time to gain knowledge from what we have experienced…to become enlightened.

One thing that took me a long time to realize was that the more aware of my actions I am on Earth, the less I will have to face in the courtyard. With the knowledge of home blocked from our memory, this is easier said than done. I have found through using my method that the more I am thinking about this right before I go down the easier this is for me to achieve.

Kaleb stood by patiently, quietly waiting for us to finish our conversation. I felt Robin relax her arms and I followed her lead, leaning back some to look at her. She had tears in her eyes like I did, and her gentle smile matched mine.

Enlightened

"There were plenty of moments where you were a great sister," I informed her. "I'm happy to say, those times were more often than not."

"Thank you, Harmony. You were a great sister too. I hope we're paired up like that again in the future. Next time, I will work harder to have your back more," she replied.

I held my kind smile. "I know you will."

Robin and I hugged each other again. This time it was a tight squeeze, like true sisters should share. We let go of each other, and both of us were smiling happily.

Robin sighed suddenly. "I guess it's time for us to mingle more."

"Yeah," I agreed.

Kaleb moved in a little closer, placing his hand on the small of my back. Robin glanced past Kaleb and I, and then she sighed again. "Yep, I already see someone else I have to talk to."

"I'll see you back in class after," I replied.

Robin started to walk away, and then I turned to look at Kaleb. The moment our eyes met, memories from our time together on Earth began flowing through my mind. I closed my eyes and smiled. "I'm happy that all of the memories I have with you from Earth are good ones." I told him.

Kaleb wrapped his arms snug around my waist and tenderly kissed my cheek. "I agree," he said, pressing his face into my hair. He took in a deep breath. I trembled when I felt his lips graze against my ear. "I am indulging in a few of those memories right now," he whispered.

Both Kaleb and I were tuned in, watching our time on Earth together unfolding in our minds. Just like a movie would play out on a big screen, each event played out in order. I couldn't help the wide smile on my face or the happiness that was flowing through me as I relived those moments he and I had shared together.

The last memory brought with it a familiar agony I had long since forgotten in the time I'd been home. A pain unlike anything I had ever experienced before in any other life until my time as Veronica. It throbbed through my veins, dragging with it a dull ache that stiffened my joints. My breathing became uncomfortable, causing me to gasp as I tried to find my natural rhythm with it.

"Are you all right?" Kaleb asked.

The pain was unbearable as it continued to surge through my body. I stood there trying hard to bring up the memories of how I managed to function through this back on Earth. But no matter how hard I tried, the combination of the dull achy pain and the gasping made it next to impossible to concentrate enough to do that. I couldn't even speak.

I felt Kaleb wipe away the tears that were now streaming down my cheeks. He held my face in his hands. "What's wrong?" he asked, his tone now saturated with worry.

Enlightened

As I continued struggling to right my breathing, I was greeted by a concentrated dose of Kaleb's sweet honey-like scent rising from his wrists. The moment his scent permeated my nose, the ache in my body began to weaken and my breathing became a little easier.

I grabbed his hands, holding them to my face, and took in a deep breath through my nose. His sweet honey-like scent relaxed my body, relieving the pain, and I was able to breathe right again.

I opened my eyes, and stretched out my arms and legs, checking for soreness like I would on Earth. "I think so," I replied.

Worry was present in his eyes as he continued to watch me. "What was that?" he asked.

I reached down and took his hand. I looked into his eyes with an empathetic smile. "This is what I went through after you died," I told him.

"Whoa." His eyes were wide. "It's no wonder you were having all of that trouble accepting our lives here after you came to me." Kaleb quickly scooped me up into his arms, wrapping me in a tight hug. "I'm so sorry you had to go through that."

"I'm just glad it's over," I replied.

I snuggled happily against his chest. I was feeling quite relieved that the pain was gone and that I could breathe right again. I couldn't help wondering in the back of my mind, though, if this kind of thing would happen again the next time I went down to Earth. Or even worse—what if it happened to him? I was shuddering on the inside at just the thought.

"I'm looking forward to going back down to Earth so I can make more new memories with you," he said suddenly. His words strengthened my current concerns about going back down there. But until he discovered what made us different, there was not much I could say or do to help avoid this. Even if he did discover that he and I were soul mates, what could he or I do to prevent either one of us from suffering like this when the other died? To my knowledge, not enough was known about extreme soul mates like us to be able to solve this. The only other pair was Charmeine and Zuriel, and no one knew what happened to them.

I composed my expression some before lifting my head from his chest to look at him. I didn't want him to worry or question me further. It was important that he discovered that we were soul mates on his own like Zipporah said, and if he questioned me further while we were in the courtyard I wouldn't be able to conceal this knowledge from him. There was absolutely no way around it here.

Once my eyes finally met his, every previous concern I had before just seemed to vanish. He had that same look in his eyes he always had whenever he looked at me. The rims of his eyes appeared wider, as they smoldered

Enlightened

with such strong, passionate affection. His stare burning a hole straight through to my heart.

The fire in his eyes sparked that familiar magnetic draw, and it was now burning strongly within me. Fueled by our intense connection, and the sweet honey-like scent coming from his breath, I quickly grabbed him by his shirt, pulling his lips to my own. He twisted his fingers into my hair, keeping me locked to his lips. The groans emanating from his throat sounded just like they had when we were last on Earth as Veronica and Seth. It was extremely deep and masculine. It was the kind of deep tone that would send chills down someone's spine and that caused most people on Earth to shudder whenever he spoke. Hearing him this way excited me. It was like music to my ears. It was sounds of him at his happiest. He was full of joy, and it was all for me.

He released the grip he had on my hair, and slowly pulled away from my lips. I opened my eyes to look at him and he laughed when I playfully pouted at him.

"Whoops, sorry." He started combing his fingers through my bangs and the back of my hair in an attempt to neaten it. "I didn't mean to mess up your hair."

"It's okay." I chuckled at him. "You can mess up my hair any time you want."

Kaleb held his finger up to me suddenly, and glanced over to the side. His eyes were glossing over, and he was staring off into the distance. I knew that look; someone had called him.

He glanced back up at me when he was finished. "Jaire called. He said he has someone with him that needs to talk to me."

"Oh… Do you want me to go with you?"

"You don't have to." Kaleb smiled kindly. "I'll call you if I need you."

I smiled back. "All right."

Kaleb kissed my cheek. "I'll see you soon," he said, and then he faded before my eyes.

I playfully pouted at first. I stood there alone, quietly helping myself to a small Zen moment. I took in a deep breath, and let it out fully, focusing myself on participating in the rest of my courtyard activities. I turned around and began taking steps, making my way deeper into the courtyard.

Chapter 21

ASIDE FROM ITS EFFECTS, THERE really isn't anything spectacular about the courtyard. There's no creative atmosphere, no pretty scenery that has been imagined by other souls, no soothing sounds either.

It's just a dull-grey boring atmosphere as far as the eye can see. It's somewhat dark in a way. Drab is a good word for it. I tried asking once why it is this way, and the only explanation I received about it was: "There is no need for it to be anything other than what it is."

Souls were scattered across the dull open field talking amongst themselves. I was wandering through, with my hands tucked in the pockets of the jacket Kaleb had lent to me for luck. I was quiet, of course, trying to be respectful of the conversations that were already in progress.

I can't say that I feel much different about the courtyard than anyone else here does. Most of the time, I would like to get this part over with too. Typically speaking, it's not all bad, but some of the conversations can be quite hard.

Billie Kowalewski

I ended up pausing for a moment when I noticed that the area I was in seemed more congested than usual. It felt like souls were everywhere, so I stopped to watch them.

I was chuckling to myself. It felt like I was standing in the middle of Times Square with the way they were all behaving. They all seemed like they were in some sort of hurry the way they were bustling through, and a few of them were shouting at each other.

It amazes me sometimes what some of them will do to try to make their time in here easier, or go by quicker. It appears these types of habits have increased over time.

Some will stand in one spot, expecting souls will just come to them. Perhaps they think they will be easier to find if they stand still. I'm not sure. Then others will run around quickly, trying to find certain souls that they think they have to talk to right away, all in an effort to get this over with.

There is nothing wrong with doing it this way. These methods are not bad and can be effective. I say, whatever makes them happy. But these souls are missing the point and forgetting a few things about the courtyard.

First, the courtyard has the ability to draw those certain individuals you need to talk to right to you. So simply wandering through like I do will have the same desired effect. Then, your time in the courtyard is tailored specifically to you. The only way to truly keep your time in the courtyard

Enlightened

short and easy is to be mindful of your behavior toward others while on Earth. It really is that simple.

Admit when you've done something wrong. Own up to your mistakes, apologize when necessary, and so on. Or better yet, always choose the high road. Face your fears instead of hiding from them. Treat everyone you meet the way you would like to be treated. Spend time with those special people in your life you know you should, and remind them of how much you love them. Controlling your own behavior is the key to your enlightenment.

Or course, with the knowledge of home blocked from our memory, this is easier said than done. I have found, though, the more I think about this before I head down, the easier this is for me to achieve.

I started walking again, examining each face that I passed by. I was looking for a familiar face, anxiously waiting for my turn. I couldn't help wondering why I still hadn't run into anyone yet. I felt like typically I would have by now.

I started to feel funny. My chest began wrenching as if someone had just broken my heart, and tears felt like they were falling from my eyes. I stopped walking and wiped my hand across my cheek and then examined my now tear-stained palm. I glanced all around me, baffled by the tears that were falling with no known cause.

Billie Kowalewski

It occurred to me what this could be when a part of Charmeine and Zuriel's story sprang to mind. Zuriel felt Charmeine's pain here when she took her life on Earth.

"But he is not on Earth," I said quietly to myself. I was mystified that this could be happening to me with Kaleb still here. I speculated that perhaps it had to do with the courtyard's ability to make us more like our Earth selves. I then wondered if Charmeine or Zuriel ever experienced this same kind of thing here in the courtyard. If they did, why did they ignore this? Why didn't they say something and insist on traveling to Earth together? Maybe they thought this was only happening in the courtyard? Or perhaps we could feel what the other was feeling no matter where we were.

At any rate, I now knew how Kaleb was doing. I stood there for a moment debating going to him. But then quickly changed my mind when I realized I would have to explain to him how I knew too. I decided to just wait for him to call if he needed me.

A while later, I finally crossed paths with a soul that I knew I had to talk to. It was a soul named Marcus, who in this last life had been named Hank. He and I had a very difficult encounter. He did apologize, and told me how horrible he had felt about himself for what he had done. I, in return, told him how that encounter had made me feel. Of course in the end, I did the right thing and forgave him for what he had done.

Enlightened

After my time with Marcus, I ended up crossing paths with Anna. She had a familiar-looking younger soul walking beside her.

"Hey Harmony, you remember Lydia, don't you?" Anna asked.

I did right away. Her name was Donna in this last life. She was my mother.

"Of course I do." I turned to Lydia. "How are you?" I asked.

"I'm well," she replied.

"I'll leave you two to talk," Anna said. "Harmony, I'll see you back in the classroom." She turned and walked away, leaving Lydia and me alone to talk.

Lydia's expression was one of remorse. "Harmony, I am so sorry for my selfish behavior in that life," Lydia began. "I feel so bad about how I was as a mother toward you. I know I should have treated you better than I did."

I smiled at her. "We all make mistakes, Lydia."

She sighed. "Yes, and for me that life was full of them. I'm just grateful you still turned out as well as you did, even if it was short-lived for you."

"Thank you." I opened my arms toward her and embraced her in a warm hug. "Had I lived, I know I would have ended up forgiving you. You were not a bad person."

"No, I wasn't. I'm not making any excuses, though. I have a lot to learn still. I haven't been to Earth as much as you have," she said.

"I know. I do remember what it was like in the beginning," I replied.

All of us who travel to Earth are at all different stages of development. The younger the soul is that is traveling to Earth, the more mistakes they tend to make as humans. The more experience a soul has tucked within their memory, the fewer mistakes they make. This holds true with anything we are learning. The more often you do anything the better at it you become.

I leaned back to look at her. She had tears in her eyes and she smiled at me warmly. "Have you seen Marcus yet?" she asked.

"Yes." I wiped my hands across her cheeks, removing the tears that were streaming down her face. "He has a lot to learn still, as well."

"He does," she agreed. "He felt so terrible for what he did to you."

"I know, and I forgave him, just like I am forgiving you."

When our time in the courtyard is up, we are automatically transported back to our classroom. This is one part of dealing with the courtyard that I like. The sudden way we find out that we are done. Then, because of our home's atmosphere, the instant relief we suddenly feel is tremendously uplifting.

Kaleb was back before I was. He was already sitting in his spot on the ground in front of his door. His guide was sitting in front of him and they were both chatting casually.

Enlightened

I took a seat on the ground next to Kaleb, where I usually did. Everyone else was back except for Robin, who ended up arriving shortly after I did.

Kaleb leaned over. "How did it go?" he asked.

"It went well." I smiled at him. "How did you do?"

"It was all right. I got through it, and that is all that matters," he replied.

Everyone took their seats on the ground in front of their doors. We were quiet as we waited patiently for instructions on what we were doing next.

Jack stood from the ground and took his place standing in front of the courtyard door. "There was an interesting discovery in this last life about one of our fellow classmates." Jack glanced over at me and smiled. "Please, stand up, Harmony."

I glanced around, feeling a little embarrassed as I rose to my feet. I wasn't sure yet what he was talking about.

"Harmony has discovered her ability with babies and children!" he announced. He started clapping and then the rest of the class joined in. "Such a great discovery! We're so proud of you!"

"Thank you…" I smiled and playfully curtsied. "Thank you," I replied, as dramatically as I could. I then bent down, trying to take my seat back on the ground.

"Wait! There's a bit more I have to announce!" he shouted at me, waving his hands. He was practically bursting at the seams. I stood back up so he could continue.

"You have been selected to work in the nursery with the newborn souls!" he shouted proudly.

I quickly placed both hands to my mouth and gasped loudly. Selected to work with the newborn souls! Me? I couldn't believe it!

"Yep!" Jack shouted. He was bouncing up and down like an excited game-show host who was telling me what I'd won. "You can skip going down to Earth this next time with the rest of the class because your skills are needed elsewhere!" He was grinning.

I stood there frozen in shock. I didn't think it was possible here, but I might have been hallucinating. Because I could have sworn he just said something that I never wanted to hear.

"Harmony?" Anna stood from her seat on the ground and slowly walked toward me. She waved her hand in front of my eyes, and she was carefully examining my face. "Are you all right?" she asked.

"I'm sorry…what?" I asked. I felt like I was going in and out of consciousness. My head was spinning from the fear that was now rocketing through me like jet fuel.

Anna took my hands and looked me in the eyes. "You were selected to work in the nursery… Aren't you excited?"

"Uh." The fear I felt consumed me. Then Zipporah's words—"The two of you should travel to Earth together. History always has a way of repeating itself."—were replaying over and over in my mind.

Enlightened

Kaleb got up from the ground and took my hand. "She's probably just a little overwhelmed."

Anna gave Kaleb a worried look. "This isn't like her."

I was now surrounded by every one of my classmates. All of their expressions were ones of concern and confusion.

"Harmony, what's wrong?" Kaleb asked. He was now inches from my face.

"You are going to Earth without me," I replied, just barely above a whisper.

Kaleb narrowed his eyes at me in surprise. "Is that all?"

I nodded.

He wrapped his arms around me, holding me tightly, trying to console me. "It will be all right."

"I have to talk with Luke now," I replied softly.

Chapter 22

I LANDED OUT ON THE street in the nighttime section of Artopia. The sounds of choppy rumbling engines roared around me like thunder. The engines were loud but did very little to suppress the other background noises. The sounds of hollering souls and energetic music were piercing through, mixing in between the rumbles.

I opened my eyes and was startled by a soul who suddenly whizzed by me on a motorcycle. Souls on motorcycles were swarming the area. It seemed like they were everywhere. They were laughing and shouting things at each other as they were pulling into the parking lot of my destination. The vibration coming from so many engines shook the ground under my feet, making it feel like an Earth tremor.

The shiny bikes seemed like they crammed the parking lot, wrapping right around the building. I had to work my way around them. I was squeezing myself through, creating my own path around the packed bikes and the crowds of souls hanging out in front.

The music and the howls of delight became more pronounced the closer I got to the building. As I

Enlightened

approached the door, I couldn't help noticing a group of souls that were hanging out by the entrance. They were standing around, talking casually, and were decked out in leather jackets and studded belts. They seemed to be staring at me, and one of them actually gave me what looked like the once-over.

That caused me to pause for a moment. I glanced over my shoulder in confusion. I couldn't help thinking that this stare must be intended for another soul. I was coming up empty-handed, trying to think of a reason why anyone here would ever stare at me this way.

I then happened to glance down at just the right angle, catching a small glimpse of what I was wearing. It all clicked in my mind right there what might be causing them to stare. I was still wearing the clothes I had put on for school, which included Kaleb's camouflage jacket.

I shook my head and chuckled to myself. I was a tad underdressed and stood out like a sore thumb. If this was Earth, this type of situation would have certainly created such anxiety. Thankfully, this isn't Earth, I thought to myself, reaching for the door handle. I opened the door and the volume from the live band jumped to a crazy level. I walked inside the coolest club in all of Artopia, known throughout our world as The Legendary Seven.

I stood in the doorway, looking around, trying to spot Luke. Hair was flying throughout the crowd of souls that surrounded the stage. They were jumping around, dancing to the wailing rock band.

Once I spotted him, I pushed my way through the crowd over to the bar. It was not very often that I sought him out this way; most of the time I just called him. But the situation that I was currently facing called for an immediate solution, one I could not come up with on my own. I stood by patiently, watching Luke serving drinks to souls, sliding frothy beers down the bar.

Luke paused for a moment once he finally noticed me in the crowd. He excused himself to the other bartenders and then leaped over the bar.

He leaned in. "Is everything okay?" he asked, trying to shout over the band.

I shook my head. "No, can we talk?" I shouted back.

"Yeah, let's go up to my office."

The noise practically disappeared once the door shut behind us.

"You can take a seat if you like," Luke said, motioning his hand toward the couch that was adjacent to his desk.

"I don't need to sit," I replied.

"Suit yourself," he said. He sat down, and kicked his feet up onto the desk. "So, what can I help you with?" he asked.

"They gave me a job," I began.

He was smiling. "I know, I heard. I'm so proud of you," he interrupted.

Enlightened

"Thank you," I replied. I started pacing a little.

He narrowed his eyes at me. He seemed confused. "Are you not happy with it?" he asked.

I was fidgeting now, playing anxiously with the linked-hearts pendant on my necklace. "Of course I am," I replied.

Luke's expression became serious as he continued to watch me. "What happened?"

"The rest of the class is going down to Earth while I work in the nursery." I looked up at him. "Luke, Kaleb is going to Earth without me!"

I flinched when Luke stood up quickly from his chair and pounded his fists on his desk. "They're planning to do what?!" he snapped. He sounded furious.

"What do we do?" I asked him.

"Why didn't they learn from the last time? They can't do this," he grumbled. Luke stepped around his desk and grabbed me by my shoulders, stopping me in my tracks. His expression was serious as he looked me in the eyes. "I'm going to go talk to Jack. I'll get him to hold off on sending Kaleb down until you're done in the nursery. You'll see. Everything will be just fine."

I nodded at him. "Okay."

"Go home now and try to relax. Don't worry; I will take care of this." Luke smiled proudly. "You need to get ready to start your new job."

"Thanks, Luke." I smiled at him. I was already starting to feel relieved.

"You're welcome."

I let the image of the rock by the stream fill my mind to take me home.

Kaleb was sitting on the rock by the stream when I arrived. His back was against the tree and he had his knees curled in, hugging them to his chest. Seeing him like this instantly took me back to when we started.

I loved him so much. Just the thought of him suffering the same way Charmeine had without Zuriel scared me. I'd had a small taste of what that was like after he died, and again in the courtyard. With Kaleb's passionate nature, and the way Earth amplifies our personalities, I can only imagine what that would be like for him.

This would be slightly different from what I'd gone through though. I, at least, knew that he did exist. He would be suffering and searching, like Charmeine had, and wouldn't know why. He would be there with the knowledge of home completely blocked from his memory. Yet another part of this that just plain-old scared me. How many Earth years would go by with him suffering like this? How long would he be able to endure that? I only had to suffer for five years like that. He had the potential of living like that for much longer. There was no telling what a human would do when they were subjected to such pain. There was no way I could allow this.

Kaleb quickly rose from the rock. "Are you all right?" he asked.

"I'm okay," I replied.

"What was all that back in class?" he asked.

You and I are soul mates, like Charmeine and Zuriel, and I don't want us to disappear, was my first thought. But I couldn't say that. I had to stick to the rules. So I decided to answer this question in a different way. "I'm worried about what might happen if you go down to Earth without me."

Kaleb flinched a little. He seemed taken aback by my answer. "Don't you think I can handle going down to Earth on my own?" he asked in reply.

"Of course I think you can. But that's not the point," I replied.

"Really." He crossed his arms. "Care to enlighten me as to what this point might be?" he asked, his tone defensive.

I sighed. "The point is that you and I just started, and there may be problems if we travel to Earth alone."

"Maybe for you," he huffed. "…I would be fine."

"You don't know that any more than I do," I told him.

"Yes I do. Other souls do it all the time," he argued.

"True, but those souls have been together for a lot longer than we have," I argued back.

He turned around, facing the enormous oak on the edge of our stream. He held his back to me as he pulled his fingers through his sandy-blond hair in frustration. I heard him breathe in and then let it out sharply before turning back around quickly.

"Harmony, don't you think you're overreacting?"

I gasped, and my eyes widened at his remark. I didn't really want to argue with him about any of this. But what choice did I have? He had yet to learn what made us different, and Zipporah had told me that we shouldn't go to Earth without each other. I knew Luke said he would take care of this, and I had no doubt that he would, but it wouldn't hurt to try to ensure that Kaleb wouldn't go. I would rather argue with him than have us end up like Charmeine and Zuriel.

Now I was the one on the defensive. "I'm not overreacting at all." I crossed my arms. "…But you certainly are," I barked back.

He took a few steps back and then started anxiously pacing and bouncing across the rock. He wouldn't make direct eye contact. "No, I'm not," he stated.

I chuckled. "Yes, you are."

"No, I'm not," he stated again.

I rolled my eyes. "Yes you are." My tone was saturated with frustration.

"No, I'm not!" he snapped.

Enlightened

"Even Luke thinks we shouldn't go down to Earth by ourselves yet. It's too soon," I stated firmly.

He narrowed his eyes at me. "Jack thinks I would be fine. Besides, it's not like we would be apart for that long."

I sighed and rolled my eyes. "It will feel that way for me, not you. You're forgetting about the time difference."

"I'm not forgetting about the time difference. I have been to Earth before," he continued to argue.

"I know you have, but that was before you and I fell in love. Things are much different now."

"Things aren't that different." He kept his brows narrowed. "You worry about me too much."

"You should just wait until I can go with you," I stated firmly.

His expression changed, softening some. He looked a little confused. "You only want me to wait until you're done?"

I narrowed my eyes at him. "Yes, what did you think I meant?"

He looked at me with a sheepish expression. "I thought you didn't want me to go at all."

I walked over to him and wound my arms around his waist. "Of course not. I just want you to wait until I'm done in the nursery, then we will both leave at the same time."

"I like that plan." Kaleb wrapped his arms around me, pressing his face into my hair like he always did. I heard him take in a deep breath. "I will wait until you are done in the nursery so we can leave together," he said on an exhale. He sounded relieved. Then he kissed the top of my head. "I'm so sorry for jumping to conclusions."

I snuggled happily, resting my head in my usual spot against his chest. "It's all right. I forgive you." I was feeling so relieved. "And I'm sorry too."

I heard him take in another deep breath. "I can't wait to fall in love with you again," he said on an exhale.

I looked up at him, smiling at the thought. "Me neither."

Chapter 23

IF ALL GOOD THINGS MUST come to an end, then I'd like to remain at the beginning. At the beginning anything is still possible. The path is a mystery, an unknown, and the potential for greatness still exists. You have choices to make, and chances to take. At the end, though, it is all gone.

Still, without an end there would be no beginning. You just can't have one without the other. Just like you can't have a negative without a positive. What goes up must come down, and so on.

Our existence is the only exception to this rule. Don't you just love that? There is always some sort of exception to just about any rule. Ways around them, to bend them, and of course to break them. I always do my best to follow the rules, but there are times when rules are just meant to be broken. You just have to use your good common sense to figure out which ones to break.

This is where your potential for greatness truly comes from. It shines from within. We all have the capability to make smart choices no matter the circumstances. It is engrained into every single one of us right from the very start. Each one of us possesses the key to unlocking our own true greatness, and no one else.

In our world, our existence is never-ending and there really is only one true beginning. It is at this innocent stage that we are taught everything we need to help start us on our journey. These basic lessons stay with us, following us through life after life.

The evidence is there, lying deep within each one of us. When we first arrive on Earth, the knowledge of home is blocked from our memory. But is it completely gone? No. Though we are all different, we all have one common trait that reminds us all that there really is more to this life than meets the eye.

Most call it a conscience. Others refer to it as a "gut instinct." Regardless of what you call it, we all have the ability to distinguish between what is right and what is wrong. We all get a sense about things we face, and then it is up to us to make the choice. A lot of times people on Earth go against what their conscience is telling them. Or think they have to because someone else is telling them to do so. Then afterward they kick themselves for not following what their "gut instinct" was telling them to do all along.

I always try to do the right thing and follow what my conscience is telling me. But there are times where I am still wrong. Let's face it, we all make mistakes, and

Enlightened

I admit I have made tons of them. You just can't get it right without getting it wrong first most of the time.

So does this mean I should stop trying? No, of course not, and neither should you. Because your life is yours, just like my life is mine. We should all be striving to be better every day. Always doing the right things regardless of what someone else thinks. Take those chances and go after all the happiness you deserve. Because at the end of your life on Earth the most important person you have to face is **you**.

✦ ✦ ✦

She stood, facing the rack in the walk-in closet, wrapped in a plain white towel. Her hair, which was still wet from the shower, draped loosely over her shoulders. She searched through her selection of clothes, making funny faces, trying to decide what to wear to her new job. I just sat on the bench with my hands folded in my lap, quietly watching her.

Normally she was not this fussy. Usually she picked something to wear pretty quickly, without giving it much thought. I sat there wondering if she was doing this because she was feeling a little anxious about working in the nursery.

"Are you nervous?" I asked her.

She finally settled on something to wear, grabbing a T-shirt and a pair of blue jeans from her rack. I paid little mind to what she chose, concentrating mostly on the expression on her face.

"A little. I've only worked with Earth children. I don't really know much about the ones here," she replied.

For someone who said that she was nervous, she didn't appear to be. She coolly got herself dressed, then sat down beside me and started pulling on her socks. The expression on her face was soft, which matched her cool demeanor. Hardly the behavior for someone who said they were even just a little bit nervous.

This is one of the things that I've always loved about her. She is one of the strongest souls that I have ever known. She faces things so easily, and if she is nervous at all, it's always hard to tell.

I smiled at her sympathetically, wanting to be as reassuring to her as she always was with me. "I'm sure they're not much different," I said in my sincerest tone.

I placed my hand on her arm. The surge I felt from touching her skin was empowering as it pulsed through my body. I held my hand there as I waited for her to look up. She glanced up at me, peeking through her long, thick lashes. Her warm brown eyes were glowing as they peered into mine and sent another energizing surge straight through to my heart.

Enlightened

It took me a moment before I was able to speak. I held my caring smile as I gazed into her eyes. "You're going to be great. I just know it," I told her in my warmest tone.

She turned and smiled affectionately at me. She placed her hand on my cheek and caressed it with her gentle touch. That irresistible floral scent that I loved so much was emanating from her wrist. I couldn't resist the urge I felt to inhale deeply, breathing her in. I know that I'll never get enough of that sweet scent and the way it travels through, relaxing my entire body, making my limbs feel a little spongy.

She leaned in close and placed a tender kiss upon my lips. I closed my eyes, savoring the soothing feeling that only her sweet lips could provide. "Thank you," she replied just above a whisper.

She stood from the bench and turned around, dramatically holding out her arms. "So…how do I look?" she asked.

Is this a trick question? I wondered to myself. I was hardly an impartial judge. She always looked so beautiful to me. But I figured she must mean her outfit choice. I looked her over, my eyes happily wandering over her frame. I took my time out of habit, lingering in a few places, trying to scrutinize what she chose to wear to work.

"Outstanding, of course…" I said at first, and then my eyes finally settled on her shirt of choice. It was a mix of reds, blues, and yellows, with a touch of green that swirled outward from the center. "Why the tie-dye?" I asked.

She glanced down and ran her hands down the front of her shirt. Her head came up slowly and brought with it a small amount of uncertainty in her eyes. "Gwen said the babies here like bright colors."

I smiled at her. "Well then, you've made an excellent choice," I replied.

"I hope so." Her brows tapered in slightly and she bit her bottom lip. "I am a little nervous."

I narrowed my eyes, surprised by what she said. "What for?" I questioned. I couldn't help sounding puzzled. I reached my hands out to her and she took them without question. "I can't think of another soul better suited for this job than you are."

She smiled at me, batting those eyelashes as she came in closer. She wrapped her arms around my shoulders, pulling my head gently against her chest. She snuggled me for a moment and then I felt her lean in and kiss the top of my head. "How did I ever get this lucky?" she asked.

With my arms wrapped around her waist, I happily closed my eyes and smiled. "I ask myself that very same question, every single moment I get to spend with you."

"It's almost time for me to go," she said softly.

I sighed. "I know. I'm going to miss you," I replied.

Enlightened

She playfully rubbed my back and then pulled back some. I looked up at her and she was looking back at me. Her eyes were full of such warmth and love for me.

"I will miss you too, of course. I won't be gone for very long, and when I come back you and I will leave for Earth."

"I'm looking forward to that." I smiled at her. "Where do you think we'll end up this time?"

"Hmmm…" She smiled and then placed her fingers playfully against her beautiful lips. "That is a good question."

"Do you think we'll end up in America again? I would love it if we were back in Connecticut."

"California was nice too. You would have loved it. I wouldn't mind being there either," she replied.

A startling thought occurred to me when she mentioned California, and I was suddenly scared. What if we don't come across each other this time? It had happened before with the others. What if this was the first life where she and I couldn't find each other?

Worry was suddenly present in her eyes. The uneasiness I was feeling must have been obvious on my face, because she was now examining it. "What's wrong?" she asked.

"What if we can't find each other?" I replied softly.

She bent down and kissed my lips. "Don't worry, we will," she said with a confident smile.

"There have been times where we didn't find the others. How can you be so sure?" I replied.

She bent down and cupped my face with her gentle hands and looked me in the eyes. "Trust me when I say this—you and I will always find each other, no matter where we end up."

She knelt down on one knee, still holding my cheeks with her tender hands, and we were now eye to eye. She still had a look of concern as she hovered an inch away, carefully studying the expression on my face. "You do understand, right? As long as we are both on Earth, we will always find each other. I will use my method, and come find you if I have to."

I took in a cleansing breath and let it out. I did my best to compose my facial expression. I didn't want her to worry about me while starting her new job. "Yes."

She became distracted, releasing my face, and then glanced down suddenly. A moment later she looked back up and smiled softly. "It's time for me to go," she said. I knew now someone must have called her.

I just quietly nodded in reply.

"I love you, Kaleb. I'll be back soon."

"I love you too. Good luck, not that you'll need it." I smiled at her. "You're gonna be great," I told her.

"Thank you," she said with a smile. Then she vanished, leaving me alone in our walk-in closet.

I remained in there, sitting quietly on the bench. I laced my fingers together and placed my hands back in my lap, continuing to stare at the spot where she'd been.

Enlightened

I let out a soft sigh. I wasn't too sure what to do with myself. This was the first time she'd left me here since she'd come home.

I know it sounds silly, but I felt strange. I didn't know why I felt this way. I shouldn't. It wasn't that long ago that this used to be my normal. I was always alone here before she came, and this was still my home.

I smiled at the thought that this was her home now too. I loved it that she lived here with me now. I started chuckling to myself and shook my head in disbelief, thinking about how she had imagined the same home for herself as I did. I always knew how wonderful she was. This made me wonder at times, though, if there was more to us than I realized.

A part of me knew I should have told her how I felt much sooner. I spent so many lives trying to figure out how to tell her, so scared that she wouldn't feel the same way. Of course, I had no way of knowing then that this would turn out so wonderfully. Thankfully all of that was past now. Spending eternity with Harmony was more than I could have ever hoped for. This may sound a little selfish, but I didn't want to have to let her go just yet. I wasn't ready to. I sighed again. I think that part of me also knew how much I would miss her if she wasn't here.

Perhaps if I had something to do while she was gone this wouldn't feel so weird? I sat there for a moment, trying to think of an activity to do. I quickly became frustrated because I couldn't think of one.

I shrugged and then sighed again. Maybe the only logical thing to do was take a nap. Who knew when I'd get the opportunity to take one of those again?

I stood from the bench and walked out of the washroom, heading straight for our comfortable bed. I sat on the edge of our hammock bed and kicked off my shoes. I scooted myself backward and swung my legs up. I fell back gently, and smiled when my head finally sank into the pillows.

"Ahhh…" I love this bed. Where else but heaven can you have a bed like this? I seriously doubt you could find one like this down on Earth. Super comfy, sways gently, and never flips you out of it! Maybe you could find something similar on Earth, but you would need to have a ton of money, I bet.

I turned onto my stomach and tucked my arm under my pillow, and then I closed my eyes. The moment I did, I caught a faint hint of my love's sweet scent and my eyes snapped open. I lifted my head up, a little excited, and looked around, but I didn't see her. I inhaled a few times, sniffing the air, trying to figure out where that sweet fragrance was coming from. I furrowed my brows and chuckled at myself once I realized what I was doing. I felt kind of like a dog.

Enlightened

I placed my head back down on my pillow. I realized the scent was much stronger when I was lying down. I quickly rolled over and inhaled Harmony's pillow. It was saturated with it. My body was rejoicing and my nostrils welcomed such a treat.

I lifted my head up and quickly switched the pillows. I laid my head back down and buried my face into the pillow. I took in a deep breath and sighed in relief as I felt each part of my body relax and melt into the bed. At least my nap would be pleasant now.

Kaleb, a familiar voice called out to me in my mind. I couldn't help groaning a little. Of course my guide was calling me now. I was just about to take a nap.

Yes, Jack? I replied in thought.

It's time to go to Earth, he said.

This struck me as kind of odd. I could have sworn I was supposed to wait until Harmony was done with work to go. Surely he must be mistaken.

I thought I didn't have to go until Harmony was done with work? I questioned.

What for? You'll all be back long before she gets done in the nursery. She doesn't even need to go... Only you do.

I rolled onto my back and rubbed my eyes. I was confused by what Jack had said. She didn't even have to go? Why would she bother, if she didn't have to? Most didn't mind skipping a life down there if they could.

She doesn't? I questioned.

No.

Then why would she need me to wait for her? I asked.

It's silly, really. She thinks you need her there, he replied.

She does? I was surprised. *Did she say this?*

Actually, Luke did. He chuckled. *Don't worry, I assured him that you would be fine.*

If I wasn't confused before, I certainly was now. Why would Luke say anything about this? He wasn't my guide, and they weren't normally concerned with any other soul except for the one they were helping. I couldn't help thinking how very strange this all sounded.

I didn't understand why Luke or Harmony would be so concerned about me going to Earth on my own either. Sure, Earth could be hard for me at times. It was that way for most of us, though. I was sure that I would be fine. Besides, I wouldn't be completely on my own. The others would be there too. I would have their support if I needed it.

Still, I did want to go with Harmony. I loved her so much. I wanted to have the chance to find her there and fall in love with her all over again. I would have loved nothing more. All of this was causing such an internal dilemma.

Stay here and wait for Harmony and leave with her like she and I had planned, or go down now with the others. I wasn't sure what to do.

Am I able to think about this for a while? I asked.

Enlightened

Jack was quiet at first. He seemed to be hesitating, which was slightly evident in his voice when he started to speak. *Yes, but don't take too long. You don't want to keep the others waiting.*

I won't, I assured him.

I felt my connection with Jack fade and I was suddenly frustrated. Every word that Jack said was playing over and over in my mind. I needed to think and try to make sense out of all of this. I got up from the bed and slipped my shoes back on. With my brows furrowed, I started walking—okay, stomping was more like it, down the path, heading for the rock by the stream.

I was so irritated that I began grumbling out loud to myself as I walked. "What is all of this about?... Why would she want to go to Earth if she doesn't have to?... Why would Luke talk to Jack about any of this?... What am I not seeing?... Why does she think I need her there?... None of this makes any sense!"

When I got to the rock by the stream, I sat down on the edge of the rock that bordered the water. I crisscrossed my legs and rested my elbows against my knees. I cupped my chin in my hands and stared down at the water that was rushing by at my feet, and I let out a frustrated sigh. I had no logical explanation for any of this.

I turned my head downward, my face cupped in my palms now. It was at this moment that a possible reason for all of this occurred to me. Slowly, I lifted my head up and smiled. "She loves me," I said aloud.

I started to chuckle. I couldn't believe I hadn't thought of this before. It all made so much sense now. She just wanted to be anywhere that I was. If she were here with me right now I would give her the biggest hug. I wanted to be with her too. I knew what she and I had agreed on, but she didn't have to go down there just because I was. It was silly of her to do such a thing. It was not like I'd gone with her to the nursery. At the same time, it was so sweet of her. Because I knew she was doing it for me. She wanted to fall in love with me again as much as I wanted to fall in love with her! I was so happy. She truly did love me, and there was no doubt in my mind that I loved her too. I would love Harmony for the rest of my existence. I could never love anyone else the way that I loved her, ever, and I knew now what I must do.

Chapter 24

OUR PATH TO ENLIGHTENMENT BEGINS the moment we do. We are all given the same essential fundamental building blocks to help start us on our journey. Individualized and structured for the newborn soul who is receiving them. No newborn soul goes without such attention. Every single one is special and is treated that way.

There has never been an exception to this rule, ever. Just like young souls like me are assigned a guide to help them, newborn souls are assigned someone to work with them too. The only difference is newborn souls lack the communication skills that young souls like you and me have. That's where souls with gifts like mine come in. I'm able to understand babies and small children in a way others cannot. Down on Earth, I always had the ability to read them in a way. I could tell just by looking into their eyes what I should do to help them learn something. This always gave me the upper hand in knowing how to teach them. I'm hoping this continues on here in the same way.

It doesn't matter where I am. Whether I'm here, at home, or down on Earth, I still find waiting equally as frustrating. I think it's funny, how this one part of me always stays the same regardless of where I am. Normally the pet peeves and annoyances we suffer from Earth are forgotten once we get home. For me, this one never changes. This is part of what makes me, *me*.

I was sitting excitedly in a big puffy blue armchair, poised on the edge of my seat. I was bouncing, tapping my foot occasionally, and allowing my thoughts to wander. There's nothing wrong with this, of course, I thought to myself as I waited in the nursery's foyer for someone to come get me.

We all have very unique personalities, after all. I wouldn't have been created to be like this if it wasn't an acceptable way to be.

This was just one of the many things I had learned about myself on my path to enlightenment. But much like the newborn souls here, though I was ahead of them, my journey had just begun. There was still much more for me to learn.

The foyer's cozy living-room-style atmosphere was doing very little to help calm me down. I was an excited bundle of nerves as I continued to sit and wait. I couldn't help it. I was eager to start my job in the nursery. It's a very special thing to discover a talent that you possess. The best part, though, is finding a way to put that talent to good use.

Enlightened

I glanced around the room, taking in the décor in an attempt to distract myself. The big puffy white sofa I sat across from had decorative throw pillows on it, and large leafy houseplants at both ends. The walls were painted a faded blue, which was just a shade lighter than my blue jeans. Photos of whales, dolphins, and other sea life hung on the walls all around the room. It was very pretty in here, but I just couldn't really appreciate it at the moment. All I could focus on was getting started and doing a good job.

"…Harmony." I glanced up and smiled the moment I heard a familiar and unforgettable voice call my name.

"Elijah!" I exclaimed happily. As I rose to my feet to greet him, I absentmindedly wiped my hands down the front of my pants. I chuckled to myself. It only took me a moment to catch what I'd done. It was not like I had to spare Elijah from my sweaty palms. Apparently, I had developed a little habit from school. We only sweat on Earth.

He walked toward me with his arms wide open. His blue eyes were alight as always. His rounded cheeks were still framed by his blond curly ringlets. His wings were still arched above his shoulders and were the soft white that I remembered.

Call them what you like, I'll leave that up to you. *Angel* is the term most often used to describe winged beings like Elijah down on Earth. I've also heard masters or spirits, cherubs too. Personally, I like to call them the divine. Any of these terms is just fine by them. They really have no preference.

There's not much of a difference between the newborn souls, us, and them. We are all the same, after all, just at different stages of development. Like a caterpillar will grow and change, morphing into a beautiful butterfly, so do we. At some point, we will become like them. We are all divine as well.

Honestly, I don't know what I was expecting. But I instantly felt such relief upon seeing a familiar face. I was so excited. I hadn't seen him in such a long time. I quickly embraced him in a warm hug. He hadn't changed a bit in the time I'd been gone. I couldn't help running my fingers in his feathers, feeling their soft silky texture, just like I used to do when I was little.

"I'm so happy you're finally joining us!" he said as he gave me a tight squeeze. He rocked me gently and patted my back.

I leaned back and playfully narrowed my eyes at him. "How did you know that I would be?"

"Oh, my darling Harmony, I've been at this a very long time. I can see the potential in a soul long before they do!" he replied with a carefree chuckle. He pulled back some, keeping me tucked under his arm. His wing was curled around me, resting gently against my shoulder. "Come on." He smiled. "…Let's get you reacquainted with this place."

Enlightened

Elijah led the way down the hall, though I didn't really need him to. I was smiling as I walked. My confidence was growing, stemming from how much I still remembered about this place. It did surprise me a little. It had been such a long time since I'd been here that I wasn't expecting to.

Walking alongside Elijah was causing memories from my own time here to start rising to the surface. I was happily reminiscing as I walked down the main corridor. I was peeking into rooms that I passed by and greeting more familiar faces. I was smiling as I realized that most of those memories included Kaleb.

It was so comforting that nothing had changed here. The walls of the corridor were still decorated with fun zoo animals and cute little bears. There were still many rooms with brightly colored cradles, each with a unique mobile hanging above. Toys and books still lined the brightly colored wood shelves in the rooms, though I could tell there had been many new additions.

It was safe to say that the way the nursery was set up wasn't much different than a school on Earth would be. There were plenty of places for the little ones to play, sleep, and learn.

"As you can see, not much has changed here," Elijah said, and then patted my shoulder. "The saying is true. If it's isn't broken, why fix it." He chuckled.

Elijah continued to lead the way down the hall. The moment we rounded the corner we encountered something that I wasn't expecting.

A baby soul was sitting out in the hall all alone. I could only assume that the baby was a girl by her purple PJs. The only hair on her head resembled peach fuzz. She was just sitting there, smiling and glancing around.

Elijah and I exchanged a glance. "Is that normal?" I asked him.

"Occasionally we have some who are a little more adventurous than others," he replied.

The moment Elijah spoke, the little one turned her head, looking in our direction. She smiled wide when she saw us, an adorable toothless grin. She waved and then quickly got to her feet. She couldn't have been more than a foot and a half tall. She was giggling, and took off running down the hall in the opposite direction. I have to admit, that took me a moment to process. It'd been a very long time since I'd been exposed to a baby soul and what they were capable of. I was expecting something along the lines of an Earth baby.

"This one has had us on our toes since she arrived," he said as he started to run.

I started to run too, following after Elijah and the little one down the hall. The little one was giggling and squealing as we ran after her. She darted into a room and we trailed in behind her.

Enlightened

Newborn souls and newborn Earth babies are similar in lots of ways. For example, they look the same. They are all very small and extremely cute. Some are bald and some have a little poof of hair on the top of their head. Both of them will stretch and stiffen when you lift them to place them in your arms.

The one real difference between the two is Earth newborns don't really do too much. They sleep ninety-nine percent of the time at first, and it is a long, gradual process to teach Earth babies basic skills like crawling, walking, and talking. Also, newborn Earth babies are not born with total control over their basic motor skills.

This is not the case with a newborn soul. A newborn soul is wide awake, watching everything and everyone. They have complete control over their arms and legs, and can even hold their head up. The one common subtle trait that both newborn souls and newborn Earth babies share is that they can understand everything that is said to them regardless of what language is been spoken to them. This is a gift that they all possess. Only, newborn souls have to be taught some basic skills so they develop a better understanding of what is being said. This gift will remain ingrained into each one of us. Regardless of what language is spoken here, we all understand each other. This gift will carry over to Earth when we are first born, but will gradually fade over time, and will always go unnoticed.

Billie Kowalewski

"Ahhh…there you are! I see you must have gone to get Elijah," an angel said as we entered the room. I remembered her the moment I saw her, along with her long red curls and her gentle voice. Her name was Lailah.

Her wings flexed outward as she bent down to speak to the little one. "You need to stay in here with the rest of the kids," she told the baby sternly.

The baby smiled. "Okay," she replied in a high-pitched voice. The baby then walked over and sat down with a small group of five other babies on a small red carpet. They had their little legs crossed and they waited quietly.

Lailah stood up and smiled when she saw me. She held her arms open to me. "Harmony, I'm so happy to see you."

I walked over and gave her a big hug. "I'm happy to see you too." I leaned back to look at her. "I'm very excited about working here."

"And we're all very excited about you working here too." She patted my shoulder. "Come sit with the kids."

I sat down on the carpet next to the baby we had chased. All the babies were staring at me.

"Kids, this is Harmony. She will be working here now. Can you all say hello to Harmony?"

"Hello," all the babies said at once.

I smiled back at them and waved. "Hi, guys."

The babies turned back, waiting for Lailah to begin. She was looking at me as she started to address the kids.

Enlightened

"We were just talking about Earth, and how short life is there," she said.

I just sat there, and nodded quietly in reply. I didn't want to interrupt what she was teaching them. I was thinking she must have known of my recent history of coming home early, too. Because it felt like she was talking more to me than the babies.

"It will seem like you have lots of time. But in reality you do not," she began. "Childhood will go by fast, and so will your teen years. Once you become an adult there, you will become consumed by mundane tasks and will forget about doing what is important. Then, before you know it, a lifetime has passed by."

Wow, she's got that right, I thought to myself. It was so easy to forget that, though, once you were there.

"My point is the most important time down on Earth is the present. Don't waste the time you are given. Make sure you listen to your heart, and do what it wants while you can. Spend time with those you love. Always do what is right for you despite what someone else says. You don't want to get to the end of your life there and have very little, or nothing at all, to show for it."

I continued to sit there, engrossed in what Lailah was saying, recalling learning these very same lessons myself, right here in this very room, a long time ago.

"You are there to learn about you. You are not there just to earn money, or to see how much more you can accumulate than someone else. It is important you don't lose sight of this. Stay strong, and stay true to yourself. This is how to truly succeed down on Earth."

She was so right. Oh, how we can become so distracted by material things down there? It is true what they say; you can't take it with you. Why do we let stuff like money consume us down there? It's so much at times that we end up forgetting what is most important in life, and we end up with more regrets at the end.

I felt Elijah place his hand on my arm, causing me to glance up. "It's time to go to work." He smiled.

I followed Elijah out of the room and down the hall. He led the way to an arched double door. I recognized it the moment I saw it. It was the room where the new arrivals came in. He pushed open the door, holding it, motioning for me to walk in ahead of him. I took in a deep breath. There's no way I get to work in here; I just started, I thought to myself. I walked in, more excited now than ever. Because I knew now that I was chosen not just to work with newborn souls, but to work with the new arrivals. These were the souls who hadn't been exposed to anything at all yet. I would become part of their very first steps on their journey. I would be the one at the start of it all.

My eyes were wide when I entered. The room was a clean, crisp white color. Ten cradles were lined up along the far wall. When I say far, I mean it. The room was

Enlightened

very big. The size reminded me of a school gymnasium. The cradles were a standard size and were spaced very far away from each other. Ten blue puffy armchairs just like the one in the foyer were positioned across the room from each cradle. I looked up as I continued to walk, and was surprised that there was no ceiling. The ceiling had the same starry effect that the courtyard door had too. This was definitely not your typical, ordinary room.

"I'm sure you're wondering why this room is so large." Elijah's question came out more like a statement.

"Yes," I simply replied.

"Well, you're about to get your answer," he said as he looked up. I followed his lead and looked up too. Just then, an angel with long flowing brown hair came flying in, holding something in her arms. Her wings stretched and flexed as she circled the room. She then landed gently by the cradle closest to us.

Elijah walked over and greeted the angel. I stood by, patiently awaiting his instructions.

Both Elijah and the angel looked up at me. "Harmony, come here please," Elijah said. I smiled and walked over to them. "This is Ophelia."

"Hello," I said, greeting her. Ophelia tucked what she had into one arm. The sleeve of her robe covered it. She then held out her hand to greet me. "It is nice to finally meet you," she said.

Billie Kowalewski

I took her hand, shaking it warmly. Like all the other angels here, she was warm and kind. She must have been fairly new. Well, new since I had been here last. I'd never met her before now.

"Ophelia, please show Harmony her first assignment."

She pushed her sleeve aside, revealing a very tiny, naked newborn soul. The baby was a soft pink color and most definitely a girl. She looked so peaceful, tucked in the crook of Ophelia's soft robe-covered arm. Her eyes were closed gently as she slept.

"This is my assignment?" I asked. I was shocked. I figured I was doing more of a preschool teacher kind of thing where I got to work with the older ones. I hadn't seen this coming. I wasn't sure what to do. Or what they wanted me to do. "What do you want me to do with her?"

Ophelia held her arms out to me, offering me the baby. I'm sure the uncertainty was there in my eyes but I took her without question. Still unsure what I was supposed to do.

"Don't worry. I'm going to explain what to do," Elijah told me as he patted my shoulder. "What do you think you should do first?" he asked.

I looked down at the tiny naked baby in my arms. I looked her over for a moment and realized what I should do first. "I should probably get her dressed?" I asked.

"Good. Of course you know diapers are not necessary here, and neither is the clothing really. They don't need them to keep warm here. This just gives them a first lesson about Earth. Clothes are important."

"Where can I find those?" I asked him.

"We keep a supply of them with each cradle." He walked me over to one of the cradles and pulled open a drawer at the end that was attached to a small changing table.

Ten cradles in the room and all of them were empty. I had this one baby. I couldn't help but wonder why there were so many cradles. "Why are there so many cradles in here?"

"Because there are more babies here than just this one. They're just not in their cradles at the moment. Souls are working with them."

"Oh." I reached into the drawer and picked out a pair of PJs for the baby to wear. It was a white one-piece with a little teddy bear embroidered on the left. I placed the baby down on the changing table and she opened her eyes. She looked up at me and smiled. She reached her hand up and was opening and closing it. I watched her for a moment and realized she might want to hold my finger. I stuck my finger out and she grabbed it quickly, now smiling even wider.

Elijah chuckled lightly. "You're a natural."

I just glanced at him and narrowed my eyes playfully at him. "What am I supposed to do with her?" I asked again.

"You interact with her, just like you just did here. This will help her discover what she already knows. She will learn what she needs to from you before she goes on to work in the classrooms," he replied.

"Oh." I'm sure I sounded surprised. This just seemed way too easy to me.

"I'll let you two get started. I'll be back to check on you soon," he said.

"Okay."

Elijah flexed his wings, flying up over our heads and out of the room. I let go of the baby's hand and started getting her dressed. I undid the little snaps on the PJs and scrunched up one side of the leg. "Okay, give me your foot," I told her. She looked at me, a little puzzled. I grabbed her foot. "See?" I pointed at it. "...This is your foot."

I put her foot down and tried again. "Please, give me your foot." The baby lifted her leg up and I slipped on one side of the PJs. I continued walking the baby through putting on the rest of her PJs, one leg and arm at a time. I still find it somewhat strange that the newborn souls have the capabilities that they do and are able to learn this quickly.

I was being silly now, making funny faces as I was doing up the buttons on her PJs, when a strange feeling suddenly came over me. I then felt something crawl slowly down my cheek and then drop down, landing on the baby's stomach, staining her PJs. I flinched a little in surprise and then wiped my cheek.

Enlightened

I pulled my hand away to examine it, and discovered my palm was tear-stained. I picked up the baby and started walking over to one of the big blue puffy armchairs. Kaleb must be upset about something, I thought to myself. I had no reason to worry, and if I went home to check on him he would wonder how I'd known to check, and I couldn't do that. The tears were flowing really heavily now and I couldn't stop them. I glanced down at the baby, and she had a look of concern in her eyes as she stared at me. "Don't worry, little one. I'm okay," I told her. I smiled as I sat down with her, tears streaming down my face. "You know what? You need a name," I told her as I sat back in the chair. "Hmm... what should I call you?'

"Harmony..."

I glanced up when I heard a very familiar guide's voice call my name. I was surprised to see Luke here. Elijah was with him. Both of them had a peculiar expression on their faces.

"What is going on?" I asked. I smiled through the tears that were continuing to stream down my face. "Are you here to see how I'm doing with the babies?"

"No, I'm afraid not," Luke replied. Elijah reached his hands out, and I instinctively handed him the baby. "I came to get you...Kaleb is in trouble."

Chapter 25

WE ARRIVED IN THE HALLWAY just outside the door of the guides' viewing area at the school. As soon as I felt the marble tile under my feet, I immediately opened my eyes, reaching for the door handle at the same time.

Luke quickly grabbed me by the arm. "Hold on just a moment."

My overwhelming need to protect Kaleb was twisting my insides, causing me to keep trying to pull out of Luke's grip. Panic-stricken, I glanced up at his face. His expression was serious, and one of concern, as he continued to hold on tightly to my arm.

"I know how you must be feeling right now, but he's all right," Luke said firmly. "I came in to prepare for your return to Earth, and was disappointed to discover that Kaleb had gone down to Earth along with the rest of your class. I had no idea he was going, and I had even advised Jack against it, just like I told you I would."

Luke knew me all too well. He held on tightly to my arm while he continued to speak, knowing full well I'd be darting for the door as soon as he let go.

Enlightened

"After I made the discovery, I sought out Jack to express my"—he smirked and cleared his throat—"disappointment. When I walked in, Jack was hunched over Kaleb's viewing screen, clutching the rim. I thought the worst had already happened…I thought I was too late."

Luke grabbed my other arm and bent down to my height to hold my attention. "As you know, Jack can be a little dramatic at times. I was relieved to discover the situation with Kaleb hasn't reached that point; he's just extremely depressed and isn't living. He is avoiding all the lessons in his life. Jack has been trying to guide him the way we normally do, but he is just not responding to any of it. Jack and I thought if we brought you in, maybe you could help us guide him better. You know him better than either one of us."

I nodded my head and was glancing around Luke at the door. I was trying to let what Luke said about Kaleb being all right sink into my mind. But my natural instinct to protect Kaleb was overruling my body, causing me to continue to try to pull out of Luke's hold.

I sucked in a jagged breath. "Please, Luke," I begged.

Luke released my arms. I had the door opened and was in the room faster than light.

Jack glanced up from Kaleb's screen when I entered. "He seems all right at the moment. He's visiting his girlfriend right now," he commented.

Billie Kowalewski

I know Jack meant well, but he didn't know Kaleb like I did. All of our personalities, traits, gifts, and emotions become intensified on Earth. It's always been this way, so we can learn and develop a deeper understanding of ourselves. So of course Kaleb's deeply passionate nature can sometimes become overwhelming for him there. Oftentimes it gets in the way of him understanding what he is in the process of learning, and causes him to lose focus.

"He has a girlfriend?" I asked softly. This information distracted me for a moment. I peered around Jack, looking into the water-filled crater to view Kaleb's life.

"Yes. His name in this life is Curtis Parker. He was born September 14, 1981," Jack replied.

I was astounded. Not since the beginning of school had I witnessed someone else's life in progress, and never had it been someone I knew. Taking young souls into the viewing area before their first time going to Earth was something all of the guides did to help give us an understanding of what Earth might be like for us. But that was normally a one-time occurrence. I'd never heard of a young soul getting the same opportunity that I was getting right now.

He looked so much like the man I'd fallen in love with on Earth, and my heart was instantly swooning. I was moved to tears as I watched the love of my existence having an engrossing conversation on a tan leather sofa

Enlightened

with a young blond woman with delicate features and thin lips.

His sandy-blond hair was replaced with a rich dark brown—instead of the jet black he'd worn in that last life. I found it heartwarming that it was cut similarly to the way he wore it when we were on Earth together last. It was hanging in his eyes and the sides and back were grown down to just past his chin. I was recalling how handsome he was then, and how much I loved running my fingers through his hair in that life.

I was disappointed, a little, that I couldn't make out the color of his eyes. I was wondering if they were the same shade of green he'd had in that last life. But I suddenly had a hard time focusing on something as trivial as his eye color anymore with what I was now watching.

He was locked in a passionate embrace with the young woman. He was holding her closely; their lips were moving in synchronization. My first reaction was shock. I know we all have relationships on Earth and that it's a normal part of the learning process. But to see the man with whom I had agreed to spend eternity with another woman was unsettling at first, to say the least.

I leaned in a little closer, carefully watching my Kaleb's body language compared to the young girl's, when I noticed him clenching his eyes shut. Her body language was passionate; she was clearly enjoying the fervent kiss the longer it went on. She was trying to press her body closer to his in an effort to push things further.

Kaleb's was clearly different. I could see his body tensing up the further they went.

"Can you listen to his thoughts at all?" I asked, deeply engrossed in Kaleb's standoffish behavior.

Jack cleared his throat. "Yes, but I didn't think that was necessary for you to hear. He's doing well now."

I snapped my head up quickly from Kaleb's screen. Luke was standing alongside me to my left, and Jack was standing across from me on the other side of the viewing screen. I'm not sure what expression was on my face, but I noticed that when I glanced up at Jack he flinched at first.

"Jack, with all due respect, I know him. He's not okay." I pointed toward the screen. "Look at his body language. I've rarely seen anyone cringe like that during a kiss, unless they're not happy. You need to turn up Kaleb's thoughts so I can hear."

Jack just stood there at first, glancing back and forth between Luke and me. He seemed to be hesitating about turning up the sound so I could hear what Kaleb was thinking.

"A person's thoughts are private and should be kept as such. I don't think Kaleb will be happy with me, knowing I allowed you to hear any of what he is thinking," he replied as he nervously straightened his solid green bowtie. He crossed his arms. "This is something I simply cannot allow. A soul's thoughts are only for them and their guide to hear—no one else."

My love for Kaleb and my need to protect him knew no bounds. It was clear to me, watching Kaleb, that there was something wrong. I was angrily gripping the rim of the crater, holding on tightly so I didn't just lose it and grip someone else by his bowtie; Luke would be greatly disappointed in me if I behaved that way. I narrowed my eyes angrily at Jack. "*Let. Me. Hear. His. Thoughts. Now*," I said slowly through my clenched teeth.

Jack and I were having a standoff. I could see he wasn't just going to let me listen to what Kaleb was thinking, just as I wasn't going to back down from doing whatever I had to to protect my love.

"We brought her in here to help us help him. She must see something that you are overlooking," Luke said, diffusing the situation. He placed one hand on my shoulder in an effort to calm me and then waved his hand over the pool in the crater.

"What is wrong with me? Why is this so hard?" Kaleb's thoughts were suddenly echoing off the pale stone walls in the room. *"She's pretty, and she's nice. She's funny too. Why is this making it feel worse?"*

"Making what feel worse?" I asked aloud, puzzled by his questioning thoughts.

"There's nothing wrong with her. Come on, Curt…you can do this…there's nothing wrong with her."

I glanced up at Jack, still puzzled by his thoughts. "What is he talking about? Jack, what is going on here?" I asked.

Jack sighed. "I'm sure it's no secret that life on Earth can be difficult for Kaleb at times. He's been struggling with a very dark depression that I've never seen in him before, until this life."

The screen went dark, catching my attention, and I was suddenly alarmed. "Jack, what is happening?! What's wrong with the screen?!" I asked, frantic.

Jack snickered. "Someone turned the lights off," he replied.

"You've been with her for four months. Other couples do this all the time. Stop thinking about it and just do it."

Jack suddenly waved his hand over the screen.

I now understood with great clarity what was going on here, so I glanced away from the screen. But his thoughts still weren't making much sense to me. Why was he trying so hard to talk himself into doing what he was doing? Why would anyone need to do that? Why would anyone try so hard to make themselves do that if they clearly didn't want to? What was even more puzzling was his statement about it making "it" worse.

The screen was suddenly lit up and I began watching again. I watched as he smiled kindly at her while getting himself dressed. I watched him as they walked together out into the small, dimly lit living room where I'd first

Enlightened

seen him sitting with her on the tan leather sofa. His face seemed a little pale but he held his kind smile. "Hey, I'm gonna take off. I'm not feeling very well," I heard him tell her.

I watched as she smiled sympathetically and casually tried to run her fingers through his hair, the way I would do to comfort him. "Aw, you can stay the night. I wouldn't mind taking care of you, if you needed me to," she said.

I saw him gently take her hands and kindly push her away. "Thanks, Shannon, but I think I need to just go home," he replied in his gentlest tone. From the angle I was watching from, I could clearly see that his smile was forced.

My stomach began twisting in knots, not paying much mind to the fact that I now had my face an inch away from the pool. "Oh my, I can feel it! This is wrong!" I began shaking my head. "There's something wrong! He's not right!"

I glanced back and forth between both guides. "How do I help him? Luke?... Jack?... What do we do?!"

I watched as Kaleb grabbed his jacket and gently kissed her cheek. I watched as he walked out of her dainty house and quickly got into his car, and as he quietly shut the door. He started the car and put it in gear. His expression was hard to discern because of the dim lighting of the dashboard. He began backing down out of the driveway and when he turned his head, the dim light illuminated the tear that was trickling down his cheek.

I quickly looked up at Jack. "Why can't we hear his thoughts?!" I asked frantically.

"Because I turned them off before. I didn't think you needed to hear *those*." He chuckled nervously.

"Well, turn them back on!" I practically shouted at him. Jack didn't argue this time and quickly waved his hand over the pool. I went back to hovering an inch away from the water.

"I'm so tired of this! What is wrong with me?!" his mind's voice was shouting. *"Why did it hurt so much?!"* His angry words were echoing loudly off the pale stone walls.

"I've had enough!" he suddenly shouted out loud. He gripped the wheel hard, making his knuckles smooth and white. His eyes were narrow and filled with anger as the car began to accelerate. *"The rock,"* he said darkly in his mind suddenly. "I'm done!" he called out as he quickly turned the wheel.

"Kaleb!" I shouted at the top of my lungs.

His car slammed hard into the large boulder. Hunks of metal were flying into the air. Glass from the windshield and shards of plastic were raining down around the car. I watched and flinched as the love of my existence was knocked in the face by a large, quickly inflating balloon, and saw it shove him hard against the side window. The glass in the window cracked in a spider-web formation

Enlightened

when his head hit it. Blood began running down from his forehead.

My head began to spin wildly, and I was screaming in horror. My knees buckled and I lost total control of my body. My head, my chest, and my left leg were suddenly in agony. Luke caught me in his arms before I hit the marble floor. "Oh dear lord," I said under my breath. I felt strangely disconnected, and very woozy. I was in so much pain, but it was nothing compared to the painful thought that was now foremost in my mind. I whispered, "We're gonna disappear like Charmeine and Zuriel, aren't we?"

Epilogue

"They have him on a stretcher." Jack let out a sigh of relief. "They're not performing CPR, and they have the oxygen mask on him… He may be all right."

"I have an idea… We need to call Zipporah right away," Luke replied.

"Yes, I see," Jack said out loud. It sounded like he was replying to something Luke conveyed through telepathy. "…Do you really think that would help?"

"It's certainly better than the alternative. Doing nothing, and taking the chance he will just do it again."

"It's not the normal. We'll have to get permission from the divine first. They will need to approve such actions."

"I'm calling Zipporah right now. If anyone can get that kind of approval, it'll be her."

✦ ✦ ✦

"We have to get him in! Jeff, quick, go around and get the door!" A man in a blue jumper leaped out of the ambulance, quickly flinging open the doors. Hospital staff quickly ran out, greeting them as they placed the stretcher on the ground.

A man in white waved his hand at the hospital crew. "Wheel him in!" he yelled. He motioned for the paramedic to follow him. "What do we have here?" the doctor asked, walking back in a hurried rush.

"A young man…looks to be in his early twenties. Crashed his car. There are concerns that this may be a possible suicide attempt."

"How do you know?" The doctor sounded surprised.

"There were no skid marks at the crash site… It's still under investigation."

"Has anyone identified the victim?"

The paramedic handed the doctor a clipboard. "Curtis Parker, born September 14, 1981, lives in Clinton, according to his I.D."

"What about next of kin? Has anyone located them?"

"Police are working on that now."

"Nurse! Let's go! We need to get him cleaned up! Keep checking his vitals, and get a drip started! We need to get this man into X-ray, ASAP!"

"Right away, Doctor!"